RAVE REVIEWS FOR
SUSAN EDWARDS!

WHITE DAWN

"A truly touching story and one that will warm your heart. Ms. Edwards has penned romance at its finest."

—*Old Book Barn Gazette*

"The story had me riveted from the first page to the last. Susan Edwards packs this story with passion and emotion."

—*Romance Reviews Today*

WHITE DOVE

"Remarkable . . . the characters worm their way into your heart."

—*All About Romance*

"A beautifully written tale. Ms. Edwards has a way of enchanting readers with her characters."

—*Romance Reviews Today*

WHITE DREAMS

"Susan Edwards has the talent of hooking her readers in the first paragraph and selfishly holding on to them until the last page has been turned! Highly recommended reading!"

—*Huntress Book Reviews*

WHITE NIGHTS

"*White Nights* leaves an afterglow long after the last page."

—*Rendezvous*

"Tender, heartwarming, touching, *White Nights* is a story you can savor."

—Connie Mason

MORE HIGH PRAISE FOR
SUSAN EDWARDS!

WHITE FLAME

"4 ½ Stars! A Top Pick! A wonderful, romantic read!"
—Romantic Times

"Susan Edwards has penned another winner. . . . Her sensual prose and compelling characters are forging a place for her at the forefront of Indian romance."
—Affaire de Coeur

"[Ms. Edwards] hooked me with an ingenious plot and held me with heart-stopping tension. Ms. Edwards's books are not just great romance; they are storehouses of knowledge."
—Rendezvous

WHITE WOLF

"Ms. Edwards's words flow like vivid watercolors across the pages. Her style is smooth, rhythmic and easy to read."
—Rendezvous

"Hop on your plush horse (your couch) and enjoy this romantic western!"
—Affaire de Coeur

"A SPLENDID story of majesty, and a very special love you can feel in your heart. 4 ½ Bells!"
—Bell, Book, and Candle

WHITE WIND

"Talented and skillful, this first-rate author has proven her mettle with *White Wind*. Ms. Edwards has created a romantic work of art!"
—The Literary Times

THE BREAKING STORM

The downpour was a silvery sheet of pelting water. The wind howled and jagged light ripped through the clouds, but inside the tipi, Small Bird hardly noticed.

"The flaps. I should close them," she finally managed to whisper.

"Leave them," her husband murmured, his voice deep, throaty and thick as box elder sap.

His gaze moved to her mouth. She licked her lips. "The fire, it will die."

"I will build a new fire." His head lowered and his breath warmed her mouth.

Small Bird's heart jumped into her throat. She didn't know this man. The stoic, cold, and even angry man of the last week was gone. In his place was a man who wanted a woman. His woman. His wife. She licked her lips again, nervous, then jumped as the tip of her tongue brushed his mouth.

Her lips parted with surprise. His mouth came down on hers, warm and moist. Soft and commanding. Small Bird responded on a sigh. She'd never known this intimacy but some inner voice guided her. Wrapping her arms around his neck, she pressed herself closer. As the shaman had merged their blood and lives, Small Bird now allowed Swift Foot to merge his mouth with hers.

SUSAN EDWARDS

WHITE DUSK

LEISURE BOOKS NEW YORK CITY

A LEISURE BOOK®

November 2002

Published by

Dorchester Publishing Co., Inc.
276 Fifth Avenue
New York, NY 10001

ISBN 0-8439-5094-3

Visit us on the web at www.dorchesterpub.com.

This one is for you, Lynn.

WHITE DUSK

Prologue

Rolling banks of wispy, cottony-white fog shrouded a band of warriors riding across the gray premorning prairie. Silent as the moist clouds concealing them, they followed the river.

Above, *Wi* rose, coloring the sky with pale pinks and golds. Taking a deep breath, the sun stretched his light and warmth upward and outward from the horizon, chasing away the last of the night. Satisfied his work was especially nice, he glanced down—but frowned when he spotted the war-painted warriors taking advantage of his absence and the morning mist. Anticipating the violence soon to take place below, he let his light dim.

Tate, the wind, howled his own protest. He rushed downward, dispersing the fog in tendrils across the rich green land. Reaching the oncoming warriors, he circled them. *Go back*, he howled. But the revenge-bent braves ignored him, pressing onward. Reaching a thick wall of trees, they dismounted and led their mounts through the silent woods.

Flowing above the budding forest, *Tate* swirled across the land until he reached the small encampment that was the war party's objective. His breath sent waves of green grass flowing across the prairie. Flames flickered in the fire pits there, and smoke from the camp's many cook fires was sucked high and far.

Unaware of the danger, the camp's men gathered to plan their day while women began the morning meal. Children of all ages embraced the dawn with the exuberance of youth. No one paid any mind to *Tate's* howls of rage.

Saddened and angry over his inability to stop more blood from flowing into the earth, he screeched upward, back into the heavens.

Pounding hooves, along with the high-pitched shrieks of the band of *Miniconjou* warriors who broke through the thick stand of cottonwoods lining the river, shattered the gentle spring-morning calm.

All in the Hunkpapa encampment, now alerted to the danger, scurried to protect themselves. Settled away from the river, away from the trees that could hide an approaching enemy, they had time to take action.

Men grabbed weapons and mounted their war ponies while women cried out warnings, grabbed their young children, and ran out into the expansive prairie. Like ants fleeing their nests, they ran low in the tall, dark grass, and hid. The aged, feeble, and ill members of the tribe had no choice but to take refuge in their tipis.

Hunkpapa warriors of all ages rode away from camp, toward the stream, to meet their enemy with lances held high and outraged shouts ringing in the air. Half a dozen Hunkpapa youths ran to their tribe's large herd of horses. As they mounted, their yells rose and sent the rest of the herd galloping to safety. Braves of a visiting tribe also joined the defense.

Despite the resistance they met, the attacking band of warriors continued on, and birds flew from the treetops, frantically beating their wings to escape the melee below. White-tailed deer froze in place for a heartbeat before leaping nimbly across the stream and away across the grassland.

A group of young boys ranging from seven to nine gathered upstream from the enemy and whirled as one at the first war whoop. Calf-Boy, the youngest, felt his heart slam into his throat when he saw the enemy riding out of the fog, heading toward them.

His uncle rode past. "Go! Hide!" the man called.

Moist earth churned up by the horse's hooves pelted him, spurring Calf-Boy into action. He and the others wasted no time in heeding the command. While their skill with the miniature bows and arrows slung on their backs might bring down a squirrel for the morning meal, they were no match for seasoned warriors.

Heart pounding against his ribs, Calf-Boy ran, his feet swiftly carrying him across the uneven ground. Fear bit at his heels. Had the enemy learned that he, the son of Runs with Wind and Sun Woman, lived? Had they come to kill him as they'd killed his parents?

Calf-Boy ran between two large rings of dwellings. A miniature tipi and two dolls lay in his path. The girls who'd been playing with them were nowhere to be seen. He jumped over the toys. Behind him, the sounds of a fierce battle raged. The enemy had chosen to attack while many of his tribe's warriors, and those of the visiting tribes, were out hunting.

Once he was far past the camp, Calf-Boy dropped flat. Dew clung to the tall grass there, soaking him. On his belly, he lifted his head, parting the grass carefully.

He trembled when he saw that several enemy warriors had managed to reach the camp. Slashing at the hide walls of tipis, they yelled in victory. When they reached the eastern horn and the largest tipi pitched there, one warrior leaned out, his knife stabbing through the hide and into the home belonging to Calf-Boy's uncle—the Hunkpapa chief.

Frightened, a woman and a young girl stumbled from the entrance, seeking safety. Horrified, Calf-Boy watched the two warriors follow. His ill aunt, one of the females, stumbled. Willow Song, his cousin, stopped to help her mother up. One of the warriors raised his war club.

Helpless and unable to look away, Calf-Boy watched the woman who'd raised him fall beneath the blow. Then the warriors ran down his cousin. All around Calf-Boy, screams of pain and victory ricocheted through the air. His uncle's warriors were fighting off the enemy, but slowly. More than one tipi fell to the hacking of a knife blade or ax. Smoke from the cook fires inside the dwellings billowed, followed by flames licking at the fallen hides.

The two warriors who had killed his aunt and cousin left the fighting behind to ride out into the grass, sending running the women and children hiding there. In that moment, Calf-Boy realized the enemy knew of his existence. They searched for him. Frantically, Calf-Boy prayed for his uncle to come, to stop these Miniconjou. He didn't want to die. He didn't want anyone else to die because of him.

A large rock dug into his knee, but he ignored the pain and remained still until a frightened cry to his right brought his head around. There, a small girl fled her place of hiding: Small Bird, a child of the visiting tribe. She ran away from the two searching warriors, right toward where he was hidden. The two Miniconjou laughed and followed.

Suddenly one of them screamed and fell. An arrow had found its mark in his back. Looking around; Calf-Boy spotted several of his uncle's warriors riding out from the camp. But they were still far away. With a cry of rage, the other Miniconjou warrior raised his club high to strike down Small Bird—a life for a life. Without thought, Calf-Boy grabbed the rock beneath his knee. He had to do something. He couldn't allow the girl to be killed in cold blood as his aunt and cousin had been killed.

Rage and grief propelled him forward. These men had killed his family. Not in battle, but for no reason. The same would not be done to this girl. He threw the rock with all his might, hitting the Miniconjou warrior's horse between the ears. The startled animal reared up on its hind legs, forcing its rider to cling to its back and use both hands to regain control.

With his blood pounding in his ears, Calf-Boy ran nimbly toward the flailing horse. He couldn't let this man kill the girl. Grabbing an arrow from the small quiver slung crosswise over his shoulder, he ducked around to the other side of the horse.

Using both hands, he stabbed the arrow deep into the surprised warrior's thigh.

The enemy screeched in pain. Calf-Boy scooped up the little girl. Tiny at only three winters, she felt light as a feather. She clung to his narrow chest tightly. "Hold on, Small Bird," he cried. Turning, he ran for all he was worth.

The pounding of hooves beating at the earth rumbled behind him. He didn't dare take his eyes off the ground beneath his feet to glance over his shoulder. He couldn't fall. Didn't dare falter. He ran—ran until he was overtaken by a large black horse. Looking up, he saw it belonged to his uncle.

They had won. They had fought off the Miniconjou.

That night, in a simple ceremony, Calf-Boy was renamed Swift Foot—and the legend of how he had at such a young age counted coup and saved a small girl of a visiting tribe would be retold by friend and foe alike long into his adulthood.

Chapter One

Thirteen years later

Standing beneath a young cottonwood near the Hunkpapa village, Small Bird leaned her head against its rough trunk, her head resting in a vee. High above, a golden eagle soared lazily across the crystal-blue sky, spiraling downward in an ever-tightening circle. The majestic bird spread the feathered tips of its wings, dipping one to glide on the dry breath of the summer wind.

The rich golden browns of the bird's plumage stood out against the pale blue sky: a calm, soothing sight for Small Bird. Lower and lower it soared until it chased its own likeness across the mirror surface of the nearby sluggish stream.

Without warning, a covey of sharp-tailed grouse took flight. The eagle let out a cry and swooped after the smaller birds. Its sharp talons shot out and snagged its prey. With a sharp downward beat of its wings, the powerful hunter lifted its head to the sun, reversed direction, and flew off.

Watching the powerful bird, which one minute gave the appearance of gentle beauty, then showed the powerful predator within, set Small Bird's heart beating as fast as that of the eagle's prey.

Around her, the spared grouse settled back into the treetops. Quiet and peace descended once more. But not in Small Bird's heart. The sight of the eagle making a kill left her feeling edgy. *Wambli*, the spirit of the eagle, presided over war parties, hunters, and battles; his appearance today, the day before her marriage to Swift Foot, did not bode well.

She closed her eyes, seeking comfort in the warm breeze, the soft rustle of leaves overhead, and the soft chirps of birds fluttering from branch to branch. All creatures had to eat. Even the golden eagle. The killing had meant nothing.

She deliberately glanced around, finding beauty in the land. But the vision of the eagle remained a dark shadow in her mind, obliterating all happiness. Seeking strength, Small Bird dug her fingers into the deep furrows in the cottonwood's trunk as she sought to anchor herself. To admit the truth of the eagle's omen.

Death.

No. It could not be.

"It is a sign you must heed." The deep, familiar voice echoed her thoughts.

Small Bird turned her head to the side. Her brother stared intently at her, worry darkening his eyes and lining his mouth. Neither sibling spoke. Both knew she understood the appearance of the eagle. She paid attention to details and listened to the spirits, and they guided the way. But this was one truth she wanted to ignore.

Regardless of her wishes, Lone Warrior voiced her fears and deepened her trepidation. Small Bird ran sweat-slicked palms down the sides of her deerskin dress. "It does not change anything."

Lone Warrior stalked over to her. "It changes everything. The spirits warn of death." Anger deepened his voice. "Do not do this!"

Small Bird kept her gaze locked to his. "*Wambli* is a great hunter." She held out one hand to stop her brother from interrupting. "Swift Foot is also a great warrior and hunter. Perhaps *Wambli* came to remind me of this." She didn't believe her own words. Had that been the truth, the eagle would not have made a kill. He'd have just shown himself.

Lone Warrior's eyes narrowed. He towered

over her. "The eagle warns of death. Yours. Are you so foolish that you would ignore this sign? The enemies of Swift Foot will seek you out."

Small Bird shrugged. She wasn't so foolish as to discount entirely the warning of death. But arguing with her brother wouldn't change anything—especially the union between her and Swift Foot. *Lone Warrior loves you,* she reminded herself. *He worries, and doesn't understand that the past has shaped your future.*

"There will be peace between the Hunkpapa and Miniconjou. I know this to be the truth. Are they not talking of peace? Many Horns of the Miniconjou brought many gifts to show that Hawk Eyes and his people wish to end the war."

Disgust filled Lone Warrior's voice. "It is a trick. They will attack and kill again. As the wife of Swift Foot, they will seek you along with him. As they killed the parents of Swift Foot, they will kill you and him." He spun away to pace along the bank.

After several taut minutes of silence, he continued, "I cannot allow you to put yourself in this danger."

Small Bird sighed. His words held truth. Over the years, the Miniconjou had tried many times to kill the son of Runs with Wind. She knew they might continue to hunt him down—and as his wife, her own life would be in danger too. Yet though it scared her, she accepted her fate. The past had set her on the path that had led to this marriage between her and Swift Foot. And the fact that the Miniconjou were willing to talk peace reassured her. Deep in her heart, she had a goal: peace would be achieved, and she would have a hand in it.

Staring out across the shallow stream, Small Bird watched leaves from the tree at her back drift down to the water and float away. Bits of dried grass in sparse patches between boulders on the other bank waved gracefully; and upstream, several small toddlers played in the water, their mothers keeping close watch over them. Yet the peaceful scene did not put Small Bird at ease. Lone Warrior's words were very troubling.

How could she convince him that it was far too late to change her mind? Her brother, and many of their tribe, had been against the marriage and the joining of these two Hunkpapa tribes from the beginning; it put them all at war with the Miniconjou.

Lone Warrior had even tried to talk her father into refusing the marriage offer. But deep in her heart, Small Bird had known this was her future. She'd turned down many suitors before Swift Foot, sure in her belief that one day her life would merge with his. And now it would—no matter the consequences.

The welfare of her people weighed heavily

on her shoulders. Small Bird's emotions whirled, leaving her confused and even a bit frightened. Responsibility could be scary. Sometimes she longed for ignorance.

Caught in the turbulence of the past like a rock or twig sucked up in a whirlwind, she pushed away from the supporting strength of the cottonwood tree at her back. Blinking against the reflected brightness of the sun on the water's surface, she allowed her sight to blur. The sharpness of the scene softened. Colors and hues merged as the stream turned silvery-white, framed with swirls of green, brown, and blue.

Come to me, she commanded. Knowledge came to her in many forms. Thoughts. Feelings. Sometimes dreams. As knowledge of this fate had.

Slowly the brown blur took on the shape of a young boy with black hair. He wore a big grin as he waved at her. The scene soothed her. This child—her child, hers and Swift Foot's—represented the future and gave her the faith she needed to believe she *had* a future. One shared with a great warrior: the warrior who'd saved her life at the age of three.

The image of the boy faded at the sound of Lone Warrior's angry voice. "This is not the time to let your mind cloud with silly dreams." Small Bird's brother glared down at her.

14

Small Bird didn't bother to tell him that what he called her "silly dreams" were visions that often spoke of the future or explained the present. She'd kept her talents mostly to herself, speaking of them only to her tribe's medicine man and her father. It was this dream of the little boy combined with her past connection to Swift Foot that had ensured her choice of husband.

Swift Foot's uncle, the old chief, and Wind Dancer, Swift Foot's tribe's young shaman, knew of her abilities as well—but she had asked them not to reveal the truth to others. She had no desire to become *winyan waken*, a tribe's holy woman. Her role lay in becoming a wife and bearing a child. *This child.*

Small Bird waited patiently for her brother to leave. Nothing he said would change the course of her future. Sighing, she put her hand on his shoulder. When it came right down to it, she really didn't have a choice in the matter. Knowing this was her destiny didn't make it easy to accept, but her brother's continual arguments made it worse.

"I must do this," she said softly.

"Then you are a fool." Lone Warrior grabbed her by the upper arms and held her firmly. "Like that small bird the eagle snagged in his sharp talons, you will be taken by Swift Foot's enemies." He released her but held her gaze. "*Wambli* warns of death. If you go through with this foolish marriage, you will

15

die." Once more, bitterness filled his voice.

Trembling beneath the heat and conviction of her brother's words, Small Bird turned away. She hated the weakness and fear his prediction elicited, yet all she could do was hold on to that bit of hope the dream-child brought her. By this time tomorrow, she'd be Swift Foot's wife.

Lone Warrior forced her to face him. "Have you forgotten that you nearly lost your life because of this man you seek to marry?" His voice vibrated with anger.

Memories intruded, blurring everything around her, flashes of remembered senses:

The screams.

The pounding of her heart, which matched the pounding of the horses' hooves carrying the enemy toward her hiding spot.

The rumble of the ground beneath her chest, the terror of being alone.

The acrid smell of smoke mingling with screams that had seemed to last a lifetime.

She'd been so young. She hadn't understood death, but she'd been sensitive to the grief around her. And confused. She remembered how scared she'd been in the days following the attack, when women slashed their hair short and cut their own flesh. She shuddered, the vision of a woman chopping off the tips of her own fingers haunting her.

Small Bird drew a deep breath and forced the nightmare away. She had to make Lone

Warrior understand. Though he was not a chief, the warriors of their clan of Hunkpapa looked to him for leadership. If he refused to give his allegiance to Swift Foot, who was to become her tribe's new chief when she married him, then the rest of the warriors would also withhold loyalty, which would only cause tension and strife.

Sliding her arms free of his grip, Small Bird reached out and took his hands in hers. "I have not forgotten that day. I will never forget. So many died. . . ." Her voice broke.

Lone Warrior jumped in. "Do you not care that you may meet the same end?"

Small Bird closed her eyes, her grip tightening on his hands. "You know I care," she whispered.

"Then I will speak to our father. I will tell him about the appearance of *Wambli*. He will agree that it is a sign." Lone Warrior turned to leave.

Small Bird grabbed his arm. She loved her brother, hated to see him so worried, but could not allow him to interfere. "No. Do not. No more fights. They will not change what will be." She tightened her hold on his arm to prevent him from leaving.

For long moments, brother and sister stared at each other. Finally, Lone Warrior inclined his head. "This does not make me happy, but I will respect your decision."

Relieved, Small Bird glanced down at the

ground to show respect. "Thank you, my brother."

Shouts to her right brought her head up. A group of five exuberant boys ran past, forcing her to step back. Smiling sadly, she longed for the carefree days of childhood.

The boys skidded to a stop when a woman appeared from around a huge boulder. Leaning heavily on a thick stick, she hobbled over the rocky ground. She wore a long shapeless dress with no decoration. Not even a simple row of colorful quilling adorned the yoke. No row of swinging fringe had been added to soften the plainness of her garment. A long length of softened deerskin covered her head and hid her face. In her free hand she clutched the edges of a wide strip of leather that encircled twigs and sticks.

After a moment's hesitation, three of the boys ran in circles around the old woman, taunting her. One youngster picked up a rock. "Show us your face, old woman," he shouted. "Show us your face."

Small Bird gasped at the rude display of the boys—they were from her tribe. The two from Swift Foot's were silently backing away from their new friends. Ashamed of the children's behavior, Small Bird rushed forward. Lone Warrior followed.

"Enough!" she said. Engrossed in their cruel game, the boys didn't hear. Without warning, one leaped forward and snatched the woman's head covering away.

Startled, the woman whirled and tried to take it back. Her crutch fell from her hand and she lost her balance. Her lame foot buckled beneath her and she fell with a cry. Staring down at the woman, the three boys froze in horror.

"*Anog-Ite!*"

"*Anog-Ite!*"

"Double-Faced Woman!"

Small Bird held her breath, her heart beating fast. Anog-Ite was a legend. She had been a very beautiful and vain woman who had married *Tate*, the Wind, and borne him four sons: the four winds. As time passed, she'd become more and more conscious of her beauty, and devoted less time to the welfare of her children.

Enamored by her face, Sun invited the wife of Tate to take the seat beside him at the feast of the Gods. *Ite* took the seat, upsurping the place of a goddess: Sun's wife, Moon.

Angered, *Skan*, the Great All-Powerful Spirit, decreed that Moon would no longer be Sun's companion. That was his punishment. But condemned for her vanity, ambition and negligence, *Ite's* punishment was harsher. She was banished to the world to live without friends—and with only half of her beauty. The other half of her face became so horribly

19

ugly that the sight of her terrified any who looked upon her.

The screams of the small boys brushing against the woman here, the fallen crone, shook Small Bird from her glazed horror. Double-Faced Woman was only a myth. Gazing down at the fallen woman as she turned her head to the side. Small Bird was caught by wonder. She'd always thought her cousin Moon Fire to be the most beautiful woman alive, but this "crone's" face held an ethereal beauty she'd never before seen. Small Bird heard a gasp from her brother.

Turning, she saw his jaw had dropped. He stared at the woman as if unable to believe what was before him. Rolling her eyes, Small Bird returned her attention to the shaking beauty on the ground. Compassion won out over Superstition. She bent down.

Are you hurt?" she asked. She reached out to take the woman by the arm and help her up.

Startled, the woman pulled back and tried to scoot away. "No! You must not touch me!" She cried out as a sharp rock cut her palm. Small Bird frowned. The backs of the woman's hands were scarred, and she gave a hiss of pain.

Small Bird couldn't help her own escaping gasp of horror. While one half of the woman's face was a study in perfection, the other had been ravaged by scars and was grotesquely misshapen. The woman rolled, using her hands to hide her face.

Lone Warrior stumbled back. *"Anog-Ite,"* he whispered.

Frozen in place, Small Bird stared down at the woman. All background noise faded. A sick feeling crept through her.

All of her people dreaded the spirit of the Double-Faced Woman. She was very cunning, and she loved to frighten women who were with child to give them pains. She lured hunters away with her beautiful face, then frightened them senseless with her horrid half. And worst of all, if a woman dreamed of *Anog-Ite,* she became a Double-Woman Dreamer—ugly and scarred and a curse herself.

Lone Warrior pulled Small Bird away. "We must go. Now."

Realizing she was still gaping at the cowering *Anog-Ite,* Small Bird slowly rose. As she did, her gaze fell on the woman's leg. Long scars and puckered skin marred the shapely limb.

Suddenly Small Bird knew who this was. "Willow Song," she murmured, staring down at Swift Foot's cousin. Everyone knew of the terrible injuries the girl had suffered the day her mother had been clubbed to death, how she herself had been close to death for many months. But Small Bird had believed the stories of her mutilation to be gross exaggeration. It seemed they weren't. She reached down to offer comfort and reassurance to the woman.

Lone Warrior gripped her harder, stopping her gesture. "Do not touch her. You will be cursed."

Small Bird shook him off. "No," she said softly. "This is Willow Song, cousin to Swift Foot." She glanced up at her brother and saw the understanding dawning in his eyes.

Small Bird called out in a gentle voice, "Willow Song?"

"Please leave," the young woman said, her voice muffled by her hands.

"No. I am not afraid." And she wasn't. This was not a Double-Woman Dreamer. Willow Song had received her injuries and scars in the same attack in which Swift Foot had saved Small Bird's life.

Compassion urged her to wrap her arms around the young woman. "Come, Willow Song. We will help you up." When Lone Warrior continued to stand and stare at the distraught woman, Small Bird glared at him. He didn't notice. His gaze remained on Willow Song, who'd hesitantly lowered one hand. The other remained to shield her scarred face.

Small Bird helped Willow Song to her feet. "Thank you," the woman said.

To Small Bird's surprise, Willow Song's voice reflected the beauty of her perfect profile; it was soft, melodious and clear. Lone Warrior's gaze remained fixed on Swift Foot's cousin as if he were in a trance.

Kicking a large stone, she aimed it at his shin. He yelped, then glared at her. She motioned with her eyes for him to come to Willow Song's other side. "We will help you to your tipi," she suggested. Her voice brooked no argument—from either Willow Song or her brother.

Lone Warrior looked ill at ease, and Willow Song looked frightened as the brave approached her mutilated and ugly side.

"No!" Her voice rose. "Do not touch me."

"What is going on here?"

Small Bird and Lone Warrior whirled. Kills Many Crows, Willow Song's brother, approached at a run.

Lone Warrior stepped forward and quickly explained all that had happened.

Kills Many Crows narrowed his eyes. "The behavior of those boys is unacceptable."

"Agreed. I will deal with them," Lone Warrior promised.

Kills Many Crows slashed at the air with his hand. "No. Our *chief* shall deal with them." The two braves glared at each another.

Willow Song reached out for her brother and clung to his arm. "They did not know," she said softly.

"It is no excuse," Kills Many Crows said.

Small Bird stepped forward. Behind Willow Song's brother, she noticed several women gathering. "You are right. There is no excuse. We were about to help your sister to her tipi."

Stepping in front of his sibling as if to protect her, Kills Many Crows scooped the young woman into his arms. "You and your people have done enough."

Stung by the man's insult, Small Bird fell back as Kills Many Crows strode past her. The crowd of collecting women scattered. Some ducked their heads, some ran, and others slunk off.

Lone Warrior glanced down at his sister with troubled eyes. "Do you need further proof of what your future with Swift Foot holds? His enemies do not care who they harm, but harm they shall. Think upon that." With that final shot, he stalked off.

Alone in the morning sunshine, Small Bird shivered. She was very much afraid that he was right. If the talks of peace failed, the Miniconjou would not hesitate to kill or maim her. She too might end up scarred like Willow Song.

Needing suddenly to be around her people to keep her worried thoughts at bay, Small Bird turned to leave. She froze when Swift Foot stepped out of the shadows.

"Your brother has no faith in his new chief," he said mockingly.

* * *

Swift Foot had heard most of the conversation between his soon-to-be wife and her brother, and it upset him. While he cared little what Small Bird personally thought, he could not allow any member of his tribe to doubt his abilities. Their faith in him made him an effective leader. His people accepted his abilities without question—and while there were less than a dozen warriors, young or old, in Small Bird's tribe, Swift Foot knew it didn't take much resentment or dissension to weaken or split a group. Regardless of how anyone felt, he was chief. And he'd earned the role by deed, sacrifice, and hard work.

Expecting Small Bird to appear uneasy at being caught discussing the wisdom of their coming marriage, Swift Foot was surprised when she boldly held his gaze. Her eyes were the color of fresh-churned earth, and wide, large, and innocent as those of a newborn fawn. They gave him no apology. Which was irritating. Folding his arms across his chest, he stared down at her.

Since her tribe's arrival more than a week ago, he'd endured the doubt of her people in silence. The two tribes were to join as one—as decreed by their two councils. But not all embraced the idea. His youth alone caused many to question his capability. And the lifelong war between him and his enemy made many doubt the wisdom of becoming embroiled.

Small Bird broke the tense silence between them. "It is no secret that your enemy hunts you. Many have died in the past." The proud tilt to the woman's head and shoulders dared him to deny what she said.

He tipped his head slightly, too, acknowledging the truth in her words. "It is a battle I seek to end, one my father began before my birth and one I will put to right before I die." The selfishness of Runs with Wind, who'd chosen to marry the white captive he loved instead of the woman he'd promised to wed, had shaped Swift Foot's future. Like the man who'd sired him, Swift Foot had been ordered to marry a woman chosen for him by the council. And like his father, Swift Foot, yearned to marry a white woman with hair of the sun. But unlike his father, Swift Foot had not given in to the needs of his heart. He'd put his people first. At great cost to his own happiness.

"My brother, along with many others, believes you are too young to lead so many." Small Bird watched him carefully.

Narrowing his eyes, Swift Foot answered, "If there is doubt regarding my ability to lead, then why did your elders agree to join tribes with me? Why did you agree to marry me?"

Small Bird's gaze slid from his. "Some choices are made despite knowing the risks." She moved away from him.

Shifting sideways in order to watch her,

Swift Foot searched her words and tone for bitterness or resentment. He found none. Yet in his own mind and heart, those two emotions swelled, growing daily, crushing the man within.

"You could have said no. My uncle would have accepted your refusal," he pursued. Then he could have married the woman of his heart, not his uncle's choice.

No, a small voice inside him declared. *Your uncle would have found another for you to wed.*

That, Swift Foot knew to be true. His future had been decided the moment his uncle decided to step down as chief. Before even. It came as no surprise to him, or to anyone else, that the council would choose him to succeed his uncle. Since the age of seven, he had been groomed for the position. But the honor came with a price: he had to take a wife of the council's choosing.

He hadn't hesitated in agreeing. Nothing was more important than restoring his family's honor and ensuring the safety of his people.

Until Emily—the white beauty who had captured his heart.

Over the summer, he'd learned the power of love, come to understand what had made his father risk everything, including his life, for a woman. Yet for Swift Foot, love had changed nothing. He had still returned here to marry.

Small Bird's soft voice drew him back from his dark thoughts. "It is an honor to marry a man held in such high esteem throughout our land."

"Honor, or lack of such, is why this marriage will take place." Fearing she'd see the anger and resentment within him, Swift Foot kept his gaze focused on a nearby group of youths practicing their skills with wooden knives. What was done was done. Except in his heart, hope still breathed through him, a small, living being struggling to survive. From the corner of his eye, he saw Small Bird turn to watch the boys.

"If you overheard the conversation I had with my brother, then you know I believe our joining must be. Do you not also believe that?" He heard genuine puzzlement in her voice.

"*No.*" A twinge in his gut accompanied the harshness of his voice. He heard her swift, sharp intake of air at his brutal honesty. Guilt rapped him smartly on the shoulder. It did no good to voice his true feelings on the matter of this marriage. But it was too late, had been before he'd even met Emily. His life had been set on its course the minute his uncle had decided to groom him to be the next chief.

Small Bird walked around to face him. "How can you not believe that our lives are meant to be joined as one? Our futures were decided the day you saved my life."

Wishing he hadn't stopped to talk to Small Bird, Swift Foot smiled without humor. "I have saved the lives of many. Should I take to wife every female I've helped?" If only it worked like that. Save a life. Marry. He thought of Emily, of how he'd saved her and lost his heart in the sweetness of her smile and the braveness of her spirit. But a future had not been possible between them.

Staring over Small Bird's shoulder so he didn't have to see the hurt in her eyes, he saw only a bleak, empty future. He felt hollow inside and could not see how his shared past with Small Bird meant that their future was tied together. If life was that simple, he'd never have fallen in love with another woman—especially a white one.

Small Bird swung her hands behind her back. Her chin went up, and her eyes flashed. "Was not the day you saved my life the one that led to your becoming the great warrior you are now? Or have you forgotten that day?"

Swift Foot lifted a brow. Forget the day he'd become a warrior? The fear that had lodged in his throat when he'd seen the enemy riding down a small, innocent child? Never. That day had set him upon his path to becoming everything he was: a man who'd somehow restore honor to his tribe, a man who'd never allow the enemy to kill another helpless member of his people. He kept at bay the terror and grief that day had produced.

His voice hardened. "I have not forgotten."

"Neither have I," Small Bird replied, hands on her hips. "You linked our lives when you acted with the courage of a warrior. It is right that we marry and join together to find a way to end this war between the Hunkpapa and Miniconjou. If you do not believe this to be so, then you are not so wise as I had hoped." She hugged her arms to her chest and turned her back on him.

He'd hurt her, something he'd not intended. Now he realized he'd been looking to pick a fight when he'd approached her, maybe to learn she truly didn't want the marriage. Swift Foot opened his mouth to apologize, but the gentle sway of her long, blue-black hair, and the way it brushed against the rounded curve of her buttocks, stopped him.

Small Bird was a petite woman with narrow shoulders and a tiny waist. With her back to him, her shoulders drawn in, she looked fragile. He couldn't help but compare her to Emily—who hadn't been much taller but was more generous in the curves of her body.

The two women were very different. One was of the gentlest dawn, the other the darkness of night. One held the rich brown of the earth in her eyes, the other the clear blue of the sky. Small Bird's hair was of blackest night, while Emily's was moon and stars. One had loved him and been willing to give up all she knew for him; this other, by her own admission felt bound by duty. Duty that bound him to her as well.

The difference between him and Small Bird was that she accepted that duty.

Clenching his jaw, Swift Foot slid his fingers up his arm and over the band of rabbit fur circling his biceps. Then his fingers trailed down to his bare chest where a rabbit's foot, dyed red, hung from a narrow strip of leather. Next they went to the narrow pouch that hung below. He gripped it tightly between his thumb and forefinger, feeling the thin strand of braided hair inside. He didn't need to take it out. All he had to do was look up into the sun to know its color. To be reminded of Emily.

"You are troubled."

Small Bird's soft voice jerked him out of his reverie. She stared up at him, a frown on her face. Then she cocked her head to the side. "No. You are sad."

Her pronouncement hung between them.

Longing to lash out, to destroy the truth of her words, he took a step back, angry with himself for allowing her to see more than he'd intended. He fought the urge to run. Far and fast. Away. Anywhere that he would not have to look upon this woman who'd soon be a daily reminder of the woman he'd lost, this woman who'd soon be his wife.

His wife.

The words sent bitterness raging through him. Once he'd viewed his upcoming marriage as a duty—nothing more, nothing less. He'd seen it as no different from any other responsibility expected of him. All his life he'd put his people first, sacrificed whatever they asked of him. Without complaint. Without resentment.

Until now. His time with the young white girl had changed everything—yet nothing had changed.

When he didn't respond to her question, Small Bird walked away. Another layer of guilt slid across his shoulders. *She* didn't deserve his anger. It wasn't *her* fault he'd changed since sealing their marriage contract.

Shaking his head, he spotted Kills Many Crows leaving Willow Song's tipi—and he remembered how Small Bird had tried to help his cousin. Fairness and gratitude made him call out after his soon-to-be wife. "Thank you for your kindness toward my cousin. Few speak to her. Most fear her." He struggled to keep the emotion from his voice. Buried amongst all his layers of guilt was the heavy weight of the disfigurement his cousin had suffered.

Obviously surprised, Small Bird turned.

"Your cousin is not to blame for what happened to her," she said quietly.

The weight grew heavier. "No. I am." His words rushed out unbidden, shocking him. Not once had he ever voiced his guilt—not to his uncle, his cousin, or even to their shaman.

Small Bird walked slowly back toward him. "No. That is not true. You are not to blame for the actions of the Miniconjou."

Swift Foot laughed, the sound harsh. "No? Your brother does not share that belief."

Small Bird brushed a strand of hair from her face and sighed. "My brother loves me. He worries."

Staring up at the wide expanse of clear blue sky above him, Swift Foot tried to roll the tension from his shoulders. Right then, his responsibilities felt too much. For so long he'd taken everything on his shoulders. After so many years of carrying it all, he felt tired and weary. His soul cried out for peace. His mind knew it would be denied. "Perhaps your brother is right to fear for you. Perhaps you should listen to him."

Surprised, Small Bird stared up at him. Then she shook her head. "It is too late. And remember, that's how all this started. When your father changed his mind and decided not to take the woman he'd agreed to wed, he started the war with the Miniconjou."

Swift Foot shrugged. "I am chief. I would not punish you or your people if you refused me." A small part of him hoped she would, even. Though he could never have Emily, at least if Small Bird changed her mind, he'd be able to live alone, without reminders of other loves.

Small Bird considered him for several moments. "Why do you not wish to join with me?"

"I have no desire to marry." *Liar*, a voice deep inside cried. He could not meet her eyes. Nor could he bear to stare up into the sky and see a daily reminder of what he'd lost.

"Do you fear for my life?" Small Bird kept her gaze on his.

Unsure if he admired her courage in confronting him or whether her refusal to back down and leave him in peace was infuriating, he spoke. "Your brother was right: marriage to me will put you and your people in danger should peace talks fall through. It is one thing for the enemy to come after me. But when they learn I have taken a wife, they will seek to kill you."

"I am not afraid. You are chief. You need someone to look after your tipi." Small Bird sounded uncertain.

Swift Foot argued, for if she chose to go through with marriage to him, he wanted her to have no false impressions. "As chief, I have many who see to my needs already." He paused for a heartbeat, then added, "*All* my needs."

Small Bird blushed when she spoke, but her voice shook with anger. "I *will* honor the spirits who saw reason to give a young boy the courage and skill to save a small girl. You may not wish me for a wife; you may even wish me to leave, but I will not. I belong here, at your side. You must accept that." The look she gave him dared him to renounce her.

They both knew he could not. With one final glare, Small Bird left.

Swift Foot watched her stalk away. Ashamed of his behavior yet desperate, he turned and followed the river away from camp. The farther he went from his people, the faster he walked until he was running.

The spirits had tested him. Just before he'd returned to his village to take up the position of chieftain, he'd gone on a quest to learn the answer to disturbing dreams he'd been having. He'd come across Emily. The white girl's parents had been killed in an Indian attack and she'd been alone. He'd saved her life. Immediately, he'd known she was the cause of his dreams. He'd been destined to find her.

The test was clear: his own mother had been white, had been a blue-eyed blonde. Like his father, Swift Foot had been drawn to the white woman's exotic coloring and beauty. But he'd believed he could deliver her to her people and return, unmoved, to take over as chief.

He'd been wrong. He'd delayed his return

by spending almost two full moons with Emily. Then had come the day he'd known he could not put off. He'd had to leave Emily behind and return to pick up his duties.

Unlike his father, Swift Foot had passed the test: he'd chosen duty over love, his people over his desires. He'd won. He'd lost. The words echoed in his brain with each pounding step.

Over hills, around jutting rock formations and across flat mesas, he ran until his legs could carry him no farther. Until his lungs burned. Falling to his knees, he leaned his head back and cried out, his hands above his head.

Staring up into the blue heavens hurt his eyes and heart; the color was the same deep hue of Emily's eyes. As he flicked his gaze to the solid rock of the bluff to his left, his breath caught in his throat. The pale tawny rocks there, some bleached nearly white, brought forth memories of long ribbons of hair flowing over his arms and shoulders and brushing across his chest. He gripped his armbands. They were soft like her flesh. So soft and silky.

Closing his eyes, Swift Foot struggled against the memories of the woman he feared he'd never forget or stop loving. How could he when he saw her in the sky and land around him?

"Concentrate on your duties," he whispered. He'd always walked his path alone, his future determined long ago. Nothing had ever been allowed to interfere with the needs of his people—not the breaking of his heart, and certainly not unhappiness at an unwanted marriage.

Nothing changed. Nothing ever would. Not until he atoned for the past.

Chapter Two

Kicking a stone from her path, Small Bird wound her way through cone-shaped tipis. A few of the women were setting up. As soon as she and her tribe had reached Swift Foot's, he'd ordered the camp moved. She understood his decision. A tribe on the move was less of a target for an enemy.

Staring around, the excitement of exploring and embracing a new land faded. Even the tales of courage and brave deeds painted on the many sun-bleached hides failed to impress or excite her.

Stopping behind a fairly large tipi, she glared at a scene depicting a crudely drawn warrior lying on his back with a gaping wound in his chest. Another figure stood over the fallen one, his war ax held high. Blue Elk had many such paintings. His wife, Moon Day, glanced over at Small Bird and grinned shyly. She was very proud of her man and his tipi—just as Small Bird had been excited to know she'd be sharing Swift Foot's. The outside of his dwelling would boast of his feats of skill, courage, and triumph over the enemy. Yet it seemed the inside would hold only unfulfilled dreams on her part, and resentment on his.

Small Bird resumed walking through camp, her mind on her conversation with her soon-to-be husband. She'd been so proud and eager to share a tipi with him. . . . She still would. Changing her mind was not an option—for either of them. Just a short while ago she'd been proud; she'd had reason to celebrate. But reality had destroyed that innocent pride and happiness. Her husband did not want this marriage.

Walking around two giggling girls playing with dolls, Small Bird fought her anger and humiliation. It didn't matter that no one else knew the truth. She knew.

Glancing toward the tipi of her parents, she saw her mother sitting amid a large group of laughing, chattering women. While Lone Warrior had reservations about the upcoming marriage, Small Bird's mother did not. The woman held court over the matronly group while proudly adding finishing touches to her daughter's wedding dress.

For months her mother had worked hard to plan this wedding. Even Small Bird had eagerly joined in by making the garments Swift Foot would wear tomorrow. She'd tanned the hides until they were soft and supple. Then she'd spent nearly two months quilling intricate designs befitting a renowned warrior. She'd painstakingly cut fringe and used large glass beads her father had gotten in trade from trappers. She'd also made matching moccasins, all to prove to her husband that her womanly skills were equal to his warrior's ability, to please him, and to make him as proud of her as she was of him.

Now she wondered if she'd done all for naught. A man who didn't want a wife would not think much of the time, work, or effort she put into his clothing.

Small Bird dodged two small, naked boys who ran around a tipi. One nearly smacked into her. She caught him, steadied him, then ruffled his black, shiny head. She didn't know everyone's names yet, or even which family each child belonged to, but it didn't matter. She loved Swift Foot's people—the children especially. "*Hau,*" she greeted. They smiled shyly in return.

Twisting a bit, she opened one of three small pouches hanging from the braided belt tied around her waist. When she pulled out two small pieces of root from the *tipsila* plant, the boys eagerly accepted the treat.

A brown dog nosed close, looking hopefully up at Small Bird. Laughing softly, she stroked its sleek head. *"Le tuwa ta sunka he?"*

The same boy who'd run into her puffed out his narrow chest. *"Mitawa!"* *Mine*, he said, answering her question as to whom the dog belonged.

"She is a fine dog." Small Bird eyed the beast's distended belly. She hoped the animal would not give birth before the wedding. By many of her tribe, boiled pups were considered not only good but perfect dishes for special occasions. She herself had avoided the delicacy.

The boys both streaked off, the dog waddling behind them.

Watching them, Small Bird sighed. Despite her reservations, this morning she'd been just as pleased, happy, and excited for her future. And she'd been under the misconception that Swift Foot felt the same way.

I believe our joining is meant to be. Do you not also? When she'd posed that question to him, she'd never imagined that he'd disagree. And it wasn't just because he'd saved her life long ago. As he'd said, he'd saved many lives over the years. But in saving Small Bird's life, he'd set himself apart. His actions hadn't been spurred by selfish motivations like pride or protection of property. He'd acted to save the child of another tribe—at the risk of his own life! His action had been an act of undiluted bravery, the mark of a true warrior. He'd put himself in jeopardy to save her. Swift Foot had first proved himself as the worthy warrior and chief he was today because of her—and his actions on that day had changed not only his life but hers.

It hurt to learn that he didn't recognize that. It hurt worse that he didn't want her for a wife.

Glancing around, she bit her lower lip. Now what? How was she supposed to act? To feel? What would happen after the ceremony tomorrow? Surely he'd at least want her the way a man wanted a woman. Or would he? She recalled his words: *As chief, I have many who see to my needs already. All my needs.*

Embarrassed heat rose in her cheeks. A lump grew in the back of her throat. Blinking rapidly to keep the tears at bay, she dug her fingernails into her palms and began to walk. She'd made a fool of herself. It hadn't mattered that her marriage was an arranged one rather than a love match. Love, she'd figured, would come later, as it did for most. At least on his part. Love on her part wouldn't take long. To be honest, she figured she'd been secretly in love with him all her life.

She stared at the unfamiliar landscape, trying to find something comforting amid all the changes of the last couple of weeks. She and her tribe had left their homeland to travel to

Swift Foot's. That, in itself, had been an enormous change.

The craggy mounds of a large rock formation at the opposite end of the Hunkpapa camp sat barren but for a few sparse trees and brush. It jutted proudly from the earth, the burnt grassland creeping up its sides. Small stands of dwarfed and dried-looking trees defiantly encircled the hillock, along with scattered scraggly bushes. She headed there.

One of its mounds rose to form a sharp peak, reminding Small Bird of her people's tipis. The others in the formation appeared to be gentler. The first struck her as incredibly beautiful, a study in opposites with its sharply carved top and pale brown sides cut as if by a keen-bladed knife or ax.

Each mound sat distinctly apart, yet all were joined at their base by smaller rocks and hardened earth. They were fascinating. Until arriving in this strange land, Small Bird had known only gently rolling prairie and the dark, thick forests of the *Paha Sapa*.

Swift Foot's world was different. It was filled with such bare mounds of earth as these, along with deep, dry gullies and flat-topped mountains. Yet the starkness of his world drew her. Its beauty lay in the changing landscape and contrasting colors of green, pale brown, white and gray. Already she loved this harsh land she would soon call her own. She always would.

Two young warriors walked past, spurring her onward. She began to climb the hillock, the question in her mind whether Swift Foot would come to realize she belonged here. If he didn't, what then?

One thing was clear: she would not change her mind. Pride demanded she forget that he'd appeared to want her to do just that. Regardless of her own feelings on the matter, she'd never do anything to bring shame to her father, mother, or brother, such as breaking an engagement.

"What a way to start a marriage," she muttered.

Brushing her hair clear of her face, Small Bird let out a frustrated breath. She reached the top of a rise and stopped. Turning, she carefully studied the large Hunkpapa camp of more than thirty tipis below. Her tribe and Swift Foot's had merged effortlessly and with almost no animosity. The positions of the new families had been decided upon by the elders: those of great importance camped on the eastern side of the camp, or horn. Her own parents commanded the southeastern position there, which would allow mother and daughter to be close to each other once she and Swift Foot wed and placed their tipi at the northeastern entrance of the village.

Surveying the village, Small Bird saw a short distance away a younger group of women surrounded by small children. Strips of antelope and buffalo hung drying on racks nearby, while cook fires steamed with chunks of meat, *tipsila*, wild onion, and greens. Nuts, and dried and fresh berries sat on squares of rawhide there, inviting anyone hungry to snack. Tonight, as they had during the last week, the two tribes would eat as one.

Moving down the hill, Small Bird avoided the group of women. Her conversation with Swift Foot was still ringing in her ears, and her heart was heavy with disappointment; she wasn't sure she could act the happy bride. Forcing a smile to her lips when an elderly woman emerged from a tipi and greeted her, Small Bird let her expression die as soon as there was no one to see the false gaiety.

Needing to be with people she knew and loved, she made her way to where three of her cousins sat. At her approach Makatah and Shy Mouse, daughters of her mother's sister, smiled and motioned for her to sit between them. Moon Fire, her cousin from another of her mother's sisters, ignored her. Close in age, the four girls had grown up together.

Small Bird lowered herself to the ground and folded her legs to the side. She tried to relax and find comfort in the rhythmic scrape as her cousins used rounded stones to grind chokecherries into a fine paste.

"You look sad, cousin." Shy Mouse, the youngest among them, eyed her with concern.

Small Bird reached out and took a berry from the pouch of water in which they sat softening before being ground. What would her cousins say if she told them that Swift Foot didn't want her for a wife, that like a young girl with stars in her eyes, she'd thought he'd chosen her because of a shared feeling about their past?

It would shock and upset Makatah and Shy Mouse. Moon Fire would undoubtedly gloat.

Makatah smiled with understanding. "She worries about sharing the marriage bed," she said. "Soon she will become a woman."

Small Bird made an expression of exasperation. That was the farthest thing from her mind at the moment.

"She has more to worry about than the marriage bed," Moon Fire said. She tossed down the rounded stone in her hand.

Makatah, the oldest, and the only one married, sent her cousin a sharp look. "And what would you know about sharing a mat with a man?"

Moon Fire shrugged, then glanced at Small Bird with secretive, sly eyes. "That is not your concern."

Hoping to head off angry words, Small Bird reached out to take the stone bowl from Makatah. "Let me do this," she said. "You look tired." She needed something to do before she drove herself crazy.

Makatah shook her head. "No. We prepare

your wedding feast. You are not to work."
Then the young woman smiled proudly and
patted the barely noticeable swell of her abdomen. "Soon your belly will grow round
with child, just as mine does."

Shy Mouse giggled and blushed. She'd just
celebrated becoming a woman, and spent
much of her time gazing at single warriors,
seeking her future mate.

Moon Fire shook her mane of shiny black
hair over her shoulder, then stood, glaring
down at them. "You are fools. Our cousin will
be dead long before Swift Foot's seed can
grow."

Shocked, Small Bird glared at Moon Fire.
For weeks the girl had been in a foul mood.
Anything to do with the wedding caused her
to get angry, sulk, or grow petulant.

"Why do you seek to cause trouble, Moon
Fire?" Shy Mouse asked.

"She is jealous,"—Makatah dismissed the
question with a wave of her hand—"that she
has no warrior courting her."

Moon Fire laughed, but the sound came
out as a harsh bark. "That is what you think.
Many brave warriors wish to court me." Her
mouth turned hard, ruining the soft fullness
of her lips.

Small Bird reached out and picked up
Moon Fire's abandoned stone bowl. Just what
she needed: Moon Fire in another of her
moods. At sixteen, the same age as Small

Bird, her cousin was turning vain, greedy, and self-centered—and lately she was becoming intolerable. "Go elsewhere if you seek to cause strife, cousin," she said.

Once again Moon Fire tossed her long, silky hair over her shoulder. "You are a fool to marry Swift Foot." She bent down, her eyes burning with malice. "They will come—the warriors of Hawk Eyes—and they will kill your husband. And they will kill you to prevent you from giving birth to the grandchild of Runs with Wind."

Makatah and Shy Mouse gasped as Moon Fire spoke the name of the dead aloud. Small Bird glared at the girl for her disrespect and insensitivity. No one needed reminding that Swift Foot's parents had been killed shortly after his birth. Least of all her.

Glancing around the sheltered area in which they camped, Small Bird felt relieved that no one else had heard. Any dishonor Moon Fire brought to herself, she would also bring to the rest of her people. The actions of the young boys of her clan toward Willow Song earlier had been shameful enough.

Her gaze swept the large camp, and Small Bird couldn't help the wave of relief that slid through her at the many guards standing watch. Not young, inexperienced braves, these were hardened, trained warriors. Some had even positioned themselves upon the mounds of rock where they had a clear view for miles around the camp. No one would be able to attack without their being alerted.

"Swift Foot's warriors are many now," she said. "We will be safe. Safer than if we were alone in our few numbers." The marriage between her and Swift-Foot would join the two *tiyospayes*, or clans of the *Hunkpapa*. The harsh winter had taken the lives of many of Small Bird's tribe, including their last chief, Moon Fire's father. With so few warriors, they were vulnerable to their enemies. But all that would change.

Moon Fire laughed harshly. "The tribe of Swift Foot will face more than harsh winters. And they do not always succeed in protecting their women and children," she reminded Small Bird cruelly. "Have you forgotten how Swift Foot lost his aunt?"

"Enough," Makatah ordered. "This is a happy time. Do not ruin it with your mean-spiritedness."

Standing tall, Moon Fire glared at her. "You call the truth mean-spiritedness? You are fools if you believe that there will be an easy peace. This war will not end until all the spawn of Runs with Wind are dead!" She pointed to Small Bird. "If you marry Swift Foot, you will bring death to our people."

A heavy silence fell. Small Bird held herself proudly. "I do not let my people down," she said, forcing confidence into her voice. "This is what *must* be." Even at the cost of her own happiness. Even if she could no longer count on her own foolish dreams and desires—like one day seeing love grow in her husband's eyes. This *was* what was best for the tribe. She knew that.

Moon Fire backed away. "You are a fool," she said, then stalked off.

Small Bird closed her eyes and fought down fear of the future. Was her cousin right? Was she condemning her people to death? Was she blindly following an instinct that would mislead her? Doubts flooded in.

The blurry image of that nightmarish day in the past came back to her: the horse of the enemy bearing down as she clung to the young Swift Foot. Running. That scene haunted her dreams still. Though she'd been young, she'd known death rode after her. With her arms wrapped around Swift Foot's neck, and her legs tight around his waist, she'd watched in terror as the enemy gained on them, coming so close—she still saw the warrior's features twisted in anger. His hatred had been so great. The Miniconjou warrior had been killed by Swift Foot's uncle, but his image was forever burned in her memory.

Yet as horrible as that image was, what had also stayed with Small Bird year after year was the way Swift Foot had comforted her afterward. For two weeks she'd followed him everywhere, as if he'd become her big brother that day. He'd ignored the surprise of his peers. During that confusing time of laying the dead to rest, and those days of wailing and lamenting, Swift Foot had taken the time to hold and reassure her—something remarkably mature for a boy his age. Which in part had led to her belief that he'd known of the importance of that day to their future. Since then, she'd seen him only at the end of summers, when hundreds of tribes came together for the Sun Dance. But she dreamed of him, and of the day when he would come to claim her.

Foolishly, it seemed. So what now? Canceling the wedding was not an option, yet going into a marriage with a man who clearly did not want her didn't hold much appeal either.

"Ignore her," Makatah said softly of Moon Fire, reaching out to touch Small Bird on the arm. "You know she seeks to cause trouble."

Small Bird gave her cousin a grateful smile. "I know." She shook off her doubts and fears of the future. Continuing to grind chokecherries into a fine powder, she reminded herself it was out of her hands. This was her destiny.

Sighing, she shifted until she sat back on her feet, her heels turned outward. It would have been different had Moon Fire truly acted out of concern for *her* safety or even the safety of the tribe, but Small Bird knew better. Her cousin's concern ran only to herself.

Needing reassurance from her family, her

best friends, Small Bird kept her eyes on her task as she said, "If I do not marry Swift Foot, I would be no better than Runs with Wind, Swift Foot's father. If he had done his duty and married the mother of Hawk Eyes, as promised, there would be no war between our tribes." Small Bird thought of Swift Foot's father, who'd chosen love over duty and, in so doing, has caused years of misery and bloodshed.

Makatah reached over and gripped Small Bird's hand until they locked gazes. "We cannot change the past. You of all people know that."

Small Bird forced a smile and a bright tone to her voice. "Forget it."

The subject was dropped. Silently Small Bird listened to her cousins discuss plans for the days of feasting to come. Absently she scanned the skies. The sight of several soaring eagles in the distance brought back her earlier fears: there was trouble ahead.

Willow Song settled herself on her thick bed of furs. Wincing at the bruise forming on her hip, she shifted, then let her breath out slowly. Beside her, Kills Many Crows watched anxiously.

"I will deal with those boys," he said, clenching his fists at his sides.

Reaching out to take her brother's tense hand, she stared at her own scarred flesh.

Kills Many Crow's was strong, brown, and unmarred beneath. "No. Do not," she said. "They did not know."

"Does it matter whether they knew or not? Had you been one of our elders, bent with age and fragile of bone, would you accept ignorance as an excuse for their shameful behavior?"

Willow Song closed her eyes. "They would not have treated one of our elders in that manner," she admitted softly.

This wasn't the first time children from a different tribe, not believing the rumors of her double face, had tried to taunt her into revealing herself. The children of her tribe knew the truth. They steered clear of her.

"They are just children," she murmured, fighting back tears. She loved children, ached to someday hold her own in her arms—but knew she'd never know that joy. Nor could she gain any comfort from cuddling another woman's child. No one allowed her anywhere near their babies.

Kills Many Crows stood. He didn't look appeased. "I shall bring you fresh meat after the hunt." He paused, the muscles in his jaw taut. "And more wood for your fire."

Willow Song gave him a grateful look. "Thank you, my brother."

Staring down at her, he shook his head. "I do not understand how you are not angry. Or *bitter*." His voice rose slightly.

"It does no good to place blame." She rubbed her arms. "It changes nothing."

"It is not right that you live alone. You are the daughter of our father, an honored and respected chief." His anger was apparent. "And is not right that our cousin becomes chief. It was his father who was responsible for the death of our mother, and for the grave injuries you suffered. Instead of rescuing you, he saved a child of another tribe. Instead of being blamed and shamed, he was made a warrior that day."

"I am grateful to be alive," Willow Song said.

"What kind of life is this?" Kills Many Crows waved his hands around him. "You, the daughter of a chief, cursed and forced to live alone, away from everyone like a *Winkte!*" His voice rose as with disdain for the men who dressed like women, acted like women, and shared their mats with other *Winktes*.

Willow Song held her tongue. They'd been over this ground before—especially since it became official that Swift Foot would take over the role of chief. She'd known that her brother held out hope all these years that their father and the council would pass the role on to him, but though he worked hard, he was not a good leader.

She'd never admit her feelings to him, though. It wasn't his fault that life had been

55

so hard on him. And Willow Song didn't know how she'd have ever survived without his help and devotion. Weary after her ordeal with the children of the other tribe, she lowered herself back to her furs. "I am tired. Go now. You have duties to do." She ran one hand over her eyes and rubbed at her aching temple, worrying that her brother's bitterness would lead him to do something rash.

Kills Many Crows hesitated.

"I will be fine," she reassured him tiredly. As much as she loved her brother, sometimes his overprotective nature and bitterness wore on her nerves.

His lips tightened, but he did not argue. "You rest." With that command, Kills Many Crows strode out the door, closing the flap behind him.

Left alone in her tipi's shadowy interior, Willow Song stared out the smoke hole to the treetops above. Her home was small but it usually suited her. Yet sometimes, like today, it felt more like a prison than a home. And in a way it was. Though she remained a member of her family and a member of the tribe and was afforded the same protection as the rest, essentially she was alone. She ate alone. Gathered firewood alone. Bathed alone. Spent each day, all day, alone. And she spent evenings and nights the same way.

Visits from her father were few and far between. And at no time was she allowed to set foot in the tipi he shared with her brother and cousin.

But Swift Foot came to see her often. She closed her eyes, a small smile lifting the corner of her mouth. Her cousin's visits were a treat to which she eagerly looked forward. Like her brother, Swift Foot brought food, water, and wood. But more important, he provided conversation filled with humor, serious talk of life, and simple everyday conversation. He offered Willow Song the chance to forget she was not like other women—and sometimes he even sought her insight. He made her feel useful and needed when he asked her opinion and took her answers seriously.

Sitting, she brushed her hair back from her face, her fingers caressing the smooth skin on one side, and the puckered, scarred flesh on the other. Frowning, she wondered if Swift Foot would continue to visit once he married.

Remembering Small Bird's kindness when she'd fallen, Willow Song prayed the girl would show the same nature by not preventing Swift Foot from coming to see her. Though Kills Many Crows took care of her, he worried constantly—which didn't allow either of them to relax. He refused to forget the past. Around him, Willow Song couldn't either. But with Swift Foot she could sometimes be happy.

Shifting her left leg from its odd angle before her, she rubbed the aching muscles of her thigh. Broken when the horse had run her down, it hadn't healed properly, and still pained her.

Outside the tipi, laughter sounded. For a moment self-pity took over. Willow Song wished she could join the upcoming festivities, but she dared not. Glancing over at a colorfully quilled parfleche, she knew she shouldn't even give Swift Foot's bride the gift she'd made. Even though Small Bird seemed kind and caring now, soon the girl might treat her as did the rest of the women—with a combination of fear and dismissal.

Willow Song scooted to the doorway and pulled the flap open a bit so she could at least watch the preparations for the celebration. Lifting her good knee, she rested her chin on her fisted hand. The other hand held the tipi flap partially open.

An approaching tall figure startled her. Lone Warrior. He carried her sling in one hand—filled. Shocked, she realized he'd picked up her fallen firewood. Holding her breath, she narrowed the slit in her door and watched as he neared. Tall, broad at the shoulders, and lean at the hips, he took her breath away.

A bittersweet smile crossed her lips. At seven, before her life-changing injury, she'd thought him the handsomest boy of their two tribes. At twenty, she still thought so. Especially after having seen him up close. A lump formed in her throat when she remembered that he'd been about to touch her in order to help her stand. He'd been the first male aside from her brother and cousin to touch her, and she'd panicked. She couldn't bear to have him see her deformities so close.

She panicked now when his gaze found hers through the opening. As if speared, she dropped the flap and held her breath.

"*Hau.*" The greeting came in a deep, vibrant voice.

Closing her eyes, Willow Song couldn't answer.

"Cousin to our chief. I have brought you your wood."

Tears leaked from the corners of her eyes. His kindness, mixed with the urge to see and talk to him, almost made her shove aside the flap. But she didn't. There came the sound of something being set just on the other side of her door.

"Your wood. I apologize once more for the behavior of our boys."

The noise of leaves crunching beneath feet faded as he left. Slowly, Willow Song pulled the flap open to see him disappear down the trail. From behind, the play of sunlight over the smooth expanse of his back, and the bunching of his thick thighs, spoke of his masculine form—as did the firm backside she glimpsed beneath his plain breechclout.

Unexpectedly, he turned and caught her gaze with his. He held it for a long moment, then continued away. Shaking, Willow Song closed her tipi's flap and put her forehead on her knee. His kindness meant nothing, she told herself. It was pity. Guilt for the way the boys of his tribe had treated her. Maybe curiosity. Nothing more.

Men feared her less than women did. Women avoided her as they dreaded dreaming of her and becoming a Double-Woman Dreamer themselves.

Willow Song's lips twisted. She was no dreamer—had never had such a vision—but Buffalo Medicine Man, the tribe's old shaman, had never believed her. He'd labeled her a dreamer. Now, though his son Wind Dancer, the new shaman, believed her, it was too late. Looks alone labeled her *Anog-Ite*.

Drying her eyes, Willow Song returned to her bed of furs. As she picked up a pair of moccasins she was making for her brother, her gaze fell upon a beautiful pouch with a small bird perched on the horn of a buffalo.

Getting back up, she took it into her hands and sat back down. Running her fingers over the quilled surface, she closed her eyes, tipping her head back. She opened her mouth, and her voice, soft as the summer breeze, lifted with the sweet melody of song. No one but *Tate*, the spirit of the wind, heard.

* * *

Swift Foot led the hunting party across dry grassland to where earlier, when he'd ridden out alone, he'd spotted a large herd of elk. At his side his closest friend, Night Thunder, kept pace. The rest of the hunting party followed respectfully behind.

"You seem troubled, my friend," the other man said.

Swift Foot glanced over at him. Keeping his voice low so that no one else heard, he replied, "There is much to be done. Many more mouths to feed now."

Giving him a sharp look, Night Thunder eased his paint pony close to Swift Foot's midnight-black gelding. "I know you well my friend. We are like brothers." He paused. "Small Bird will make a good wife to a powerful chief."

"More so than a white woman, you mean." Swift Foot's voice deepened, pitched so low he barely heard the words himself.

Night Thunder sighed. "If you seek the truth, then yes. And you know that in your heart, or you would not have given the white woman to another."

Remaining silent, Swift Foot knew there was nothing he could say; his friend spoke the truth. Aside from Wind Dancer, their shaman, Night Thunder was the only other person who knew about Emily. And he knew of her only because he'd known Swift Foot so well that Swift Foot had not been able to hide his pain or resentment. Had anyone else known of Emily and his feelings for the white woman, they'd have been starkly reminded of his father, and Swift Foot's role as leader would have been questioned.

"Do not worry, my friend. I will not do anything foolish," Swift Foot reassured his friend, glancing over at the other man.

Night Thunder lifted one brow. "I never thought otherwise. I seek only to ease your pain so that you may enter into your joining without bitterness. There is already too much of that." He shifted his gaze to the right, where several Hunkpapa warriors rode half a horse-length behind.

Swift Foot glanced over and spotted Kills Many Crows and Lone Warrior riding among the hunters. He grunted. Both resented his position as chief, and Lone Warrior had made his displeasure over the joining of the two tribes clear. "That, my friend, may be asking far too much. Of both others and myself."

Spurring his mount faster, Swift Foot headed for a low rolling hill. Silently and single-file, the hunting party urged their horses up the slope after him. At the top, they fanned out without instruction, lining the rise. To their left and right, rounded hillocks dotted the landscape. Some cut sharply from the earth; others rose like the spine of a buffalo; while others still, like the one they stood upon, rolled gently from one grassland to another.

Less than a hundred feet from them, the river continued on its sluggish way, winding and cutting a path through the rocky land. Here there were no trees to provide relief from the hot rays of the sun. The banks along the river varied from steep, rocky shale to patches of short green grass and clumps of shrub.

In the midst of the greenery, a large herd of *hehaka* grazed, rested, and took their fill of water in the heat of the afternoon. Opposite the herd, the bank rose sharply upward. Using hand signals, Swift Foot split the hunting party in half. The elk, once warned of the hunters' presence, would either run to the right or left; Swift Foot and the rest must make their kills before the elk managed to cross the river through the flatter land on either side of the adjacent rock wall.

Putting all thoughts of both the future and the past from him, Swift Foot squared his shoulders and lifted his chin. He had responsibilities now. Others to think of. Glancing at the herd, he adjusted a gauntlet made of stiff deerskin. Brown rabbit fur edged the cuffs.

Preparing, he pulled his bow from the case inside the quiver resting slightly behind him on his horse. After adjusting the quiver's shoulder loop so that it rested at his left side, he pulled out five arrows. Taking one in his right hand, he kept the others in his left with his bow, their points down and feathers up for quick retrieval.

Before giving the signal to attack, he offered a silent prayer for success. Each warrior did the same. Making a kill was not the joyful sport white men seemed to believe. The act of taking a life, even that of an animal, was *Wakan*—mysterious, holy. A pipe was smoked before an organized hunt, and an offering given before eating. A good hunter relied not only on skill, strength, and organization, but also on the power obtained from the spirits.

Nocking his arrow so its blade ran from top to bottom—the same alignment as the rib cage of the animals he hunted—Swift Foot gave the command: *"Hoka he!"*

His warriors' horses rushed down the slope toward the herd. The silence of the afternoon was split with the cries of his men as they tried to confuse the elk. By the time he hit level ground, Swift Foot had already fired off three arrows in a high arc. Those three shafts were followed by two straight shots. All five arrows struck at the same time.

In seconds it was over. Several elk were down. The rest of the herd split in two, fleeing so rapidly the animals appeared a brown blur flowing across either side of the rocky bank, jumping across the river to rejoin as one brown mass far from the reach of the hunting party.

Swift Foot reined up. His horse, Kastaka, displayed displeasure at being forced to halt by crow hopping, tossing his head, and snorting.

"Later, my friend," Swift Foot said, patting the horse on the side of his neck. "You have more work to do this day."

A quick count of a half dozen fallen elk confirmed that the hunt had been a success. Moving among the beasts, the warriors checked the arrows imbedded in each to see who'd made the kill; the meat, hide, antlers, and all other parts of each animal belonged to that hunter.

Pleased to find that two of his arrows had found their mark, Swift Foot called over a warrior who had not made a kill. "I give you first choice, Matoluta."

The man nodded solemnly and chose the smaller of the two animals. "My wife will be pleased," he said.

Swift Foot knew that Small Bird's cousin, Makatah, was with child. By giving her husband enough meat not only to feed his family, but his wife's, he'd shown selflessness and generosity to the other tribe. And proven his skill to them.

In a short time, all the elk were loaded onto the backs of the warriors' horses. Night Thunder mounted at Swift Foot's side, the elk he'd killed tied behind him. Swift Foot's uncle had also made a kill, and Small Bird's brother had made two. There would be plenty of fresh meat for the wedding feast.

The hunt over, the warriors rode back to camp in loose formation. Lone Warrior rode past without acknowledging Swift Foot. Two other warriors of Lone Warrior's tribe did the same.

Night Thunder shook his head. "That one may give you trouble. He is not happy you are to marry his sister."

Swift Foot lifted a brow. "It is not his concern."

"The happiness of a sister is always of importance to a brother, my son," Charging Bull, Swift Foot's uncle, said, riding up beside them.

Swift Foot kept his gaze trained on the horizon and on the thin trails of smoke rising from his tribe's camp. Thinking of his cousin Willow Song, he gave his uncle a respectful nod. "My future wife will be taken care of. Lone Warrior has no need to worry. She will have food and a place to live in safety."

Frowning, Charging Bull gave him a sharp glance. "What about love?"

Swift Foot grimaced. "Love does not guarantee happiness, Uncle. Happiness did not last long for my parents, or even you."

Seeing the brief flash of pain cross his uncle's features, Swift Foot cursed his own anger and resentment. He had no desire to hurt the man. "I am sorry, Uncle. I have no right to talk to you in such a disrespectful manner."

Charging Bull grunted. Swift Foot kept his silence, hoping the subject would end. His uncle didn't know of Emily, he knew only that Swift Foot's feelings had changed toward this joining. Before going away for much of the summer, he'd been indifferent to the marriage. The council had ordered him to take a wife, and he'd complied. Simple.

At one time, no sacrifice had been too great for his people. But since meeting Emily on his journey and falling in love with her, he knew he was giving them the ultimate sacrifice: his life. And not physically, though he would gladly die honorably in battle to protect his people. He was sacrificing the life of his heart, his soul. For him, joy or happiness was not something he would ever again experience.

Kills Many Crows flanked his father and interrupted Swift Foot's inner battle. "Perhaps Lone Warrior fears you bring dishonor to his sister as your father brought dishonor to us. Perhaps he fears she will die as my mother died." The young man's voice was filled with resentment.

Charging Bull's head whipped around. He stopped his horse and glared at his son. "What is past is past."

Kills Many Crows and Swift Foot also came to a halt. "No, Father. The past will repeat itself. More will die. More will be maimed as my sister was. Lone Warrior has reason to be concerned. As do we all!"

Swift Foot interrupted: "Are we not talking with our enemy instead of fighting? Many Horns has come to us three times now to discuss peace." Swift Foot stared his cousin down. Progress *had* been made toward peace between the two tribes. "There have been no raids, no attacks since the *maka* turned green," he reminded Kills Many Crows.

"You are a fool. There will never be peace. Not as long as you walk upon the earth!"

"Enough," Charging Bull thundered. "You show disrespect not only to your brother, but to your chief."

Eyes filled with fury, Kills Many Crows slashed the air with his hand, startling all the horses. "It will never be enough, Father. The war will continue—the attacks and the deaths of innocent women and children." He paused and drew in a deep breath. "He is not my brother, yet you regard and treat him as if he were your son."

Furious with his cousin for his pettiness, Swift Foot tightened his hands on his reins, causing Kastaka to shift uneasily beneath him. Like water off the back of a bird, he ignored Kills Many Crows's denial of fraternity; his cousin had resented his presence among their family all his life. Instead he addressed the issue of peace.

"Am I not doing all I can to find the path of peace between our tribes?" he repeated.

"How can there be peace when you are the reason for the war? How can you lead our people when you are the one our enemy seeks to destroy!" Kills Many Crows's voice rang out, drawing the attention of every warrior within earshot. "Like your father, you will bring death to our people."

Chapter Three

Swift Foot clamped his jaw shut as Kills Many Crows whirled and rode away. Beside him, his uncle's shoulders slumped.

"My son has allowed grief to cloud his emotions," the man explained. Sadness and disappointment lined his voice.

Swift Foot remained silent. There was nothing else to add. His uncle had never held him responsible for either the death of his wife or the injuries to his only daughter.

"I do not know what to do for him," his uncle admitted, his face filled with defeat.

For the first time, Swift Foot noticed how old his uncle had become. The man's face shone with the look of oiled leather. Age had pulled the brown skin around his eyes and mouth downward, while wrinkles carved deep grooves down the center of each cheek, around his eyes, and across his forehead. His hair now had more white than gray. Even his sharp gaze had dulled with age. He was a proud man who'd seldom shown emotion, but now sadness clung to him. Without another word, the old chief dropped back as if ashamed to ride at the side of his brother's child. The side of his new leader.

Swift Foot drew in a deep breath. He vowed to avoid any more confrontations with Kills Many Crows within his uncle's hearing. Kills Many Crows was now his problem. As chief, he needed to have the trust and loyalty of all his warriors, yet he knew he'd never have those from his cousin. Too much resentment and hatred stood between them. And it didn't stem just from the war Runs with Wind had started.

Kills Many Crows hated Swift Foot because of the status his cousin had earned that he himself hadn't—and because Swift Foot's status had come on the day of the death of his mother and so many others. Before that day, Swift Foot had been Calf-Boy—just another boy in the tribe aspiring to become a great warrior. But at the age of seven, Swift Foot had achieved what many warriors to this day had not—including Kills Many Crows—counting coup by touching the enemy, causing harm to the enemy by touching him. In his cousin's eyes, Swift Foot had compounded his crime in the years following by becoming a great warrior and earning Charging Bull's respect and loyalty, and the title of chief—things that were due to him.

As the dead elk weighed down his horse, the weight of so many lives settled across Swift Foot's shoulders. Once more he found himself yearning for those few weeks during the summer when he'd been carefree and truly happy. For the first time since saving Small Bird's life, he'd felt responsible for only himself.

Of course, he had quickly taken on more responsibility—that of the life of a young white girl stranded in the wilderness after an Indian attack had killed her parents. But no one had any raised expectations. No one had expected him to train harder or ride to war with grown warriors. During those few blissful weeks with Emily, he'd been able to leave everything behind. For the first time since boyhood, he'd savored each day, each moment as it came—not worrying about being the best, but simply living. As the mounds of rock near his people's camp came closer, along with thin wisps of smoke carrying the scent of food, Swift Foot tried not to think of what could not be. But with the lingering sorrow of his uncle, the resentment of Small Bird's brother, and his own cousin's hatred, Swift Foot's inner spirit flagged. Starved, wounded, and desperate, he needed to re-member—to dream, if only for a moment. He closed his eyes, his horse needing no guid-ance from him to find his way back home.

The bright afternoon sunlight burned through Swift Foot's eyelids, lighting his in-ner mind. His gaze turned inward, seeking the dark, shadowy recesses of his heart, in-viting a petite figure to emerge from his mem-ory. Long hair the shade of a new sun framed her shoulders and fell over one breast. Her eyes, as bright a blue as the sky after a rain, smiled at him. She held out slim arms, beg-ging him to come to her, to bring her fully out into the light. Back into his life.

She danced around the edges of his heart and mind, carefree, filled with life and laugh-ter. He saw himself running to her, grabbing her, twirling her around. He saw the two of them falling to the ground, arms and legs tan-gled, lips merged as one, his body sliding into the slick warmth of hers. He heard her cry of pleasure, felt her trembling, heated warmth, and shook with fulfillment he'd never known. He reached for her, needing to hold her close, but the sound of high-spirited warriors in-truded. In the blink of an eye, she was gone.

Swift Foot's eyes flew open, and he cursed *Mato*, the spirit of the bear was in charge of love and hate, bravery and wounds, and many other powerful medicines—but he was also the patron of mischief.

He took a deep breath and struggled with the tide of emotion racing through him. Nothing was amusing about his current situation. Though he'd proven his bravery many times over, the elders still demanded that he marry before he'd be allowed to fully take over as chief. At twenty, he was the youngest chief his tribe had ever appointed.

Holding the exalted position of chief had meant everything to Swift Foot: it was the means for him to restore honor to his family. Thus, he'd agreed—having no idea what he'd have to give up.

Riding back into camp, Swift Foot guided Kastaka to the place where Small Bird sat with her cousins. Dismounting, he untied his kill and pulled it to the ground. Around him, cries of joy went up at the amount of fresh meat he and the others had brought. But for Swift Foot, there was no joy. Only duty. Without meeting Small Bird's eyes, he left. For him, there was only a broken heart and no hope of love or happiness.

Smoke-gray skies hid the dawning of the new day. Rough, jagged thunderclouds rose above moisture-laden air propelled by blustery wind. Kneeling at the bank of the stream with the other women and children, Small Bird ran a wet square of cloth over her skin to clean herself for the wedding. The water was far too shallow at this time of year to actually bathe. Warm and murky, some days it barely seemed to move at all.

A breath of cold air nipped at her. Small Bird's skin roughened with tiny bumps of raised flesh. Shivering, she glanced up into the dreary sky. The impending storm matched the confusion and anger in her heart. That the weather, which had been hot and dry for weeks, should suddenly turn, worried her. It was as if the elements were in tune with the confusion in her heart.

Or with her anger. All during the night she'd gone over her conversations with Swift Foot, examined each event leading up to his announcement that he would marry only because he had no choice.

This marriage was *meant to be*. She'd thought that Swift Foot believed it as she did, that he was the one who had sent his uncle to offer for her. True, she'd known his council had told him to marry, but she'd foolishly thought Swift Foot had chosen her because of their past.

Swift Foot's uncle had, in fact, along with a few of the council members who'd accompanied him to present the marriage offer, reminded Small Bird's father of that very thing. And their shaman, Wind Dancer, had spoken of their future. That was why, though her brother had wanted to refuse, she'd agreed. All her life she'd known that she and Swift Foot were to become as one—and she'd been eager and happy to fulfill her destiny.

Learning he did not share the same vision was a blow to not only her heart and pride, but to everything she was. It rocked her world and left her feeling like a fish landed by the swift swat of a bear's paw. Her heart squeezed painfully.

Rocking back on her heels, Small Bird stared pensively out at the flow of the land. Nothing had changed, yet everything felt different. Scanning the riverbank to her left and right, she focused on a group of women belonging to Swift Foot's clan. The wind whipped their laughter and the shrieks of their small children to her ears. She smiled.

She spotted her mother and cousins mingling there, as if they'd been a part of the tribe for years instead of a week. Sighing, Small Bird admitted that she was entirely at a loss. When her mother waved at her, she waved back, wishing she could confide her doubts to the woman. But speaking of her anger wouldn't change anything, for there was too much riding upon this marriage: the survival and continuation of her tribe, her aunts', uncles', and cousins' and friends' lives.

To back out now would destroy their future—not by war, but by the very nature of the world. Their tribe had suffered greatly over the last few years: warriors had left to find mates in other *tiyospayes*, as was the custom, but few new warriors had joined. Deaths due to illness, old age, and a harsh winter had left the clan vulnerable and without enough men to hunt or protect it. Allowing her people's fears or her own desires to get in the way of this union would be disastrous. There was only this solution.

Standing, Small Bird put her dress back on and decided to return to camp. There was no way out. This was to be her future. In spite of the anger and disappointment weighing her down, she knew this was truly the only hope for her tribe.

A small voice in her head whispered, *Then Swift Foot's feelings shouldn't matter to you.*

But they did.

The sound of feet running gave her pause. She turned just as Makatah raced up to her.

"Aren't you excited?" Makatah linked arms with her.

The girl looked so eager. It was on the tip of Small Bird's tongue to lie, to play the part of the happy bride, but right then she needed to confide in someone. "No," she said. Sliding her arm free, she reached out and grabbed her cousin by the hand and pulled her off the trail.

Makatah raised her brow at Small Bird's unexpected action, then smiled wisely. "You *are* afraid of mating with him," she guessed, a gleam of humor in her light brown eyes.

Small Bird rolled her eyes. Several days ago she'd certainly been nervous about becoming a man's wife, especially a man of great importance like Swift Foot. And yesterday—which already felt like a lifetime ago—she'd been as excited and eager to become a woman as any young bride-to-be. Today, the thought of giving herself to a man who didn't even want her left her depressed.

"He doesn't want this joining," she blurted, stopping. She couldn't meet her cousin's eyes.

Makatah touched her arm. "What are you talking about? He chose you."

Lifting her gaze, Small Bird couldn't hide her anger and sadness—didn't want to bear the burden alone. She needed advice, comfort, and support. "That's what I thought—what we all thought—but the truth is, he wants *no* wife."

"But the council came and said he had to have a wife, and he chose you," her cousin repeated.

Small Bird stared down at the ground. She kicked a small stone loose from the hard-packed soil. "He did not choose. They chose for him. Yesterday he told me. He had no say in the matter." She stared with moist eyes past her cousin. "Unlike me, he doesn't believe that the two of us have come full circle from a shared past to a shared future." The last was said in a soft whisper as tears clogged her throat.

Frowning, Makatah took Small Bird's hands in her own. "Still, you are the one who is to marry him." She smiled gently. "Look at me, cousin." When Small Bird complied, she continued, "I was not in love with Matoluta, and on our wedding night I was very afraid."

Small Bird felt a wistful tug in her heart at her cousin's soft smile and the love shining in her eyes. Right then, with all her heart, she wanted to see that same look in Swift Foot's. But she was very sure that was one wish she'd never have granted. "Matoluta loved you. He offered for you. He *wanted* to join with you."

Makatah's smile broadened. Her hand lowered to lovingly cup the gentle swell of her own abdomen. "Yes. And now I love him. As you love Swift Foot. He will grow to love you, cousin."

Small Bird bit the insides of her cheeks. Did she love him? She'd thought herself in love, but . . . How could a woman love a man she didn't know? Learning Swift Foot's true feelings had made her feel as though she'd been in love with dreams, not reality. "How can you love a man you don't know?" she asked.

"But you do know him. We all know him."

"No," Small Bird argued, shaking her head. Fear skittered up and down her arms. "We know *of* him. We know his courage. His greatness in battle. But none of us know *him*." Saying the words, she realized it was true. She least of all knew the man who would become her husband.

Yes, she'd always been attracted to Swift Foot. At the end of each summer when the Hunkpapa joined together for the Sun Dance and the last of the buffalo hunting, her eyes had eagerly sought him out. But the two of them hadn't conversed since she'd left childhood behind. Each year his greatness had grown along with his responsibilities.

Yet, she recalled many summers when he'd greeted her, treating her like a younger sister. He'd even taken time to speak to her or to give her a small gift despite the teasing of his friends. That had been long ago. Somewhere along the way, she'd grown too shy to approach him, and he'd become aloof. A stranger.

With sudden clarity, Small Bird saw that she'd foolishly convinced herself that she loved him, that he would offer marriage and love her in return. Or at the very least, that he would desire her for his wife.

Unfortunately, it hadn't taken but a few words to clear the stars from her eyes.

I have saved the lives of many. Should I take to wife all I've helped?

Small Bird felt her cheeks burn. *No,* she wanted to shout. *Just the one who set you upon your path, the one who will fight at your side for peace!* She shook her head. *Want the one who wants you.* From deep inside, the words burst from her heart. She wanted Swift Foot to love her. As if sensing Small Bird's inner turmoil, Makatah remained silent as they walked back to the ring of tipis.

Glancing up into the roiling clouds gathering over her head, Small Bird stopped. Fingers of cold threaded through her hair, tossing the drying strands around her shoulders.

"*Mahpiya* shows his displeasure by withholding good weather," she noted. As with the eagle, Small Bird knew this was another ill omen of the future. The spirit of the heavens, clouds, and sky heard invocations, and if he was pleased, he sent good weather. He was displeased. The question was, with whom: her, or Swift Foot? She shivered when the breeze swept over her arms and face.

Slipping an arm around Small Bird's shoulders, Makatah tugged her gently. "Come. Swift Foot will soon see that you are a good wife."

When they arrived at Small Bird's tipi, Shy Mouse ran toward them. "Hurry. We are waiting for you."

Small Bird allowed herself to be pulled inside, where her mother, her aunt, and her cousins and friends waited to dress her. But even as she smiled and laughed, a storm in her heart raged. As sure as she knew rain would soon pelt the earth, and that the Thunder Beings would make loud noise, she knew she'd fight for this marriage. Not even the bad weather, the eagle, or Swift Foot's displeasure could sway her from her conviction that the journey of her life had led her to this day. What she had to do was prove it to Swift Foot and make him believe.

And, she mentally added as hands tugged at her hair, make him love her.

Swift Foot brooded over the same dark horizon that Small Bird had noted. He'd angered the spirits. What had possessed him to confess to Small Bird his feelings? He'd never be able to tell her the reason he didn't wish to marry. He'd never be able to tell her about his love for Emily.

Guilt at his own selfish desires slid deeper into his heart. For the first time in his life, he rebelled against his duties. Not outwardly; but rebellion in one's heart and mind amounted to the same thing. The driving need to lead his people had always kept his path clear. He'd always done what he needed to do thoughtfully, deliberately, and with no emotion. Until now. Unfamiliar resentment threatened everything he'd striven to achieve.

Scenting rain in the air, he knew soon the Thunder Beings would light up the sky, toss their jagged bolts to the ground, and fill the air with bellows of rage. Around him, voices rose with excitement as water was fetched from the stream, but they were difficult to hear over the growing assault of the wind. Fires flickered, the flames dancing violently in a struggle to remain alive. Members of both tribes mingled as everyone prepared for the wedding of their chief, a chief who'd given his all for this day. For them.

There was nothing he could do to stop it.

Accept your fate.

Swift Foot grimaced, then turned on his heel and walked away from camp. He kept his head high, his eyes clear of emotion. He had agreed to this marriage, and would go through with it. Was that not acceptance? Was this not enough? He prayed for it to be so, for he feared it was all he had to give.

His lips twisted in a grimace. Though his mind had long accepted the inevitable, his heart still sought a way out like a rabbit trapped in its hole. His heart and soul longed for Emily and lamented as though grieving for the dead.

A cold whisper of air crawled across the back of his neck when the wind lifted his hair. Emily *was* dead to him.

Swift Foot stumbled. His heart pounded in denial. But it was the truth. He'd never see her again. Quickening his steps, he ran into the storm as if defying the elements. A droplet of rain hit his cheek: a tear falling from the heavens. Inside, his heart shed tears too.

Blinking against the wind and the downpour from the heavens, Swift Foot smiled with grim humor. It seemed only fitting that his day of marriage begin with the crashing of thunder. After all, violence between the Hunkpapa and Miniconjou had begun with the wedding of his father and mother. His marriage was just one more unhappiness.

Small Bird's cousin stared into the flames of the fire while the storm raged outside. Smoke flaps rattled and the wind bounced off the hide wall behind her. The dew cloth, the tipi's inner lining that kept cold, moist air from condensing inside it, was keeping her warm. A thick layer of old hides and furs placed on the ground around the fire and beneath the beds kept the floor dry.

Glancing furtively at the closed flap, she turned and lifted up the edge of her bed to reveal the base of the dew cloth. Tied two palm-lengths up the tipi poles, it left a lower edge that her mother had turned under. With the layer of furs on top of it, dust and drafts were kept out.

Using her fingers, she carefully peeled it back to the poles, searching the space beneath for a sign. She found nothing. No painted pebble. No notched stick. Nothing but sticky mud already forming from the rainstorm. Sighing with disappointment, Moon Fire fixed the lining and her bedding. Where was Many Horns? It had been more than fourteen moons since he'd come to her. The last time she'd seen him, he'd promised to find a way to stop the wedding of Small Bird and Swift Foot.

She paced. With all the places of concealment in this unfamiliar, hot, and hostile land, one warrior should be able to slip past the guards by keeping to ravines and following the river until he got close. Many Horns was more than cunning enough to come to her without being spotted. But Swift Foot moved his people often—seldom did they stay in the same place for more than a week or two.

Yet Many Horns was clever. He always found them. He always appeared with talks of peace, or slipped unspotted into the camp to be with her.

As they'd done the last time he'd come to visit, he would leave her a sign that he was near. Then all she had to do was get out of camp and wait for him to find her. Since that first time he'd come in peace, they'd been drawn to each other. She'd found ways to approach him.

Closing her eyes, Moon Fire remembered his bravado, his courage, and the boldness he'd shown in riding into their camp, risking his life. That had pleased her. His fine form doubly pleased her. He was a worthy warrior.

The second time he'd visited, he'd waited until everyone thought he'd left. He'd stayed nearby for more than a week, but no one had known. It had been the same the last time, except he had come to her *before* announcing his presence to the rest of the tribe.

Many Horns was sly. Clever. He'd never failed. And he'd promised to come to her again before the marriage took place. He had to stop it. Otherwise he and Moon Fire would not be able to marry. She tipped her head back.

"Where are you, Many Horns. Come before it is too late." Biting her lower lip, she resumed pacing. The fire snapped and the small tipi glowed with warmth despite the storm bursting all around. Frustrated, Moon Fire returned to her bed and threw herself onto its thick furs. With her chin resting on her fisted hands, she thought of the future.

Many Horns loved her. He wanted to marry her, and she him. But they'd never be allowed to marry. Not with him belonging to the Miniconjou tribe. Not with her tribe joining Swift Foot's. Once the two tribes merged, their enemies became hers.

"I knew we should have just run off," she muttered. Then both tribes would have had to recognize their right to be man and wife. Or they could have just run off alone and joined another tribe. But Many Horns refused to shame her.

Wait, he'd said. *Let me bring peace to our tribes.*

And if you cannot? she'd asked.

Then you will not have to worry about your

cousin's marriage to Swift Foot. It will not take place.

Restless, on edge, Moon Fire paced to the altar at the rear of the tipi, then back to her sleeping pallet, then to her younger sister's bed of furs, past the door and onto the side of the tipi where her parents slept. When she reached the other side of the altar, she retraced her steps.

She kicked at the furs of her bed in frustration. She'd tried once to speak of her interest in Many Horns. She'd said that perhaps by her marrying him, the two tribes could know peace. But her father had violently forbidden her to even think upon joining with the enemy. Many Horns was Miniconjou. She was Hunkpapa. *Your cousin's enemy is your enemy,* he'd reminded her.

She repeated his words, her voice low and bitter. It wasn't fair! Why should she be punished for something that had nothing to do with her or her family? Back and forth she paced. Where was he? He'd promised to come for her if he could not achieve peace between the tribes. Did this mean the Miniconjou planned to attack?

The thought chilled her, but only for a moment. Many Horns would protect her. He'd ride in and take her with him. He'd never allow anything to happen to her.

Going to the doorway, she peered out. All seemed quiet. There came no shouts from the warriors guarding the camp. Slapping the hide door closed, she kicked a fur to the side. Anger had risen to quash her disappointment. Let him come. Let the *enemy* come.

She felt no guilt for her traitorous wish. No one cared what she wanted. Besides, hadn't she tried to warn her foolish cousin? As for Swift Foot, it mattered not to her whether he lived or died. What made him and Small Bird more important than herself and Many Horns?

Her mother burst through the tipi flap, startling Moon Fire as they nearly collided. Dripping wet, Yellow Quail grabbed a length of softened deerskin, which she used to wipe the rain from her face. "Ah, so much to do before the wedding and the feast," she said.

Moon Fire returned to her bedding and sat, staring at the fire while her mother stripped down and began dressing in her finest garments.

"You did not come help ready your cousin, daughter," Yellow Quail said. Disapproval filled her voice.

Moon Fire shrugged. "My cousin had more than enough help." She plucked at the feathers she'd tied above her ear. She too had dressed her best—for Many Horns.

She still believed he would come. He had to! If he did not, her father would marry her to another. Every night some warrior came forward with a marriage offer. The single men of Swift Foot's tribe were many, and Moon Fire was smart enough to know her looks were more than pleasing to the eye.

Restless, she stood and returned to the door. People, young and old, hurried to the lodge on the other side of camp; with the rain, the ceremony would be held there. Their laughter, shouts, and the buzz of many conversations rivaled the noise of the Thunder Beings. Moon Fire closed her eyes, resting her forehead against the edge of the tipi.

Where are you, my love? You promised to stop this wedding, she thought.

Yellow Quail touched her shoulder. "Soon we will hold a wedding for you," her mother said, smiling gently. Her eyes were eager and proud. "There are many fine warriors in our new tribe. Already we have offers of many horses."

Moon Fire moved away from her mother. She clenched her hands tightly. She was growing to hate being reminded of her duty to marry. "There is no one here whom I wish to wed."

There was only one man she wanted, and she'd wait for him. With or without the approval of her parents—she didn't care.

Yellow Quail sighed. "Daughter, your sister has found a man she wishes to marry." She looked pleased. "Your father has accepted his offer. All that remains is you."

Waving her mother's concern aside, Moon

Fire turned away. "Let *her* marry then. I shall wait," she said.

Her mother's voice firmed. "You will marry first—as is your right and your duty. By the next full moon." She paused. "Your father has accepted a very generous offer for you."

"What?" Moon Fire whirled to face her mother. "He cannot!"

Yellow Quail went to the doorway and shoved open the flap. "It is done. We shall have two weddings. Two daughters to two brothers." Then she left.

Stunned, Moon Fire stood where she was. A crack of thunder across the heavens spurred her to run after.

Her mother had already joined a half dozen other women working beneath a shelter. Frantically, Moon Fire glanced around. The warmth of her tears mingled with the cold rain. Many Horns had to come. And when he did, she'd demand to go away with him. It was the only solution.

Chapter Four

As suddenly as it started, the storm abated. The elders sitting around a warm fire inside the lodge smiled at one another, then left the structure. "It is a sign," they told all whom they passed, a very good sign that the spirits were pleased with the marriage that would soon take place.

The wind carried the message from tipi to tipi. *Mahpiya* had heard the Hunkpapa and answered by giving the People pleasant weather—at least for a few hours, at least for the wedding.

Charging Bull left his tipi. He stopped to have a word with his nephew, who was grooming a horse right outside the doorway. "*Anpetu waste*. Good day. It is a good day, and right that the heavens smile down upon my son on it." He drew crisp, clean air into his chest. Time had narrowed that chest, but age had not stooped his shoulders.

Swift Foot stared into his uncle's wise gaze. No matter his emotions, he'd never do anything to hurt this man who'd raised him as his own. "Yes, *Ate*."

Ate. The title echoed in his head. It meant "uncle," on the father's side of the family, *but* it was also the same word for "father" and very fitting, for this man had been a father to him—the only father he'd known.

His uncle narrowed his eyes, suddenly serious. "Do not try to hide your true feelings, my son. This man knows you do not go into marriage with a happy heart."

Swift Foot didn't deny it. He chose his words carefully. "I will do what is best for our people."

Tipping his head back, Charging Bull gave a soft, low laugh that brought Swift Foot's horse's head closer for a rub. He obliged as he regarded his nephew. Taking his time, he finally replied, "Yes, my son. You have always put our people first." His gaze turned sad. "Even at the expense of your own happiness."

Startled, Swift Foot tried to hide his emotions. He hadn't mentioned Emily to his uncle, or falling in love and losing his heart. "I have family and friends. I am a feared warrior and will be a respected chief. Is that not enough to make any man happy?"

"Yes, you have all those things, and more." A wistful expression crossed Charging Bull's features. "But you also knew love. And lost it."

Swift Foot swallowed hard. He did not dare say anything, for he could not deny the truth. Nor could he admit that he'd nearly fallen into his father's footsteps—steps that would have led to dishonor and the loss of everything he'd worked hard to become and achieve.

His uncle spoke: "A man who has known love—and maybe even more so, a man who has had that love, his beloved, ripped from his life—stands a good chance of recognizing the shadow that dwells in others' hearts and soul. I see the pain you try to hide." Charging Bull gave Swift Foot a knowing look, then paused once more to gather his words. "I knew when you came back. You did not bring this woman with you, but she was there in your eyes. I wish things could be different. Had I known . . ."

Swift Foot sighed and glanced up into the sky. "You could have done nothing different. This love was not to be."

His uncle nodded. "Sometimes it is so. But you've known the deep joy of love, the completeness when two hearts join. You are a better man for it." Charging Bull's melancholy look faded. He drew himself up. "It is a gift. One that remains with us for the rest of our lives and will go with us to the spirit world."

"I hope that is true, Uncle," Swift Foot said. Realizing he'd spoken the telling words aloud, he shifted uneasily.

In an uncharacteristic display of affection, Charging Bull grabbed Swift Foot's shoulders with his hands and pulled him in for a crushing hug. Then he stepped back, his eyes moist. "My son. My *cinksi*," he whispered. "Son of my brother. He would be proud of you this day."

Hearing the words, Swift Foot felt regret. He knew very little of the man who'd given him life—or of the woman. But the anger and resentment he'd always felt toward his father faded. He now understood how his father could have chosen love over his duty to his tribe. He wanted to himself.

His uncle started to walk away, then turned back. "Give this woman you marry a chance. The pain of losing my wife was such that I chose not to marry another—and now I am a lonely old man. Do not be afraid to let someone new into your heart." And with those words, Charging Bull briskly strode off.

Swift Foot resumed his grooming of the mare. He examined his uncle's words. "I am not afraid," he said to the restless horse. "I cannot fear losing what I do not want."

With quick, efficient movements, he finished combing and cleaning the mud from the gray beast. Taking a pot of red paint, he drew a small bird on its rump, adding black slashes and yellow zigzags. Next he tied braids of dried sweet grass to the long mane, along with small puffs of eagle down. He left the tail loose and flowing, but added a thick pad of sewn-together rabbit furs onto the mare's back. Fur and claws dyed yellow, red, and black hung from each side. The horse's rawhide bridle, too, had been carefully lined with rabbit fur.

Taking hold of the lead rope, Swift Foot closed his eyes, praying for the strength to go through with the dictates of his elders. He reached up and fingered the tiny hide pouch that hung over his heart, rubbing the softened leather together and staring up into the sky. The clouds above him had parted slightly, allowing a thin sliver of blue to peep through.

Scanning the horizon, seeing the approach of another late-summer storm, Swift Foot knew that the bit of clear sky wouldn't last. Just like the love he'd known. In Emily's eyes, he'd found a ray of happiness—happiness that honor demanded he destroy. Forced to return to his tribe and his duties, Swift Foot had left his true love to be found by a trapper. She'd tried to run after Swift Foot, but like a shadow he'd slipped away.

He hadn't left, though. He'd waited. He'd watched over her as she screamed and cried for him to return. His own tears had fallen with hers. He'd remained nearby, hidden in the early dawn, until she was found by the other man, one he knew would care for her. Then he'd left to return home.

Each night he fell asleep remembering those weeks of bright, happy days with Emily. But when the night turned its darkest and loneliest, his dream turned to nightmare. Her screams haunted him. And he woke with guilt a large stone in his stomach.

Her pain had been his fault. When he first found her and saved her life, he had planned to return her to her own people. But after just one look, he hadn't been able to resist. He'd wanted her, and he'd selfishly kept her with him for most of the summer, knowing full well that he could not return to his tribe with her at his side. Not with his wedding to Small Bird already arranged. His breathing quickened. Just thinking of that final day added another arrow of guilt to the quiverful he carried lodged in his heart. It had been in his power to spare her the pain. He hadn't. His hands shook as he replaced his pot of paint in his pouch. Drawing a deep, steadying breath, he put his guilt and shame away too. Picking up the reins, he led the mare through camp. As he made the walk to Small Bird's tipi, children shouted and fell in step behind him. By the time he reached his destination, a crowd followed. Head high, shoulders back, he halted a respectful distance from the tipi of her parents. From inside he heard women giggling. Soon this whole ordeal would be over.

Give her a chance, his uncle had said. But the blinding truth was, Swift Foot himself didn't deserve a second chance—at happiness or love. He taken those gifts from another and destroyed them. He had no doubt he would pay for his selfish and cowardly behavior for the rest of his life.

Lone Warrior came forward, snapping him from his depressing thoughts. Neither man spoke, not even the traditional *Hau* said in greeting. Small Bird's brother finally broke the silence, speaking in low tones: "You marry my sister this day. She is no longer my responsibility but yours. Do not allow harm to befall her."

Swift Foot tipped his head back. "I am a warrior of name. Your sister will be taken care of. This day she becomes part of my family and tribe—as do you, and your mother and father." He met Lone Warrior's stare with a steady gaze of his own.

Finally the other man nodded. "I will hold you to this."

"As I hold myself responsible for the lives of every member of my tribe," Swift Foot pledged. Holding out his hand, he offered Lone Warrior the lead rope of the mare he'd brought. "As your sister's *Hakatakus*, I give you this horse that you may bring my wife to me."

99

Though it had actually been Swift Foot's uncle and Small Bird's father who had agreed upon the terms of the marriage price, along with the merging of the two families and tribes, Lone Warrior was her *Hakatakus*. As such, he was entitled to her bride price. Swift Foot had given him twelve horses. Surprisingly, many of those horses had already been given back to Swift Foot's people as gifts—which showed the family of Small Bird was generous.

Swift Foot saw the struggle taking place in Lone Warrior's eyes. He waited in the gusting wind. Finally Lone Warrior took the reins.

"I will bring my sister to you as arranged."

Swift Foot inclined his head. All that needed to be said had been spoken. Turning, Swift Foot strode back through the crowd.

Kills Many Crows stalked after him. "She is to become a beloved member of this tribe, but my sister is treated as if evil spirits live in her heart," he hissed. Bitterness filled his voice.

Swift Foot didn't break stride. "Your sister is taken care of, provided for, and offered the same protection as all." The words sounded hollow, but there was nothing he could do to change Willow Song's status in the tribe. Being chief did not mean he could tell his people what to believe or force them to accept things they would not. He led by example. In Willow

Song's instance especially, that was all he could do.

"It is not right!"

"No, it is not. In this we are in agreement, cousin. But you know that there is nothing I can do."

"No. It is too late. You've done enough. Your family has. If not for your father, my mother would be alive and my sister unharmed. We'd have been *whole*."

Swift Foot whirled around and came to a furious halt. "Choose your words carefully, cousin. I tire of your bitterness toward something that happened long ago when we were but children."

Kills Many Crows stepped back, but the anger still burned in his eyes and voice. "My father made you a warrior the day I lost my mother, yet it was your father who destroyed our family. Your actions were celebrated in the midst of her death. Death has continued to come to our tribe because *you* live."

"*Henakeca!* Enough. You go too far."

"What will you do? Force me to live with the *Winkte's?* With the old women or my sister on the edge of camp?" Spinning around, Kills Many Crows stormed off.

Another stab of guilt hit Swift Foot. He slowly made his way to the northeastern horn of the camp, regretting deeply that Willow Song had been ostracized due to her looks. It wasn't her fault. It wasn't anyone's. It just was. Bitterness would not change the past. Only wisdom could bring about a peaceful future.

Arriving at the new dwelling erected by Small Bird's female relatives, Swift Foot hesitated. It had been dedicated yesterday by a group of old men who each struck the south door pole with a stick, then recited a coup before entering. Swift Foot had held a special feast for the men afterward.

Entering, needing to be alone, he stared at the interior. Larger than most tipis for a newlywed couple, it seemed empty and hollow. His shield, three lances, a bow and quiver of arrows, and his war ax hung from two poles at the back, along with his feathered bonnets.

On the floor behind the fire an altar had been fashioned; and a pile of food stores, pouches, and other cooking and housekeeping implements waited for a new mistress to make this shell a home. Alone on another slanted wall, several brightly quilled parfleches were hung for easy access.

Across from him, on the other side of a glowing fire, one sleeping pallet waited. Piled high with furs, it was meant to invite. Swift Foot felt only dread at the sight. Running his hands over his jaw, around to the back of his neck, he approached it. Tonight he'd be expected to share this bed and make Small Bird his woman.

In the center of the bed a bundle of clothing

lay neatly folded. Kneeling, he picked up the moccasins on top. He studied the skillfull, brightly colored quilling. Setting the shoes aside, he held up a shirt. Fringe edging the yoke, the seam under the arms, and along the bottom, swayed from his shaking hands. He rubbed the material. The buckskin had been tanned to a soft, creamy yellow, and felt soft as the fur bands around his upper arms.

He marveled at the softness. With no woman in their tipi since his aunt's death, he, along with his uncle and cousin, had received clothing in exchange for providing meat to other families or widows. But nothing he'd ever owned felt this soft. Not even the gifts from Willow Song were tanned to this degree.

He ran the pads of his fingers along the rows of decorative quilling covering the yoke. The same black, red, and white design ran down the sleeves from shoulder to wrist and bordered the bottom above the long fringe.

Next he examined the leggings. Again he found no fault with the workmanship. Like the shirt, long fringe and a swath of red, black, and white quills ran down the sides.

The last item was a matching breechclout. Reluctantly, Swift Foot admired Small Bird's skills. To be honest, her quilling was better than any he'd ever seen—even that of Willow Song.

Hearing the sound of a drum beating outside, Swift Foot stripped off his clothing and slid into the garments made by the woman he would soon call his wife. With each heavy beat of the drums, the heaviness in his heart grew. The time had come. His people for his heart. A future decided by his past.

Stepping out of his tipi to await the arrival of a woman he didn't know or love, he spotted a small brown spider crawling along the outside bottom of the tipi. It was looking to get out of the water.

Iktomi! A spirit who it was said resembled a man with the many legs of the spider. *Iktomi* delighted in pranks and jokes on the People. He used his powers to work magic on his victims, and sometimes included his friend coyote.

Squaring his shoulders, Swift Foot looked out over his people. This was no game, no joke to be laughed over. It was real. And it was forever. But as if *Iktomi* were actually there, on the hide of the tipi, Swift Foot heard the taunting laughter of the mystical spirit. Though he had passed the test the spirits had put him through by leaving Emily behind, it was a hollow victory.

Swift Foot might have earned his place as leader, but Iktomi had had the last laugh.

Pressed on all sides by the crowd of chattering women, Small Bird smiled, laughed, and endured. Makatah and Shy Mouse tugged, braided and yanked as they tried several different hairstyles.

"No," Shy Mouse said. "Try this." Half the voices in the tipi agreed; the rest urged Makatah to leave it.

Feeling a strand of hair pulled from her scalp, Small Bird finally exploded. "Enough!"

Makatah poked her gently. "You will be wife to our chief. You must look your best."

Small Bird rolled her eyes. But with so many surrounding her, she couldn't argue with her cousin. Around her, those women who were married smiled indulgently, assuming her nerves stemmed from simple bridal jitters.

Small Bird gave up. She just wanted it to be over, to *get through the day. But then there will be the night* a small voice whispered. Unwilling to think that far ahead, she put her fear aside. Across the tipi, throaty giggles drew her attention. Yellow Robe, surrounded by new friends, was also being dressed and groomed—as mother of the bride, she too had to look her best.

Trying to act happy and excited, Small Bird knew that a week ago, or even two days ago, she wouldn't have had to pretend. She'd have eagerly participated. Today she endured. To her relief, her cousins finally decided to leave her long, blue-black hair loose and flowing except for two tiny braids on each side of her head. Thin, colored leather thongs had been woven around the braids, and pure white feathers were left to dangle at the ends.

A young woman came forward. Small Bird didn't remember her name, but she remembered the woman's two children. The young mother smiled shyly. "For you," she said, holding out two armbands.

Makatah took them for Small Bird and held the bands up, and the tipi full of women exclaimed over them. Made of rabbit fur, each had been delicately decorated down the center with white, brown, and black quills. Once donned, each hugged Small Bird's upper arm perfectly.

Yesterday she'd have been thrilled with the gift. Today they were a reminder that soon she'd be tied to a man who didn't want her. Keeping her feelings and thoughts carefully concealed, Small Bird sent the woman a grateful look. "Thank you for the lovely gift," she said. "I am honored." And deep down she found some happiness. She had many good friends, some new, some old. And family who loved her.

"You are beautiful, my cousin." Makatah wiped the tears from her eyes.

Small Bird reached out to hug her. "Thank you for the new garments." Glancing down at herself, she marveled at the creamy whiteness of her tunic top and leggings. The beauty of the clothing lay in its simplicity. The yoke, worked with bleached porcupine quills, added texture. Along the seam, a tiny row of brown birds in flight were sketched, adding grace and beauty The sleeves bore only fringe, but the edge of the tunic and the skirt sported a simple bird-in-flight vee-shaped pattern.

Shy Mouse came forward. "I too have something for you."

"You have all done so much," Small Bird protested. Slightly embarrassed, with all eyes on her, she took the proffered square of hide. Pulling the edges open, she gasped. "It is . . ." Words failed her as she stared at the palm-sized medallion.

The center featured a brownish-black bird sitting between the horns of a black buffalo. A braid of woven grass formed an outside circle, and the background had been quilled with yellow. White rabbit fur backed the round piece of deerskin, and a tuft of fluffy spotted down had been sewn to the bottom. Three leather thongs ending in long feathers finished the piece.

Tears gleamed in her eyes as she glanced up. Many a moist eye met hers. These women believed in her, and in her marriage. They had confidence that she'd be a good wife to Swift Foot, a wife of distinction and honor.

Handing the gift back to her cousin, Small Bird turned and allowed Shy Mouse to tie it around her neck. The other women's sudden quiet after a morning of constant talk, laughter, and good-natured advice warned that it was time. Each woman came forward to hug her and kiss her on the cheek.

She sniffed when everyone but Yellow Robe went out the door. "You will make us proud," her mother said, tears running down her cheeks.

"I shall do my best," Small Bird promised. And at that moment, she knew she would. It no longer seemed to matter what Swift Foot believed or wanted. All that mattered was her own belief that she was doing the right thing. The support of these women of her people— her people now included nearly four times the number of her old tribe—added to her belief that she followed the true course.

When her father entered, she walked straight to him. Though he said nothing, the pride in his eyes made her stand taller and lift her chin. He reached out and slid the backs of his fingers down her cheek. "Are you ready to meet your future, daughter?"

The future. Her father had taught her to carry herself tall through everything.

"Yes, Father," she said simply. "I am ready."

Ducking out the door, she walked proudly to Lone Warrior and nimbly mounted the mare he held, sitting with her legs to the side, her fingers fisted in the beast's silky mane. She was ready for whatever the future held.

Chapter Five

Lone Warrior halted Small Bird's horse in front of a bright, new tipi with a fire burning before it, and she swallowed hard. This was now her tipi, one she'd share with a man who didn't want her. Remembering her resolve of just a few minutes before to fight for this marriage and the man she'd been fated to wed, Small Bird straightened proudly and waited. People formed a semicircle around the dwelling, with her, Lone Warrior, Swift Foot, and Wind Dancer in the center. Staring at her tipi, Small Bird couldn't help but note with pride its size, which indicated Swift Foot's wealth. He'd provided, as part of the marriage price, the many hides needed to make this new home. The workmanship, the wrinkle-free sides, and the curling ribbon of smoke floating through the smoke hole, all looked inviting. Her mother and the other women had worked hard in the last week to finish this, and it showcased their skill and knowledge.

The inside—the housekeeping, the level of comfort and decorations—would be an opportunity for Small Bird to display her own skills. Pride rushed through her. This was now her home. *Hers*. Her eyes shifted to the man standing to one side of the open doorway. Hers and her husband's.

Lone Warrior spoke, his voice loud and clear. "I bring to you your new wife."

Swift Foot stepped forward. The aura surrounding him frightened Small Bird as much as it drew her; he looked more like her chief than a man who was as good as her husband from this moment on. Her brother's words gave her to him. The words to come from Wind Dancer were only a formality.

From her perch on the horse, she noted the short headdress her mate wore. It was made of eagle feathers, and she knew he'd earned each one for a brave deed.

He stopped below her, feet planted apart. As he reached up one hand to signal his acceptance of her, she took a deep breath. He looked unapproachable. And undeniably handsome.

He wore his hair parted down the middle, bound on each side with leather strips starting just below his ears and ending at his strong, smooth jaw. Small, downy feathers swung back and forth from his hair, blown by the wind.

He wore the shirt she'd made for him, and it pleased her to note that it fit like a second skin. When he crossed his arms, rows of fringe swayed. The cut hide moved with him. It was part of him—fluid, free, yet fierce.

His greatness was apparent: he'd been a brave, strong child and had been nurtured into a courageous and powerful leader. His wide forehead and the intensity of his gaze bespoke intelligence, while prominent cheekbones, a proud, hawkish nose, and firm lips were outward signs of his power and authority.

But Swift Foot had also once been a kind, concerned, and tolerant boy. As Small Bird searched the dark depths of his eyes, she wondered where that boy had gone. Was he there, hidden deep inside, or had the warrior completely devoured him?

She swallowed nervously, her mouth dry. It had been easy to convince herself of the rightness of this moment when she'd been alone in her tipi, but facing her future was more difficult.

This is right. You know this is right.

And soon Swift Foot would see the truth. Perhaps he worried that a wife would interfere with his tribal duties. She would prove that a wife would be a great asset.

Taking a deep breath, Small Bird held out her hand. When Swift Foot closed his warm fingers over hers, she twisted on the back of the mare. Swift Foot's other hand reached up to swing her down, and her free palm instinctively landed on his shoulder. The rope of muscle there bunched—hard flesh covered in soft deerskin. The contrast made her long to run her hands up and over her husband's shoulders, to marvel in his strength and enjoy the soft feel of the shirt she'd made for him.

Her fingers dug in for a brief moment before she realized what she was doing and pulled her hand away. For a long moment, Swift Foot and Small Bird stared at each other. Harsh slashes of red, black, and white paint across each cheek and his forehead emphasized the warrior in her husband. The hard man. Then Swift Foot turned and led her to the fire, where Wind Dancer waited.

Following slowly, with head held high, Small Bird felt pride in her betrothed's appearance. The long rows of fringe on his clothing trailed back and forth as if a plaything for *Tate*. To tease her, the wind lifted the back of Swift Foot's breechclout, revealing glimpses of the smooth, golden skin there, the rock-hard flesh. Small Bird's pulse jumped, surprising her. She knew what he looked like—or at least most of him—as she'd studied the sculpted strength of him each

114

time their tribes came together over the years.

Somehow it was different, studying him now. Maybe because soon she'd have the right to touch those wide shoulders, to trace the powerful muscles across his chest, back, and upper arms, and to explore his very male body. Even fully clothed, he set her heart to hammering. Maybe even more so fully clothed. Now, when he was not walking around wearing just a simple breechclout, less was visible. But each step, each swing of his arms or lift of his head, hinted at the potent power hidden beneath garments she'd fashioned for him. Small Bird had to refrain from running her tongue over her suddenly dry lips.

Swift Foot turned and took his place near the fire. The wind ruffled the feathers in his headdress and whispered over Small Bird as she took the last few steps to stand at his side.

Around the couple, friends and family of a united People gathered. The air grew quiet, and Wind Dancer lifted his arms high. For the first time, Small Bird got a good look at the medicine man in his full regalia. While she'd been focused on Swift Foot, the young shaman had finished preparing for the ceremony.

He wore a breechclout, the front emblazoned with the head of a bear. A ring of bear teeth sewn to a strip of otter skin encircled his neck, hanging low in an arc from his collarbones to his breastbone. Around each wrist and ankle, bear claws spiked outward.

Most impressive was the bear head he wore; Wind Dancer's eyes barely showed beneath its snout. The slits where the bear's eyes had once been were sewn-together dark spots, and the ears sat perked on the shaman's head. The rest of the bear hide flowed around his shoulders and nearly down to the ground.

Small Bird stared at the young Shaman in awe. She'd seen him many times over the last week from a distance but had never seen him in full glory. She was now impressed. As a young brave, he'd repeatedly dreamed of a bear. The next morning, he'd come face-to-face with one.

Without a weapon, Wind Dancer had been unable to defend himself. Bravely he'd stood his ground, showing no fear, even when the animal rose on two feet to tower over him. Speaking softly despite the animal's roars, the boy had calmed the beast. It had unexpectedly dropped to all fours as armed warriors arrived to aid him, then, to everyone's surprise and shock, the bear left.

That night, the spirit of *Mato* returned to Wind Dancer's dreamworld. This time the bear spoke and told him he'd given his life for him, and that Wind Dancer was a Bear Dreamer who would one day walk with the spirits while still roaming on the *maka*.

The next morning, warriors found the bear dead, lying in the spot where Wind Dancer had encountered it.

Wind Dancer now belonged to the Bear Society. He was considered *Wakan*: a wise man who had power, spoke to the spirits, and did many strange things.

Small Bird felt insignificant as she met his gaze through the eye slits of the bear mask. When he turned away, she released her breath and tried to relax.

Without warning, Wind Dancer bent down, picked up a leather pouch, and straightened, throwing his arms high once more. His voice rose, as he sought to gain the attention of *Wakan Tanka*, the Great Spirit, the one who was all. He shook his hands, the claws on his sleeves jangling and matching the pitch and rhythm of his voice.

Moving slowly around the fire and behind the bridal couple, he chanted. Sprinkling a mixture of sweet grass and other medicines known only to him, he formed a circle separating them all from the rest of the tribe. He then tossed herbs to the sky, the earth, and to the four winds. Four times he repeated action and prayer, one for each of the four kinds of gods as he prayed to *Wohpe*, the Mediator. Then he turned and pulled a knife from the sheath strapped to his ankle. He still chanted, but in a low, soothing, magical tone. It washed over Small Bird, and she allowed him to take her hand in his.

Tipping his head back, the shaman stared into her eyes and spoke. "You bring the gift of words to this tribe. It is words that often cause war, but it is also words that can end it. This you bring to our people and to your husband. You will walk at his side, be of comfort to him, care for him and be his helpmate."

Mesmerized by the medicine man's words, by the validation he gave to her own feeling of the rightness of this joining, Small Bird barely felt the tiny cut he made in her thumb. Keeping her eyes on Wind Dancer, she watched him turn to Swift Foot.

He said, "You have fulfilled your destiny, one begun when you were but a boy. This path has led to greatness and given you wisdom and courage. But remember this: it takes a wise man to keep to his chosen path." He paused. "And many sacrifices."

Small Bird didn't have much time to wonder if he referred to her or to the marriage, for the medicine man quickly continued. "It is your duty to care for this woman, make her yours, and live as man and wife. You will protect her and consult with her—for her words hold truth. It is through this woman that peace for our future will be fulfilled. Questions of the past will be answered in time. Join now your future to hers. Let the path of yesterday and today become as one, as you and she become man and wife."

Taking Swift Foot's thumb, Wind Dancer sliced the skin. A bead of blood formed. The shaman took both Swift Food's and Small Bird's hands, pressed them together at the palms, then joined their thumbs so that their blood mingled. As he bound their thumbs together, he lifted his voice. "You are now as one, just as your blood is one. I command you to live as one flesh ever after."

Swift Foot drew a deep breath. It was done. He was now married to this woman—forever. Keeping his face devoid of emotion, he held up their hands for all to see. Cheers rose high and loud, coming in waves. His gaze met hers. His mouth opened but he didn't know what to say. What did a man say to a spouse he did not know?

"My wife." The words came out low, harsh, a barely audible whisper.

Her head tipped back and she boldly met his gaze. "Yes," she whispered. "Your wife."

Firming his lips and clenching his jaw, Swift Foot glanced away when the sound of drums reverberated through camp. The crowd that had encircled them now dispersed amid excited chatter. Unbinding his thumb from his wife's, he couldn't help but note her long slender fingers, their pads rough from long hours of sewing. His eyes traveled from her hand to her wrist, lingering on the soft, fragile skin there before skimming up and over the finely tanned sleeves of her shirt. Of their own accord, his eyes absorbed her, taking in the short, nervous breathing that lifted her breasts and warmed the air between them.

Standing before him, her head barely reaching his shoulder, his new wife seemed small and fragile. She looked younger than sixteen winters. But he should not judge her so; he himself often felt double his twenty years of age. He'd seen more in his lifespan than had some men his uncle's age. And he'd lost so much.

What did he have to give this woman? he found himself wondering. Protection? For all his brave words, he couldn't even guarantee that. Her brother had been right: now that he had a wife, his enemy would target her.

"You are not pleased," she said softly.

Meeting her searching gaze, he saw unexpected wisdom there—along with compassion and determination. And something else in those dark, depthless eyes made him feel uneasy. As if she saw clear down into his heart.

"Any wife of mine is in danger," he explained. It was the truth. Not all of the truth, but all she needed to know.

She shook her head. "Our joining is for a

reason, and it is not fear for my safety I see in your eyes. It is sadness. Grief."

"Have I not lost much? Do I not have reason to grieve?" His lip curled, but with difficulty he kept his voice dispassionate.

She did not flinch. "Have you not gained much as well? This is your wedding day. And I do not believe the pain I see in your eyes is the pain of past loss. It is too fresh, this agony I see." She reached up as if to touch his face, then slowly lowered her hand to take his.

Her warmth stole into him. And Swift Foot, frightened of no man, not even his most feared enemies, felt true fear in the face of this small woman with more compassion in her eyes than he deserved.

Had he not met Emily, nor fallen in love with her, he might have been open to giving his heart to another. He'd at least have gone into this union with the same acceptance with which he'd agreed to it. If not for Emily, he might not have resented Small Bird's place at his side. But he had met Emily, and he had loved her.

Deep down, he knew he wasn't being fair to Small Bird. It wasn't her fault that he'd given his heart to another. She was beautiful and kind in her own way, and in a different time or place . . . Needing to dispel the gloom growing inside him, he turned.

"Come." Tugging at her hand, he led her to where two willow backrests had been positioned before the fire; then he let it go. *For show,* he told himself, to prove to his people that he accepted this woman as his mate. But the minute he released her hand, he felt strangely lost, like a small child who'd forsaken the comforting grip of a parent and wandered off alone.

Shaking such foolishness from his mind, he took a seat beside her. The willow chairs had been placed so close that, as she reclined, her shoulder touched his. He shifted slightly to put a measure of space between them. Her sudden stiffness said she'd noticed.

His people returned slowly, and food was brought, and gifts. Sighing with relief, Swift Foot turned his attention to these guests. But through the distraction of their conversation, he couldn't help noticing the gentle manner of his wife. He listened to her soft, gracious voice and observed the smiles she elicited from his people, old and young.

As she accepted each gift, she motioned for its giver to enter her home where her mother, aunt and cousins had retired. Each left with a small gift in return and a huge smile on his lips. His people were pleased. In just over a week, she'd won their hearts. Not that they'd had any reason to resent her, or her tribe merging with his. All—except for Kills Many Crows, who resented everything that came to Swift Foot—seemed happy to see their chief take a wife.

The hard part would be in his winning the respect of her tribe. But he would. The two tribes were joined now. As they were wed.

Shifting inward slightly at the same time as his bride, Swift Foot felt their shoulders brush. Small Bird's head turned slowly. A wispy strand of her blue-black hair feathered over his cheek.

Taking a deep breath, Swift Foot inhaled her clean, sweet scent and stared into her eyes. Black lashes and brows framed irises the same shade as the golden-eagle feathers in his bonnet. Flames from the fire danced within those eyes and glowed over the smooth brown skin of her cheeks.

Aware of his perusal, his wife lifted her chin with an expression he already recognized: one of determination. Once more he met her gaze. This time she lowered her lashes, looking away. She turned to greet the next guest—a small girl—and he jealously observed the way her arms wrapped gently around the child's shoulders. A moment later, Small Bird threw her head back and laughed at something the child said.

Mesmerized, Swift Foot stared at the delicate flesh beneath her jaw. His wife was a study in contrasts: Strength with fragility, stubbornness with compassion, gentleness with determination. And, oh, yes, beauty.

With a start he realized Small Bird was truly ravishing. Again came a shiver of fear—

and guilt. His thoughts made him feel traitorous to his earlier love. But when Small Bird touched her forehead to the child in her arms, he too longed to feel her tender touch.

Grateful for the sudden arrival of food; he accepted a bowl of steaming elk, jerked tongue and rabbit. Another woman set before him a bowl of pemmican, wild potatoes, onion, and prairie turnips. A third presented a bowl of gooseberry mush.

Taking a small piece of meat, Swift Foot held it up, then tossed it into the fire. As he did, he recited, "Recognize this, Ghost, so that I may become the owner of something good." Then he offered the bowl of fresh hot meat to Small Bird.

She took a piece. *"Pilamayan."*

Accepting her thanks, Swift Foot took a chunk for himself and set the bowl down on the square of hide that lay before them. They were soon joined by others. The women sat on the same side of the fire as Small Bird, the men before Swift Foot. Typically, when in groups, each sex remained apart—together yet separate.

Children ran about. One small boy stopped near Swift Foot. Smiling indulgently, he handed the child a tender piece of meat. The youngster shyly grabbed the morsel, then ran off.

Taking up another hunk of elk, Swift Foot tried to eat—but he was too aware of the woman beside him, his wife. The knowledge of their union made his stomach clench. At least the two of them weren't expected to speak.

Night Thunder directed a question toward him. "When do we leave?" he asked.

"In two days." Swift Foot had already made plans to move camp. With summer coming to an end, it was time to leave and join the other tribes as they gathered together out on the plains for buffalo hunts and Sun Dance ceremonies.

Soft laughter drew his attention back to Small Bird. She looked happy, pleased, but he noticed tension in her shoulders, a slight strain around her mouth. She hid it well, though. Unlike him, she ate, sampling everything that had been brought as gifts.

Unwilling to offend the many women who'd worked from sunup to sundown for nearly a week, he resumed eating, forcing the food down. His fingers collided with his wife's as they both reached for the same piece of rabbit. Both he and Small Bird drew sharply back from each other, and across from them, several women smiled and two girls on the verge of womanhood giggled.

Sighing, Swift Foot tore the chunk of meat into two pieces, then handed one to his wife. Embarrassed, she accepted it.

Again, he noted her graceful, delicate movements: the way she turned her head, the dainty way she ate, the way she sat with the poise of a confident woman with legs to the side, back straight, not leaning on her backrest as he did. Even the sway of her hair when she turned to converse drew him, and her voice, silky and fluid, held an elegance and maturity that washed over him. It held the warmth of sunshine and the freshness of rain. He could make no more pretense at eating, longing to jump to his feet and run—it didn't matter where. He longed to run from the fear nipping at his heels, the guilt burdening his shoulders, and the pain in his heart.

At the sound of drums, everyone rose. The singers began their chants and pounded on drums. Warriors, braves, and young boys took their places on one side of them, females danced on the other. The two sexes were separate yet together, two halves making a whole.

Swift Foot noted the young braves and warriors eyeing the young maidens, saw protective mothers move closer to the edge of the dance circle to watch over their daughters. Knowing it was expected, he stood and led Small Bird forward.

He tried to lose himself in the beat of the dance, the rumble of song, the strong shouts followed by softer ones. But when Small Bird began to move, he could think only of her. Watch her.

Her stance was like that of the other

women. Unlike the men, who whirled and danced with energy, with knees lifted high and arms flung out, the females kept their legs together, their arms crossed over their breasts, while moving their feet in small steps. The two groups moved toward each other, and soon were separated by only a few feet. Swift Foot's gaze locked with Small Bird's. His breath caught.

In her eyes he saw dark shadows, thunder clouds reflected from the sky. The wind picked up and gusted around them, bringing the smell of rain. Bits of grass mingled with wood smoke. Still the newlyweds stared at each other. Swift Foot's steps slowed to the pattern of hers, his arms crossed over his chest as they danced.

Her hair, unbound, swirled around her face. As the singers increased their tempo, their beats stronger, harder, the wind did too. Like the black of the evening falling across the sky, it surrounded her. In her eyes, Swift Foot saw the lightning playing across the clouds.

Small Bird looked as wild as the elements. Her beauty remained, her grace and gentleness. But along with those, Swift Foot saw something else: power. Untapped energy.

The first crash of thunder rolled through the camp, followed by others, as if the gods were trying to break the tight weave of magic that held the two newlyweds' gazes locked to each other. With his heart hammering, Swift Foot tried to tear his away. But he couldn't.

The wild tangle of her hair, as black as the night mixed with the storm in her eyes, contrasted with features that looked too fragile to withstand such ferocity. His eyes never left hers, yet he took her in. All of her.

Where Emily's hair had been of the palest sun, Small Bird's was of jet. Blue sky had shone through Emily's gentle eyes, soothing him with cool comfort. A storm brewed in Small Bird's. Emily had been desperate to please. Small Bird's steady gaze promised challenge.

Swift Foot admired the purity of her garments, and his eyes went to her medallion: a small bird perched fearlessly on the strong head of a buffalo bull. It symbolized the relationship of the animals—strength, acceptance and even need. The symbol suited her, became her.

Catching himself, Swift Foot attempted to shake off his new wife's allure. Why was he suddenly noticing this woman? He'd seen her many times over the course of his life. Never had she held him as she did now.

His time with the white girl had been happy and peaceful, yet bittersweet, for those weeks had been stolen from the very people he'd vowed to serve. He'd known his days with Emily couldn't last, that his life's path demanded sacrifice. That was why he'd left her to return to marry this woman, chosen for him by others. Chosen because he had saved her life long ago.

Watching the storm brewing in Small Bird's eyes, he recognized that his life would never be peaceful or complacent. The elements lived within this woman, were a part of her. And no matter what he might once have wished, they were now part of him.

Chapter Six

Lone Warrior followed the stream away from camp, away from the feasting, joking, laughter, singing, and heavy throb of drums. Worry churned his gut like the wind moiled the stream. In the few short hours of rain before the wedding, the water level had risen drastically—as had his fear for his family's future. And the storm looked like it was about to return.

How could his father have agreed to this? He couldn't argue the fact that Swift Foot was a great warrior; the man had proved himself in countless battles. But one fact remained: Swift Foot was hunted. And as surely as Lone Warrior knew water flowed downstream, he knew that sooner or later the enemy would target his sister.

Rounding a bend in this river that twisted and turned, went from slow and shallow to deep and flowing, he leaned into the wind surging against him. From the camp, the sounds of celebration had faded to a low hum.

Lost in his worry and fear for the future, it took a few minutes for Lone Warrior to realize that something sang in his ears, sweetly and softly. He stopped to listen.

Behind him, drums pulsed. The fading evening light illuminated the stream as it slapped against rocks, and birds and insects fluttered and buzzed in the rain-freshened air. Yet one thread of sound didn't seem to belong. Turning slowly, he tried to locate the light, sweet noise that seemed part of the wind, yet not.

Closing his eyes, he found a melody as pure as birdsong stealing into his heart. It promised warm, summery nights beneath a clear night sky. So clear, so compelling it was, he knew the song was a message from the spirits. He concentrated. Listened. Allowed it to flow through him and become one with him until he felt not only the beauty but a deep sadness.

Realizing it came from somewhere just ahead, beyond the rocky bend, he followed the trail of notes. As he reached a large pile of boulders, the song faded into a whisper. Then it disappeared.

Lifting his face to *Tate*, Lone Warrior

begged for the return of the music that spoke to his heart. He didn't understand why or how, but he knew he needed it.

Wind answered with the return of the light, airy sound. Lone Warrior climbed. The haunting notes called him, pulled at him, held him in its magical grip. Over stones he pulled himself, climbing the rock pile until he was several feet off the ground. Afraid that the unseen spirit would disappear, he moved as stealthily as he could.

Then he saw his spirit. She stood in a small indent in the bank, upon a flat boulder slightly above him. Long black hair streamed behind her, and her lovely features were lifted to the heavens. In a voice as pure as the very air he breathed, she sang softly to the sky. To the world around her.

Mesmerized, Lone Warrior could only stare. The perfection of Willow Song's profile, the compelling movements of her hands, the sway of her body—he'd never seen anything so beautiful, nor heard anything so . . . otherworldly. He'd never heard a voice like hers. Slowly, as if his body no longer belonged to him, he climbed toward her. Then he waited. And watched. And listened. Taking a deep breath, he drank in the sight and sound of this woman who was both beauty and beast in looks, but gifted with a voice of perfect purity.

When her voice faded, he silently waited

for her to sing again. But apparently feeling his gaze upon her, she opened her eyes and cried out. Bending down, she scrambled to retrieve her head covering, then took two unsteady steps away.

Lone Warrior rushed forward and steadied her. "No, do not run," he implored, his voice low and soothing.

She froze, then ducked her head and turned away, re-covering her head as she did. "Go," she said. "Do not look upon me." Fear, sorrow, and pain turned her clear singing voice to a husky plea.

Lone Warrior gently turned her to face him. He stared down at the ugly hide draped over her head. "Do not be afraid."

"You should not be around me." Her voice was panicky.

Yesterday Lone Warrior would have agreed. Yet after hearing her voice, and seeing again the perfection of her profile and the grace of her arms as she danced and sang to the spirit world, he no longer feared her. "You have a beautiful voice," he whispered.

"I am cursed!" She tried to move around him.

"No. You are beautiful." The words spilled from his lips, startling him as much as her.

Her head shot up, her face still hidden. "What joke is this? You seek to make fun of me? Do you think I do not know the truth?"

Lone Warrior wasn't sure what had come

134

over him. But he couldn't walk away. "What I heard is a gift. Your voice is not a curse. It is not evil. It is sweet and innocent. Sad and haunting. Never have I heard such a gift."

Willow Song laughed, the sound harsh. Without warning, she tossed her head back and yanked off the covering, revealing her full face to him. "This is what goes with that voice." Anger burned in her eyes.

Unable to help himself, Lone Warrior sucked in his breath. Words failed him.

She shoved him out of her way. "The gifted was cursed." She scrambled away, over the rocks, but her lame leg slowed her and caused her to stumble.

Springing forward, Lone Warrior caught her. This time he was prepared. He made himself look at her—really look at her, and not just what was beautiful. This time he took her in fully, his gaze roaming over even the puckered and distorted flesh.

When she tried to bury her face in her hands, he held her chin up. Yes, one side of her was beyond scarred and ugly; it was hideous. But beneath the obvious defects, he saw the heart of this woman. While one half of her face held perfection, that was not her true beauty. Only a woman of pure heart and soul could be gifted with a voice like hers, and therein lay her worth.

"There is beauty in you that none has seen before."

"You jest," she whispered, tears shimmering in her eyes.

He shook his head. "No. I think I am falling in love with you." The shock in her eyes mirrored his own. But it was true. He hadn't been able to stop thinking of her since yesterday.

Picking up her walking stick, he handed it to her. Then he took the head covering from her grasp and placed it gently over her. Leaving her face free, he wrapped the ends around her throat. "Walk with me."

Stunned, she could only stare at him.

"Walk with me, Willow Song. Please." Lightning flashed overhead.

Slowly, she nodded.

Lone Warrior took her arm, placing her hand on his arm as he led her over the rocky ground until they reached the bank. There, when she tried to pull away, he tightened his hold. Their gazes met. Hers was filled with confusion and fear of rejection, his with the desire to get to know her.

When she glanced down at her hand resting on his forearm, his gaze followed. The back of it, puckered from her old wounds, felt hot, as though a fire within burned.

As if struck by the earlier bolts of lightning from the sky, Lone Warrior knew fire smoldered within her. And it was that spark of life that electrified him.

The storm broke.

*   *   *

The downpour was a silvery sheet of pelting water, and the wind howled as jagged light ripped through the clouds. The beat of drums, the singing, the feasting, and the gaiety of Swift Foot and Small Bird's wedding all ended with mad dashes to warm, dry tipis. Hobbled behind each gently glowing dwelling, warhorses shook their heads and swished their tails. The outside fires sizzled in their pits, while the inside fires provided warmth for the newly united Hunkpapa tribes.

With early-evening fury, the earth had turned violent, primitive. Staring up at her new husband, Small Bird saw those same elements in his eyes. A crash rumbled across the sky. Startled, she realized she and her husband were the only ones remaining outside; everyone else had sought shelter.

Swift Foot seemed to realize it too, for he grabbed her hand and pulled her toward their tipi. Bending at the knees, he swept her up into his arms and carried her through the flapping doorway.

Inside, she waited for him to set her down, to break contact and turn away in distaste and anger. She waited for him to reject her. To her surprise, he did neither of those things.

Against her right breast, his heart beat with resounding thumps. Hers responded by speeding up, like the wings of *Tanagila*, the tiny hummingbird who flitted from flower to flower.

Her lips parted as she worked up the courage to ask him to release her, but the intensity of his gaze sent Small Bird spinning downward like an eagle making a steep, curving dive. The dark brown of his eyes turned orange-yellow in the dancing firelight. Mesmerized, curious, and just a bit scared at the emotions shimmering in his gaze, Small Bird shivered. And then she saw something else.

Something undefined. Something that frightened and fascinated her. Desire?

Her breath hitched. Her lungs felt tight, as if she'd just run many miles or danced the most sensual dance of her life—which she had. For the first time in her life, she felt primitive desire.

Longing to form a bond between herself and Swift Foot, Small Bird ran the tip of her tongue across her dry lips. She just didn't know what to say. What did one say to one's husband? Was he waiting for her to drop her eyes in respect? She tried, but his gaze held hers. Not that she minded. Her husband was *tanwaste*—handsome.

"The flaps. I should close them," she finally managed to whisper.

"Leave them," he murmured, his voice deep and thick as box-elder sap.

His gaze moved to her mouth. She licked her lips. "The fire will die."

"I will build a new fire." He moved nearer to her.

Small Bird's heart jumped into her throat when she felt his breath warming her lips. She didn't know this man. The stoic, cold, and even angry man of the last few days was gone. In his place was a man who wanted a woman. His woman. His wife.

She licked her lips again, nervous, and was shocked when the tip of her tongue touched his mouth. She gasped in surprise. His mouth came down on hers, warm and moist, soft yet commanding. Small Bird responded with a sigh. She'd never known this type of intimacy, but some inner voice guided her.

Wrapping her arms around Swift Foot's neck, she pressed herself closer. When his lips moved over hers, she imitated his actions. As the shaman had merged their blood and lives, Small Bird allowed Swift Foot to merge his mouth with hers.

Lost in the heavenly feel and taste of her first kiss, Small Bird settled into her husband's arms, tipping her head back. A throaty groan escaped her. Swift Foot broke off the kiss, allowing her time to recover.

Her eyes darted to his, fell into bottomless pools of emotion. She lifted her face—inviting, begging, needing more from him. Much, much more.

With a groan he lowered one arm, allowing her to slide down the front of him. The hard length of his body, the soft feel of his skin, even the wetness of their clothing added to the moist heat simmering between them.

Without releasing her, Swift Foot again bent his head down for a kiss. Small Bird's lips parted on an anticipatory sigh. Once more his mouth covered hers.

Their passion started out slow and tender, as before. Small Bird took her time tasting him, stroking him, exploring him as he did her. But when he paused to kiss the corner of her mouth, she moaned. His tongue slid along her lower lip, making her grip his shoulders tightly to keep from falling. Deep down inside her, a strange feeling was brewing. She felt weak yet exhilarated.

Suddenly, with the swiftness of a thunderburst, Swift Foot took the kiss to a new level. Passion erupted in a wave of heat that left Small Bird shaking. On her husband's part, all the careful control he'd ever shown fled. His hands, hard on her shoulders, slid up to cup her face, then they slipped down over her waist. He pulled her flush against him. His mouth pressed tighter against hers.

Feeling the hard length of Swift Foot's manhood press against her belly, Small Bird gave herself up to her husband's loving. Everything would be all right now. The past, the present, the future—all had come together as she'd known it would.

At her feet, the fire continued to crackle and

pop as the lashing rain found its way inside. Swift Foot's hands traveled back up, skimming the outer swells of her breasts, and Small Bird leaned into her husband's hands. Knowing what would come, she felt grateful that the tipi's inner lining, aside from keeping out drafts, also prevented their shadows from being visible to the rest of the camp.

Swift Foot felt the storm within him burst. Need raced through him. He forgot the past, the future. Now was all that mattered. Small Bird's warm skin, her hot breath, her sweet taste drew him to her.

The primitive abandon with which she gave herself to him—her eager yet sweet tremors whenever she touched her tongue to his—drove him to claim her. Swift Foot felt only that wild desire racing through him. Small Bird tasted like the storm—and he'd never tasted its fury before. He'd never felt his control slip so easily, so recklessly as it did now.

Scooping his wife up into his arms, he carried her to their bed and lowered her to the soft furs. Her arms refused to release him. Sliding close, he held her face in his hands. His mouth touched hers briefly, then trailed down her body.

Using lips and tongue, he skimmed a path along her jaw, nipping gently at her feather-soft earlobe, then retracing his path, veering

141

off to explore her smooth, soft throat. Feeling the wild beating of her pulse, he dipped his tongue into the delicate hollow there, then scraped his teeth back up her neck until she pulled his mouth to hers. Her hands tangled in his hair. She became the aggressor.

Beneath the sweet, hesitant licks, the bold thrusts of her tongue, and the playfulness she displayed by teasing his mouth into following hers, Swift Foot felt himself spiraling into oblivion. Her passion blotted out everything. He had no past, no future. No guilt, no responsibility. Only this. There was only Small Bird and the storm she unleashed within him.

He slid one hand down the soft wet deerskin of her dress, over the ridges of quills, and ran his fingers through the long, silky strands of its fringe. Past her belted waist and lower he went, until he encountered bare skin. Hooking his fingers beneath, he drew her knee up, baring more flesh to his seeking palm, which stroked the softness there. It slid up the inside of her thigh with slow, measured movements. Small Bird's breath came faster and faster until she turned her head, overwhelmed by the assault to her senses.

Burying his face in the nape of her neck, Swift Foot tasted her, his tongue flicking over her collarbone, teasing the flesh beneath her tunic. When his fingers reached the apex of her thighs, he drew in a deep, ragged breath. She threw her head back and moved restlessly beneath him, pushing her soft womanhood into his palm.

Swift Foot groaned.

So long. It seemed so long since he'd let himself go. Since he'd given himself over to his primitive side completely and without maintaining a thin layer of control.

Always in control. Always thinking. Always planning. Even with *Emily*.

Emily.

The name burned through his brain and shattered his haze of desire with the same intensity that lightning ripped across the sky. He rolled off Small Bird, shocked at his loss of control.

Even during his mating with Emily, he'd never been able to completely lose himself or forget who he was. The past retained its presence in all he did. Until now. For once he'd forgotten who he was, what he was, and what his duties were. He'd forgotten everything. He'd lost himself so completely in Small Bird's arms that it shook him to his core. He felt as though he'd been slammed into the ground and left there to die.

"What am I doing?" he whispered, sitting. His manhood was swollen. It throbbed, ached for release. Minutes ago he might have given in to that need. Now he could not.

Guilt churned deep in his heart. In its shadowy corners, he imagined condemning blue eyes filled with shimmering tears. Once again he heard Emily's desperate pleas for him to return to her. She'd loved him. He'd loved her. He'd fallen asleep to the memories of warm summer nights beneath the moon and stars as he made gentle love to her. Peace and quiet had followed those sessions and left him relaxed for the first time in his life.

With Emily, there had been none of this wild torrent of emotion. He had loved the white girl. With horror, Swift Foot realized he'd used the term in the past tense. He swiped a hand over his jaw. That wasn't right.

He loved Emily still.

I love Emily, he repeated over and over in his mind.

Then how could you have lost yourself so completely with Small Bird? Swift Foot felt confused and angry over the extent of the passion he had just shared with his wife. He ran his hands through his hair and stared into the fire. "What am I doing?" he asked again harshly.

Whatever reaction Small Bird had expected to the wild and wonderful lovemaking between herself and Swift Foot, it wasn't the deep shadows of pain darkening his eyes. Waves of anger radiated from him. His voice held harsh fury. The sweep of cold air blowing in from the tent flap brushed over the heated thigh he'd just touched.

Sitting quickly, she stared at her husband.

Grabbing a fur, she pulled it around her shoulders. "What is wrong? What did I do?" She reached out and softly touched his shoulder. He'd seemed to want her. He'd enjoyed their kisses, she knew he had. He couldn't deny the evidence of his desire.

He jumped to his feet as if she'd burned him. He stared down at her, his eyes hard as arrow tips. "This should not have happened."

Getting to her knees, Small Bird clutched the buffalo robe to herself, more for comfort than warmth. She didn't understand. "Why?" she asked. "We are man and wife. It is right we share the marriage bed."

Swift Foot turned to go.

Panicking, Small Bird dropped the fur, jumped to her feet, and ran after him. "Don't leave. Tell me what I did wrong?"

"You did *nothing* wrong." The words were torn from him.

He looked at her with such pain, Small Bird fell back. "Then why did we stop?"

Before Swift Foot could answer, a loud cry sounded outside. It echoed as if it came from far away. The call repeated then, as if from one person to another. Or one guard to another!

Small Bird sucked in her breath. The shrillness of the calls signaled trouble.

Swift Foot rushed past her, discarding his shirt and leggings. As if she weren't there, he whipped off his breechclout, unashamed of

145

his nakedness or the undeniable evidence of his desire for her.

Working fast, he redressed. When he was finished, his fine wedding garments lay in a heap at his feet. Then he grabbed his weapons, brushed past her and dove through the door. Small Bird followed, scanning the distance and looking for trouble. Rain poured from the sky. Warriors ran from their tipis with weapons in hand and mounted their warhorses. Several warriors rode into camp, shouting out warnings that a group of riders were heading toward them—fast.

The enemy had found them. And this wouldn't be a wedding party.

In minutes all the warriors were assembled. Swift Foot faced them on his own black warhorse.

"Break camp. Take the women and children to safety," he ordered one group. "You know where to go. The rest come with me to meet the enemy."

As he whirled around to ride off, he stopped to stare at Small Bird. "Go. You will be safe."

Small Bird, like the rest of the women, rushed into action. She didn't doubt the need to hurry. The attack of Swift Foot's enemy so many years ago, the one she'd lived through, spurred her to work faster. In one minute, the perfectly taut and straining tipis were waving and flapping with each gust of wind. Another minute had more than fifty tipis flat on the ground. As soon as the women began taking poles down, the boys and older men who had run to fetch horses returned. Belongings were made ready for travel. Families who owned dogs called the animals. Horses and dogs were loaded.

As Small Bird secured her belongings, she glanced up. A bolt of lightning ripped the heavens apart and illuminated the drops of falling rain. She was soaked, her new wedding garments splattered with mud.

Considering the omens with which her marriage had started, despite the brief moment when all seemed well, this ending to what should have been the happiest day of her life seemed fitting.

Two warriors rode over and urged her onto her horse. She mounted and set off. A young boy had been put in charge of the steed carrying her belongings. With a warrior on either side, as befitting her status as the chief's wife, she rode in the opposite direction from her husband.

Earlier, she'd told her father she was ready to meet her future. With a quick glance behind her, she sent a prayer to *Wakan Tanka* to watch over her husband and give her a chance to lead the violent past to a peaceful future.

Chapter Seven

Swift Foot rode away from camp. At the first warning cry, his mind had reverted to its training. Emotions and problems were set aside, and nothing mattered but his people. At that moment he was nothing but a warrior— a chief and a leader of his tribe. Protecting that tribe overrode everything else.

He'd planned long for this moment. Confident that his orders for the evacuation of the village would be followed, Swift Foot began thinking of the forthcoming confrontation with the enemy.

Leaning low over his warhorse's neck, he let his mind work furiously. Who approached? Were these the warriors of Hawk Eyes? Or were these riders from the Mandan tribe?

He discounted the latter idea. Over the years, raids and skirmishes with neighboring tribes had occurred, but they were mostly meant to prove stealth and skill as each side sought to steal horses or other goods. Those raids were also carried out with small bands to keep from being detected, not with large war parties.

Deep in his gut Swift Foot knew his enemy had finally come after him, and it caused him a pang of disappointment. He'd hoped there could be peace. Hawk Eyes had sent Many Horns to speak to Charging Bull three times now. Though his uncle had feared that the offer of peace talks was a trick, he could not discount the opportunity to end the feud. Now, if it was indeed the warriors of the Miniconjou riding toward them at night, it was clear that their chief had other intentions than ending the fighting.

Above Swift Foot, the rumble of thunder continued. Rain lashed down through the darkness making it hard to see. The air carried with it an acrid smell, burning. The very atmosphere hummed with violence.

Swift Foot allowed himself a moment to think of his people. His wife. Though he hadn't wanted one, she was now his. And the enemy, if they knew of her, would seek her out. But he'd anticipated this day. His tribe would head south. There, after many days of travel, they would see the land undergo a dramatic change: it would become dusty and inhospitable, with deep canyons, little water, little vegetation, and the earth filled with jagged rocks and peaks that would make good places to hide.

Ever since his uncle had led them to this place—to hide the son of Runs with Wind—Swift Foot had explored each canyon, ravine, and gully. He knew each bend in the winding river, and each of the smaller creeks leading away from it. He knew the land his people referred to as the badlands. There were many places to hide. Food and pouches of water had even been hidden in many places in case of an emergency.

At the base of the hilly mounds, Swift Foot's warriors split into two groups. The young chief himself went around to the left. Beyond the rocks' gently sloping base, he saw the approaching tide of shadowy riders, in the far distance, he heard their war cries mingling with the howl of the wind. His warriors had been spotted.

He firmed his lips and prepared to meet the enemy. Angling his horse slightly to the right, he moved to rejoin his split war party. Those warriors who had been on lookout atop the high peaks joined them as well. Swift Foot's men came together, then rode out onto the plain.

Close enough to see his foe's number, Swift Foot held up his lance and came to a halt.

Warriors surrounded him. Soon each man shifted until they all formed a long, intimidating line stretching out on either side. Overhead, the rain pelted the earth, soaking the horses and the warriors. Flashes of light jittered from cloud to cloud.

Swift Foot kept his gaze trained on the enemy riding out of the night. Behind him, another row of Hunkpapa warriors formed, then a third row, each line stretching out into the darkness. Their numbers were many now. Since the attack so long ago that had killed his wife, Charging Bull had set about preparing for this day. Each year, at the summer gatherings, he had sought out the best warriors from other tribes and enticed them into marrying into his own. Under his wise leadership, the Hunkpapa tribe had prospered. But judging from the large number of Miniconjou, that tribe had also grown.

Beneath Swift Foot, Kastaka shifted. "Easy, boy," he murmured. "Soon we will ride to meet our enemy."

Kills Many Crows's voice rang out behind him. "And how many more will die this day, cousin?" the man asked in a loud voice.

Beside Swift Foot, Night Thunder shifted. On his other side, Charging Bull angrily turned.

No one spoke, though. The question had been directed at Swift Foot, who chose to ignore his cousin's bitter question, even if his mind could not. *How many will die because of me?* Over and over the question circled like two snarling wolves.

"*Amayupta yo.*" Answer me. Kills Many Crow's voice was taunting.

Night Thunder's horse shifted. Swift Foot felt his friend's fury. With a small movement of his hand, he warned Night Thunder not to act on that anger.

"*Hecetu sni yelo,*" Night Thunder said in a snarl, his voice low and harsh.

"No, it is not right," Swift Foot agreed. He knew his cousin was questioning the tribe's leadership, something that would never have happened while Charging Bull was chief. But now was not the time to deal with Kills Many Crows's resentment. He glanced over at Night Thunder. "Clear your mind, my friend. Anger directed at anyone besides our enemy will only distract you and get you killed."

"You are right. It is only out of respect for you and your uncle that I do not challenge and humiliate your cousin by revealing his cowardly nature," Night Thunder explained.

Swift Foot nodded. "That day will come, my friend. But the matter will be settled by me." Lifting his lance high, he attempted to clear his own mind and heart. He could not afford distractions—yet for the first time since becoming a full warrior, he couldn't focus.

In one day, so much had changed. He had

a wife now. This war was no longer just between him and his enemy. He kept seeing that day so long ago, the murder of his aunt, when his father's foes had been willing to risk so much to get to her, as well as to the son of Runs with Wind. Families were weaknesses.

Waiting for the right moment to signal his warriors to attack, Swift Foot could not throw off the heavy cloak of worry that threatened to smother him. He'd always known he'd pay for his father's actions, and now he had his own sins to atone for. Though he'd done his duty by marrying the woman chosen for him, Swift Foot was no better than his father. He'd fallen in love with a white woman, and had nothing to give the woman he now called wife except the danger of being his bride.

Hawk Eyes cursed the summer storms that had taken him and his men by surprise. Their suddenness and intensity had blinded and slowed his war party, and ruined his plan. He'd intended to arrive during the wedding ceremony, when the Hunkpapa were off guard.

Many Horns had done well; alone, he'd been able to remain close and spy on the enemy. And when he'd returned with the news of the wedding, Hawk Eyes had ridden hard to attack. But the weather had changed, slowing him. He should turn, abort this battle, and return another day—but the enemy had already been alerted. And all peace talks had been ruined.

Across the wide, flat sweep of dirty brown grass that had become mud, he spotted the strange mounds of which Many Horns had spoken. He also saw movement: a gathering of mounted figures.

Slowing, he halted to study the land. As he'd discovered, the *maka* in this part of the world was unlike any he'd seen before. It had many faces, many moods. Today anger vibrated through the air. Still, he refused to back down. He could not allow his enemy to survive. There were deaths to avenge.

He thought back to the last bloody skirmish, when he'd lost a brother and friend. It was infuriating. Last year he'd tried to exact his revenge, but had not been able. The peace talk had been a fine idea; if nothing had come of them except perhaps the slackening of the Hunkpapa's guards. Now that it was down, he'd seek his revenge on the treacherous group.

Lightning flashed, and Hawk Eyes saw the lay of the land. Without warning, the smooth, flat ground dropped away into deep, brown gullies that twisted and turned and snaked before him. The sight reminded him of prairie dog tunnels above ground. Just beyond, he spotted flat earth perfect for battle.

Following Many Horns, who saw the same,

he raced ahead of his warriors. Where the gullies narrowed, he and Many Horns jumped from their horses and led them across to the other side. His men did the same; then they all remounted.

To his right, in another lightning flash, he saw jagged spheres spike the horizon among tall, flat-topped patches of land. A winding river cut through the earth. He'd never seen a land so filled with drama. Even the banks of the river shifted, from soft earth and green growth to steep banks of rock and overhangs. There was beauty in such land, and Hawk Eyes was suddenly overcome with doubt.

Many Horns called out over a crash of thunder. "Our enemy comes. We are many. We will destroy them." The young brave flexed his shoulders, loosening them.

Hawk Eyes said nothing. His mind and heart warred. This feud had gone on so long. The first life had been taken by his father, avenging the pride of his mother in having been jilted by Runs with Wind for a white woman. Then Charging Bull had retaliated. On and on it had gone, the two tribes' leaders striking at each other's heart and the deaths from each attack fueling the next, and the next. So many lives had been lost in the name of honor, pride, and revenge. This was a vicious cycle of war that he feared would never end.

Take a life. Lose a life. When would it end?

It would not end by his killing Swift Foot and his new bride. Logic and the past told Hawk Eyes this. Yet he had no choice. Did he?

Let it be, son, his mother had counseled him just last night.

Do not take more lives, Seeing Eyes, his wife, had added.

Let peace begin with us, both had begged. *You have begun peace talks. Let them be in earnest.*

As if he sensed his chief's weakening resolve, Many Horns tightened his hold on his horse's reins. "They do not want peace," the brave said. Fury tightened his voice.

Hawk Eyes glanced over at him. The warrior was a few years younger than himself, and he had been the one risking his life in the faux parleys. Did this youth so want to see bloodshed? He sighed. "Do they not? I am suddenly afraid that this attack will do nothing but destroy us all."

Pausing, he thought of his own small son. At the age of four, the boy was already eager to become a warrior. Over and over, young Golden Eagle begged to hear the story of Swift Foot. Though his tribe felt anger and hatred for the enemy, there was also grudging respect. That day long ago had indeed been a blight in the history of their Miniconjou tribe: not only had they failed to kill the son of Runs with Wind, but the attack had given birth to a legend.

Hawk Eyes still remembered his own fascination with the tale of Swift Foot. And his admiration and pride in the knowledge that someday he would face the boy who had earned such fame.

It was only recently that his mother, weak and fragile with age, had begged him to reconsider. She wanted to die in peace. To know her son lived with peace, not hate and war.

Unfortunately, Hawk Eyes could not give her this. The peace talks had been a trick to set the Hunkpapa off guard, but perhaps something might have come of them. Perhaps. But not after hearing from Many Horns that Swift Foot carried the rage of revenge within him and had sworn to take the life of Hawk Eyes's son.

Many Horns shifted restlessly. "We will not allow them to kill your son," he called loudly. The angry buzz of agreement whipped through Hawk Eyes's warriors like a swarm of angry bees.

Hawk Eyes drew in a deep breath, flaring his nostrils. He released the air through parted lips. "We *will* protect our own," he announced, then divided his group into two.

"Go," he called. He watched one group ride off to the right. He led the rest to the left. Only by forcing Swift Foot's warriors into smaller groups could he hope to win. It would also give him a greater chance of breaking through the barrier to attack the tribe—to harm Swift Foot's family as that chief had intended to do to his.

As if holding its breath, the thunder stopped. Even the rain stopped, as if something had suddenly dammed up the clouds. An eerie silence fell as heavily as the rain had moments before. The moon came out, lighting the battleground.

The faint glow of *Haani* was a sign. Swift Foot gave the signal to meet the enemy. Instead of dividing his warriors in two, he split them in three. He charged forward, confident that none of the enemy warriors would break through and reach his fleeing people.

Grabbing a fistful of arrows from the quiver hanging at his side, he began loosening them. His shrill war cry burst forth and echoed through the night air. The sucking sound of hooves kicking up mud accompanied his warriors' shrieks and whoops of fury.

Two of his shafts lodged in the chests of oncoming warriors, and Swift Foot smiled grimly when he saw. His third arrow took down a horse. All around him, missiles flew back and forth. The whiz of a shaft close to his ear made him bend low. A loud cry came from a warrior behind him who'd been struck.

Rage welled up in his heart as the distance between him and the enemy closed. Shouldering his bow, he grabbed his buffalo-horned war club and his shield. When the warrior whose horse had gone down rose and swung an ax at him, Swift Foot retaliated. The enemy, sliced by his club's wicked horn tip, fell in a bloody heap.

The battle continued. Horses tired. Arms ached. Bodies fell. Warriors chased, maneuvered, evaded, and clashed. Fighting broke down into groups of two against three. One against one. Four racing after five.

Over and over, Swift Foot alternated between swinging his club and using his shield to deflect blows as he guided his horse through the vicious melee. Smaller groups broke off, and he rode after them, a tight band of warriors at his side to aid him, and keep him safe. He would not let the Miniconjou through to the tribe.

He fought to catch up. Following the four warriors racing past his men, he urged his horse faster. Soon he was alone chasing his foes. One fell when struck by his club. The other three turned to fight.

One of the enemy, dressed and elaborately painted, shoved the horse of another man circling Swift Foot out of his way. "He is mine," he said in a snarl.

Swift Foot smiled grimly. He recognized Hawk Eyes. "We meet. You will die this day," he promised. All his years of anger and guilt were forged into a will of steel against this man. He would avenge each loss of his tribe, each injury.

"It is the son of Runs with Wind who will die," Hawk Eyes shouted.

The two men swung at the same time. Hawk Eyes wielded a club with a large stone head. The force of its blow against Swift Foot's shield jarred the nerves in his wrist. Pain traveled up to Swift Foot's elbow. Brought down in a swift arc, his own club tore through Hawk Eyes's shield.

Again, both chiefs lifted their clubs and brought them down. The weapons slammed against each another. The sharp horn tip of Swift Foot's embedded itself into the thick wooden handle of his opponent's club. The force unbalanced both warriors. As one they fell onto the muddy ground, their horses skittering away but well trained to stay close to their masters.

Hawk Eyes stood first, whipping out a knife. Swift Foot did the same. The two men circled each other.

Swift Foot eyed his sworn enemy. "You spoke falsely of peace. It was nothing more than a trick." He crouched and waited.

"Ha! It is you who lie. You do not want

peace. We came to you." His dark eyes burned with rage.

"Yes, you came to us. But if you want peace, then why are you here with clubs and arrows? Actions speak louder than words." Faster than a striking snake, Swift Foot's knife flashed out, cutting his enemy on the arm.

"I will do whatever it takes to protect my people and my son." With the same speed and skill, Hawk Eyes jabbed back.

Swift Foot dodged the blade but it nicked his shoulder. Feeling it burn across his flesh, he reminded himself who he was. He was Swift Foot. Powerful. Courageous. No one would ever kill the innocent women and children of his tribe again.

Around and around the two men circled, striking out and slashing at each other. Around them, similar hand-to-hand combat took place. The skies once more filled with clouds. Reflecting the violence on the ground, lightning exploded overhead. The white-hot fury of the heavens matched the bloodred rage on the ground. Rain burst through the clouds, turning the ground scarlet.

A jagged bolt of light slammed into the earth, blinding Swift Foot. Its force threw him to the ground. Overhead, a menacing rumble grew to a low roar as if the very spirits were ready to vent their wrath. Warriors on both sides shook their heads and glanced fearfully up at the flashing heavens.

Slowly Hawk Eyes backed up until he reached his horse. Swift Foot did the same. While he didn't fear his enemy, he did fear the wrath of the spirits. A second sizzle sounded, followed by the bolt of heavenly fury slamming into the earth. All the warriors scattered.

Hawk Eyes mounted. "We will finish this at another time," he promised. Then he whistled, a shrill sound.

At the given signal, the Miniconjou scooped up their dead and injured and rode off while Swift Foot's warriors retrieved their horses. Swift Foot mounted, ready to go after his foes, but the driving rain made it hard. Then he took note of the number of injured and dead.

He bellowed in anger. Instinct made him reach for his bow, but he stopped himself and got himself back under control. It was too late. The slick ground and the blinding rain made it unsafe to pursue the enemy. He might ride into a trap. And the exhausted state of both his men and their horses made it a bad strategy even without the rain and darkness.

When they were sure their enemy was gone, Swift-Foot and his men fanned out and collected their fallen. Breathing heavily, the young chief jumped down from his horse each time he came across a wounded member of his tribe. Pain tore through him. *More lives lost.* He'd seen the enemy littering the ground; they had lost a large number as well. That should have given him a small feeling of victory, but all he felt was an empty, hollow ache.

"So much waste. So much loss," he murmured after calling a warrior over to load up several of his fallen comrades.

By the time all of his men were accounted for, Swift Foot's mood had turned black. The loss to his people had been great: ten dead, four injured so severely, he knew they'd die of their wounds. And of the others, just about every man had an injury—some small, some great. One man's wounded arm would render him useless for fighting forever.

Kneeling in the mud with the storm pounding angrily over head, Swift-Foot felt his tears mingle with the rain. His chest hurt; his lungs burned. Grief left him paralyzed.

"Get up, my son," a voice commanded.

Swift Foot glanced up at his uncle. "Is my life worth so much loss?" he asked.

"It is not for you to put a price on." Charging Bull's eyes closed wearily. The man's shoulders slumped with exhaustion.

"Is it right that one person cause so much pain, my uncle?"

Charging Bull drew himself up. "You were chosen a long time ago. You have no choice but to do the job you were born to do. You are a leader."

The smell of mud and blood stung Swift Foot's nostrils. "Yes, I am a leader. I've led my people to their death." Without another word, he stood and walked to his horse.

As he mounted, he heard another ravaged cry of grief. Another warrior had been found.

"Nooo! Nooo!" The cry rivaled that of the howling wind.

Swift Foot rode over, through the rain, to a group of warriors kneeling on the ground. Lone Warrior was there, bent over an older man. The brave threw his head back and bellowed with the red rage of a buffalo bull.

Swift Foot sucked in his breath. Lone Warrior's father, Tall Shield, lay there. The man was still, his lifeless eyes unblinking against the steady downpour. Staring at his father-in-law, Swift Foot bowed his head. Small Bird's father had died in battle.

"He is dead." Kills Many Crows's harsh voice brought a hush to the battle-weary men.

Swift Foot motioned to three of his warriors. "Load him. Carefully."

"This is your fault," his cousin continued. "You brought bad spirits to our people—and now to those who joined us. Many die because of you." Hatred blazed in the young man's eyes.

Night Thunder nudged his horse between him and Swift Foot. "We have wounded who need to be treated. Now is not the time to lay blame. This war began before the birth of our chief."

Kills Many Crows glared at Swift Foot. "Yes, but he is the one who will destroy us all. Think upon that." He jerked his horse around and rode off.

Swift Foot dismounted to help the other warriors and his brother-in-law lift the body of Tall Shield.

Lone Warrior shook his head. "No. Do not touch him. I will take care of him."

Nodding, understanding the other man's pain, Swift Foot turned his attention to the others and supervised the last of the loading of the dead and wounded. When it was done, they all started back.

He sat his horse tall as he rode, trying to lead his exhausted warriors with a show of pride, but inside Swift Foot felt defeated. At the moment, it all seemed too much for one man to bear; the war, the resentment, the hatred. As he stared up into the clouds, blinking against the assault of rain, even the storm seemed too much.

Sunshine. Peace. Gentleness. Love. He yearned for those things—needed them, or he feared he'd break like a dead, dry twig under a boot.

"The enemy retreated. They ran from us," Night Thunder said.

Swift Foot stared at his friend. "They re-

Join the Historical Romance Book Club and GET 4 FREE* BOOKS NOW!

A $23.96 Value!

Yes! I want to subscribe to the Historical Romance Book Club.

Please send me my **4 FREE* BOOKS.** I have enclosed $2.00 for shipping/handling. Each month I'll receive the four newest Historical Romance selections to pre-view for 10 days. If I decide to keep them, I will pay the Special Members Only discounted price of just $4.24 each, a total of $16.96, plus $2.00 shipping/handling ($23.55 US in Canada). This is a **SAVINGS OF AT LEAST $5.00** off the bookstore price. There is no min-imum number of books I must buy, and I may cancel the program at any time. In any case, the **4 FREE* BOOKS** are mine to keep.

*In Canada, add $5.00 shipping/handling per order for the first shipment. For all future shipments to Canada, the cost of membership is $23.55 US, which includes shipping and handling. (All payments must be made in US dollars.)

NAME: _____

ADDRESS: _____

CITY: _____ **STATE:** _____

COUNTRY: _____ **ZIP:** _____

TELEPHONE: _____

E-MAIL: _____

SIGNATURE: _____

If under 18, Parent or Guardian must sign. Terms, prices, and conditions subject to change. Subscription subject to acceptance. Dorchester Publishing reserves the right to reject any order or cancel any subscription.

The Best in Historical Romance!
Get Four Books Totally FREE*!

A $23.96 Value! FREE!

PLEASE RUSH MY FOUR FREE BOOKS TO ME RIGHT AWAY!

Enclose this card with $2.00 in an envelope and send to:

Historical Romance Book Club
20 Academy Street
Norwalk, CT 06850-4032

treated, yes. But they ran from the wrath of the spirits. They will return."

Victory was theirs today, but death had made it hollow.

Chapter Eight

Small Bird rode for what seemed like hours. The storm continued to unleash its power, as if in retaliation for the battle taking place somewhere behind her. As she had so many times she'd lost count, she glanced over her shoulder. Where was Swift Foot? Was he all right? She also thought about her brother. And her father. And the others.

Shortly after leaving camp, they'd headed away from the river, which flowed deeper and faster from the rain. The land rose, then fell into shallow gullies that were starting to fill with water, then rose again up and out of them to become more flatland. Finally, when Small Bird feared she'd fall asleep on her horse, the group stopped at the ridge of a deep, dark ravine. The rain had stopped, but the moon had not returned. They made their way carefully.

The two warriors riding on either side of her dismounted and rolled away three huge boulders. To Small Bird's surprise, a hidden path led down into a chasm. One of the warriors remounted and urged his horse first down the trail.

Small Bird urged her mount forward to watch his progress as he skillfully made his way down the side of the ravine. At the bottom he rode off. They waited in silence. A few minutes later he returned and signaled.

The warrior beside her nodded. "It is safe. Go, wife of my chief."

The rain had slicked the earth. The path looked treacherous. Small Bird took a deep breath. Huge boulders on either side of the trail made the cleared area just wide enough for her animal. As the rest of the ravine was rocky, this one path seemed out of place; she realized that Swift Foot's warriors had cut it.

"Go now," the warrior behind her said.

Small Bird nodded and gently coaxed her mare to descend. The horse slipped halfway on the slick ground but quickly regained its footing. It faltered once more before they reached level ground. At last safe, Small Bird let out a huge sigh of relief and glanced around. The moon had come out of the clouds once more.

Tall cottonwoods grew along yet another

river. Although narrower than the stream they'd camped along that morning, this one looked deeper. She moved onward, following the warrior ahead of her. Drenched and sick with worry, Small Bird tried to keep her attention on the rock-strewn ground. She hated not knowing what was happening with Swift Foot and the rest of the men.

Behind her, women, children, and the elderly or maimed continued to descend into the hidden valley. Their horses' hooves churned up the narrow path, turning it into a sticky quagmire, and the long journey had shortened tempers of both beast and human. Children fretted and bickered, mothers snapped, dogs whined, and horses tossed their heads in protest. The two warriors in charge sent fierce looks to everyone to reinforce the need for silence. The enemy could be near.

A collective gasp behind Small Bird made her stop and look back. A long line of refugees stretched up the side of the ravine as yet more of the large Hunkpapa tribe continued to pick its way down. Small Bird held her breath when she spotted a horse sliding midway down. The animal struggled to regain its footing. At last he did, and a great sigh of relief feathered the air.

Turning back to the seemingly endless ride, Small Bird tried not to think of her husband, or any of the others. She rounded a bend and stared. The land dipped gently and widened into a full canyon. "Is this where we will camp?" she asked.

One of the warriors answered: "Yes. Our enemy will not be able to find us. There is also a secret path out, should we need to flee. The ground is also far from the top. We will wait here for the others."

Small Bird nodded. But before she could again set off, she heard a shrill scream from somewhere behind her. More cries followed. She whirled around, but was out of sight of most of her refugee people.

Without a thought to her own safety, she nudged her horse in the sides with her heels and rode back. She ignored the shouts of her guards to stay put. Rounding the bend, she scanned the slope where everyone was descending. The women there were rushing toward the bottom, where she saw a horse scrambling to its feet with no rider.

Small Bird spurred her mount forward. Stopping near the crowd, she jumped down and rushed forward.

"Who was injured?" She pushed her way through. As wife to the chief, she had duties.

Reaching the fallen rider, she came to a stunned stop. "Oh, no," she said under her breath. It was Makatah, and the girl lay deathly still. She was white-faced, her eyes were closed, and a line of blood dribbled down her temple.

Kneeling, Small Bird called her cousin's name and gently patted her bruised face. "Open your eyes, cousin," she commanded as she ran her hands over her cousin's body. She didn't feel any broken limbs, but she did find a large lump on the back of the girl's head.

Moving her face close to Makatah's, she felt the warm stir of air and noted with relief the rising and falling of the girl's chest. "Wake, cousin. Obey me in this!"

Finally, and slowly, Makatah's eyes fluttered. Her face dark with pain and confusion, the girl tried to sit.

Small Bird kept gentle hands on her cousin's shoulders. "No. Rest. Tell me where you hurt."

"I—I am fine," Makatah said, her voice faint. Ignoring Small Bird's orders, she sat, then tried to get to her feet. No sooner had she stood than her knees buckled. She cried out, doubling over and clutching her belly.

"Oh, no," Small Bird said again.

The two warriors had followed her. One said, "We must continue. We cannot stop here. It is not safe." But they looked worried as they stared at Makatah.

"She needs to rest. She cannot ride," Small Bird implored. She feared that moving her cousin any farther than to a safe, dry shelter would cause her to lose her babe—if it wasn't already too late. Once more she glanced up at the slope of the moonlit ravine and saw the mire and the huge boulders. She also saw the fearful faces staring down at her, filled with fear as they glanced back and forth over their shoulders, then down to Small Bird and her cousin.

Small Bird knew they couldn't stay where they were. But she also knew Makatah couldn't go far. "Help me get her onto my horse." Her voice brooked no argument.

Cradling her cousin before her, Small Bird shuddered with every cry of pain Makatah gave.

"We must find shelter. Quickly," she said.

An elder walked up and stared at her with wise and knowing eyes. "It will not matter," he said. Then he turned, his gait awkward as he hobbled back to his horse.

As she resumed her ride toward the canyon, that was their final destination, Small Bird feared he was right: her cousin had already lost her child.

Though the storm had entirely fled, it left the air heavy with moisture and an unrelieved quiet that settled across the hidden canyon like banks of early-morning fog. The moon had disappeared again, and though they'd managed to rebuild their camp, the blackness of the night surrounded and suppressed everyone. Women and children huddled close for warmth, as there was no dry wood for fires.

With the warriors still gone, all present quailed at the uncertainty of their future. Would the guards posted on the hidden path down the ravine and at the canyon's mouth send the signal that the enemy had found them? That fear kept most adults awake, staring blankly, waiting. Most were silent. But in the unnatural quiet, there was one sound that, though faint, set hearts to pounding: a young woman's sobs.

Makatah had lost her unborn baby.

She wept, inconsolable. Shy Mouse cradled her sister's head in her lap, trying to muffle her gut-wrenching sobs. Moon Fire paced near the doorway, where Small Bird's mother and her aunts huddled close for warmth. Moon Fire's younger sister sat beside Small Bird.

Outside the tipi, nothing moved. Small Bird glanced toward the door. Where were the men? Where was Swift Foot? Had their tribe been victorious, or had the enemy won? The soft sound of mud sticking to moccasins broke the silence. The women all stiffened. Then it faded, and they relaxed slightly—just one of their own warriors standing guard.

Moon Fire stuck her head outside.

"Sit, daughter," her mother commanded when a gust of cold air rolled over them. "Your cousin needs to be kept warm." Moon Fire tossed the tipi flap down. She refused to sit. Instead, she paced restlessly.

When the toe of her foot brushed Small Bird's thigh for the hundredth time, Small Bird snapped, "Sit, Moon Fire. Pacing will not bring our warriors home faster."

The girl snarled at her, but she did as she was told.

Where were they? Listening to her cousin's sobs, seeing the worry and fear on Shy Mouse's and the others' faces, the stoic expressions her aunts wore, Small Bird knew it would be a very long night. It had been already.

Closing her eyes, Small Bird sent prayers to the spirits: to *Wamble* to watch over the warriors. Thanks to *Mahpiya* for ending the storm. A plea to *Sungmanitu*, the wolf in charge of war parties. *Cretan*, the hawk, for swiftness and endurance.

Recalling her dreams of a child with him, Small Bird held on to the hope that Swift Foot would not be killed in battle. Their child represented the future. The image of the boy in her mind gave her hope. She wanted a life that promised peace.

"Where is Matoluta?" Makatah sobbed. "Where is he? I cannot lose him as well."

"He will return, cousin. Our warriors will prevail," Small Bird said. Tears slid down her cheeks. Her cousin had lost a male child, and Matoluta would be devastated by that when he returned. She only hoped she wasn't giving false hope that he would return. But they all needed hope. *She* herself needed reassurance that her husband would return.

Moon Fire glared at Small Bird with contempt. "This battle is not ours, yet we have all paid. Do you see what grief your actions have caused? See what your selfishness caused?"

Shy Mouse snapped her attention to Moon Fire. "Our cousin has always thought of others before herself. It was *for* our people that she married Swift Foot. His tribe provides much that we did not before have. This marriage is also meant to be—did not our medicine man say so before he died? Even Wind Dancer, when he came with Swift Foot's uncle to speak to the elders of our tribe, said the same thing. All agreed it should be so."

"You are a fool," Moon Fire spat. "Why must we all sacrifice what we want for her? I could have married—" She broke off.

Spotted Deer, Moon Fire's sister, glanced up. "Who could you have married? There were no males in our *tiyospaye* that were not relatives. It is here, among Swift Foot's warriors, that there are many seeking mates."

Moon Fire hugged herself. For a moment she looked lost and forlorn, worried, even lovesick. Then her features hardened. "I will not marry a man in this tribe. It will never be safe. *We* will never be safe. And what warrior would wish to join this tribe and put all he has at risk?"

Ignoring the harsh rejoinders from her

mother, Moon Fire ducked out of the tipi.

Small Bird hung her head. Maybe her cousin was right; maybe she'd brought about the destruction of her family—of her tribe. Everyone in her tribe was family, either by blood or by marriage.

A hand on her arm tugged her back to the present. "Do not listen to her," Makatah said, her voice raw with grief.

"How can you tell me not to listen?" Small Bird asked. She paused, her throat closing, choking her words. "She may be right."

"You cannot blame yourself." Makatah said. She lay back and closed her eyes as exhaustion took over. It had been an incredibly hard night of travel fraught with fear—all after the wedding.

"But I do," Small Bird said softly, stroking a tear-soaked hair from her cousin's cheek.

Anger threaded its way through her pain and grief, and the flood of emotions left Small Bird feeling trapped in a whirlwind. Her joy and eagerness toward marriage had soured upon learning Swift Foot's true heart, and his confession had left her angry, hurt, and confused. But this afternoon she'd replaced those emotions with the conviction of rightness; determination to fulfill her destiny had given her the courage to ride through the camp to marry him. And all her dreams had returned to life when he kissed her. That kiss, his desire, had confirmed the rightness of her decision.

Then the attack had shattered everything.

Once more, anger burned inside Small Bird. But toward whom? Swift Foot? Her enemies? Or at herself for what her cousin had now suffered? Maybe all three. All Small Bird knew was that somehow she had to make everything right.

A small crest of moonlight and a sprinkling of stars provided little relief in the black night. His progress slowed by the darkness, the wounded, and his warriors heavy hearts, Swift Foot led the way toward the new campsite. Tired, the group plodded toward its loved ones. Horses stumbled with fatigue, and their riders swayed.

Keeping his gaze fixed forward, Swift Foot went over each of his decisions in the battle. Though his warriors had declared it a victory, Swift Foot knew there had been no winner. Deaths and injuries had been suffered on both sides and had the spirits not brought the violence of the storm to stop the battle, he knew it was likely that the fight would have lasted much longer. The suffering would have been greater.

His shoulders sagged. It didn't matter either way. The damage had been done.

Suddenly a call, soft as a breath of air, sounded. Tears formed in Swift Foot's eyes.

There was no sound sweeter. The call of home spurred both man and beast.

His warriors drew close, staying in formation though each was eager to return home. Yet they all dreaded the grief and the bleak days ahead, Swift Foot especially.

He glanced to his right. Night Thunder cradled a young warrior whose injuries were so severe, he'd died a short time ago. Each mortality rested on his shoulders. For each serious injury he blamed himself.

Slowly they picked their way down the hidden trail and followed the river to the canyon, the thought of safety and peace drawing him. Even if the enemy pursued, they wouldn't find this place. The canyon, surrounded on three sides by deep ravines and gullies, would provide a safe haven. Unfortunately, safe didn't make up for the loss of life.

"I should have been ready," he murmured.

Beside him, Night Thunder reached out to grasp his wrist. "We *were* ready. Our guards notified us in time to get our women to safety. None of them were hurt."

Hearing the first welcoming cry coming toward them, Swift Foot shook his head. "You are wrong, my friend. Their pain and injuries aren't to their physical bodies but to their hearts, minds, and souls."

Night Thunder lapsed into silence. There was nothing he could say against that truth. Swift Foot knew he should have moved his

people before the wedding, found another se-
cure location, taken his tribe far away. There
were several other places, he saw in hind-
sight, that would have kept them all from destruction. But it didn't matter now. It was too
late.

In the distance, Swift Foot picked out the
darker shapes of tipis. No fires added their
warm glow to this new home, but now that
he and his warriors had returned, they would
be built. Then the wounded would be tended.

Entering the camp, Swift Foot stared
straight ahead. The welcoming cries of the
women and children, and the warriors left behind to guard them slowly changed into wails
of grief. Each scream, each woman who fell
to her knees in anguish, stabbed Swift Foot
in the heart. Little by little, the part of him
that held hope and happiness died.

He watched the mother of Brave Bear
Walking rush toward Night Thunder, her face
lined with shock, her voice shrill with agony.
Seeing her pain, Swift Foot clamped his jaw
tight to stop his anguish from escaping.

He was chief. Their leader. He could not
lose control.

*A leader does not show fear. A leader is cou-
rageous at all times. No matter what.*

The words his uncle had spoken to him the
day his aunt died and Willow Song was injured echoed in the hollowness of his soul.
He'd been angry and afraid that day. And

181

guilty. Though only seven, he'd known the deaths of his tribe's people were because of him. Because of him, and because of his father. But he'd shouldered that burden and borne it in silence. Today would be no different. Yet the loss of life had been enormous this time. Worse than any since his seventh year.

Weary and disheartened, he dismounted. A tall youth strode forward to take his horse. Normally Swift Foot groomed his prized warhorse himself, but tonight there was still much to be done. Turning, braced to confront the grief he heard all around him, he came face-to-face with his wife. Her eyes scanned him, looking for injury, lingering on the gash on his arm, the cuts on his thigh, and the bleeding wound on his shoulder.

"You are injured," she said. Her voice, soft as a summer breeze, drifted over him. Staring into the shadows of her face, he saw compassion, concern, and a calmness of spirit that was inspiring. For the first time since leaving Emily, Swift Foot did not picture the white girl's loving features. In Small Bird's presence was all the comfort he needed.

"My injuries are nothing," he said. But the fact that she was willing to fuss over him eased his pain somewhat.

Around him, married women tended to their men. It didn't matter that warriors were expected to be stoic; the battle had devastated spirits, including his own. And Swift Foot felt himself near breaking. Yet his duties were not over. Another wail of grief rose, and his wife turned her head. Looking over to where she looked, Swift Foot saw Lone Warrior progress through the camp. His father lay across his lap.

Swift Foot heard his wife gasp, her instinctive cry of denial cutting through him. She started forward, but he reached out, halting her. She glanced over her shoulder, her eyes wide with shock and denial.

Though he'd been so angry at her before, at their assigned marriage, he had the overwhelming urge to pull her into his arms and shield her from grief. He longed to offer words of comfort—but there was nothing to say. He'd promised her brother he'd keep all his people safe. He'd failed. Married not even a day, and he'd failed.

He released his wife suddenly and she stumbled back.

"Please, no. Tell me he's not dead," she cried.

"I am sorry, wife," he whispered.

Small Bird's fingers flew to her mouth and stifled her sorrow. She turned and ran, leaving Swift Foot standing there, his arm still out in front of him as if begging her to return and be comforted.

At last, with a heavy heart, he lowered his hand. The wounded needed tending, guards needed to be posted, and his people needed reassurance that they were safe. He would have to take care of these things.

Entering his tipi, he gathered clean garments and donned them, then stood staring down at his dwelling's cold fire pit. Piles of belongings lay there waiting to be unpacked, a mixture of his possessions and his wife's. He noted that she'd hung his war bonnet, but nothing else. The sight of the feathers of the headdress fluttering in the drafty tipi reminded him how he'd earned each one. The flowing bonnet belonged to a courageous man. A wise man. Or it should.

"So much waste," he whispered. He would give up every feather to end this bloody war. He'd gladly give up his position too, if it meant that no more of his people would die. Yet they would not want him to give up. They believed in him.

But what if he no longer believed in himself. The warrior who'd earned those feathers had been arrogant and filled with his own importance. With dreams of achieving the impossible.

Tearing his gaze away, Swift Foot drew in a deep, calming breath. Something inside him felt close to cracking.

Alone.

He felt so alone.

He closed his eyes and imagined a cozy fire. He saw gentle eyes filled with the dark mystery of the night sky, hands that soothed and a voice that understood. These were the things he wanted.

A sudden wailing from nearby brought reality crashing back. *"Foolish,"* he chided himself. *"Foolish."* He didn't deserve the peaceful and loving dreams he wanted. Not now. Not ever. He'd been born of a union that had mocked his father's responsibilities, and he would pay for that until he died.

Leaving his tipi, he walked away from the close ring of the other dwellings. Though many of his tribespeople saw him, none stopped him. No one said anything.

There was nothing to be said. Each death, each injury, had only proven him a failure.

Chapter Nine

Small Bird held her wailing mother in her arms and wept. This was all too much.

Yellow Robe had been screaming for some time now, and her voice cracked on each long sorrowful cry. Blood caked her arms from where she'd scratched herself, and she would occasionally scream and tear at her shorn hair.

Small Bird shuddered. "No more, Mother. No more."

Her mother didn't respond; she buried her head in her hands and began scratching deep furrows down the sides of her face. Unable to bear any more, Small Bird physically restrained her.

Across the tipi, Lone Warrior stared into the glowing embers of the fire. A moment later he glanced up, his face a twisted mask of grief and hate. Though he'd said nothing since laying their father onto his pallet of furs, Small Bird knew he blamed her for the death of their father.

He hadn't said anything; he didn't need to speak words to remind her of all the ominous signs before her marriage. The memory was there, burning in his eyes and twisted in the hard set of his mouth.

"Forgive me, Mother," Small Bird whispered against Yellow Robe's head. "Forgive me."

The loss to her own clan in the fighting had been comparatively small: only her father had died. But there had been many serious injuries. And then there was the loss of Makatah's unborn child, which was a bad omen for the future.

Small Bird closed her eyes. Swift Foot's clan had lost many more warriors, had suffered more injury. Yet the loss of a child . . . Grief vibrated through her, twisting and merging with guilt until her mind cried out for relief. But there was none to be had. Outside the walls of the tipi, the crying and wailing over the dead continued. There also came voices, shouts of anger and rage. But what stabbed her most deeply was the crying of small children. They were frightened at the storm of emotion raging around the camp; and Small Bird understood, for it was unlike anything she herself had ever experienced.

No, that wasn't true. Deep inside, Small Bird recalled how frightened she'd been at the age of three during the first Miniconjou attack. She remembered hiding from what she hadn't understood, and recalled her silent sobs.

Fighting those same nightmares all over again, Small Bird longed to have Swift Foot comfort her as he had done so long ago. He'd found her, small child she'd been, saved her. He'd offered comfort to her. And that day, he had planted the seed of love deep in her heart and mind.

Staring toward the tipi's closed door, she wondered where her husband would be now. Offering aid to others and keeping the tribe from falling apart, no doubt.

Slowly rocking back and forth, rubbing her cheek on top of her mother's head, Small Bird thought of the future. It was terrifying. She'd been so sure that she knew what would occur, so sure that she knew the truth. She'd believed so strongly that between herself and Swift Foot, they'd achieve peace. But now they wouldn't.

How full of herself she must have seemed. Especially to her brother. Small Bird took a deep breath, striving to keep her fear and guilt from making her heart pound out of control. Lone Warrior had been right. This morning she'd been so sure of herself. Now she wasn't sure of anything. Even one life extinguished in this bitter feud was too many for her people, and now, between their combined clans, the number of dead, maimed, and injured took her breath away. Hope and the belief that she could make a difference dimmed with the dying fire. After all, what could one woman do?

Turning her head, she stared at the body of her father. It lay so still on the pallet, covered with furs, that she could almost believe he merely slept. A fresh wave of tears trailed down her cheeks from the corners of her eyes.

Father, she cried out in her mind. *You believed in this union. You wanted it. But it took your life. Will it take my mother's? My brother's?*

There was no question; if a way to end this war was not found, it would surely take Swift Foot's life and her own as well. She now believed her brother regarding that. Had the enemy been able to reach their camp, many innocent women and children would have died as well—the same way Charging Bull had lost his wife, and Swift Foot his parents.

Small Bird thought of the child she hoped she'd one day have. Would she give birth to a new life just to die herself? It hurt unbearably to think that any child could be left without parents to face life, hunted by their enemy— as Swift Foot had been.

As if a child already grew inside her, she

covered her stomach with one hand. "No," she mouthed against her mother's head. Yellow Robe had finally fallen into an exhausted slumber.

"I will not allow it," she continued, promising herself. "This will end. Somehow it will end, and my child will never know this pain and fear."

As she sat there, her resolve grew. At last, Moon Fire's mother entered the tipi, and Small Bird glanced up.

"Go, child. I will remain with my sister this night, "the woman said." You have a husband now to tend."

Small Bird eased her mother down, then stood up and headed for the door. As she left the tipi she'd never sleep in again—her family's—part of her resisted, but suddenly she needed to find her husband and make sure he was all right. He too had suffered and needed comfort. And she wanted to give that to him. She had a different family now.

Not once as she hurried back to the hastily constructed dwelling did she consider not going to him. Swift Foot belonged to her as surely as she belonged to him. They were tied. Bound together forever, as they were meant to be.

Entering, she found their tipi dark and cold. Of her husband there was no sign. Running out of the tent, she hurried through camp. From nearly every tipi came the hushed voices of wives caring for and fussing over their mates—or the gut-wrenching sobs of the grief-stricken. Small Bird knew such lamenting would continue for many days.

Nearby, a crying woman rushed to a tipi, calling out for the woman inside, begging for the woman's help with her husband's injuries. Small Bird watched as the two headed off; then she resumed her search for Swift Foot.

As she walked, she avoided the part of camp where her cousin and Matoluta mourned the loss of their firstborn. Men passed her, their features stoic but their shoulders bowed. Off to the left, several of the dead had been laid out. Staring up at the sky, Small Bird saw the stars blur into one bright glare. Wiping the tears from her eyes, she moved slowly, seeking her husband's form among the shadowy figures. He was not there.

Recalling the profound desolation in Swift Foot's eyes, Small Bird suddenly suspected her husband had gone off alone. She turned down toward the stream. The low conversation of several warriors to her left, talking about the battle, caught her attention.

She didn't recognize her husband's voice among them, and instinct told her he wouldn't be. She wasn't sure how she knew this, except that in all her years of observing him, and in all the time she'd spent this last week watching him closely so she'd have some idea of what manner of man he had become, she'd noticed that though he seemed a part of everything going on in camp, he also seemed alone. That sense of solitude in him had touched her heart.

Following the line of trees away from the voices, she'd just about given up on finding her husband when she spotted a lone figure standing in the middle of the rushing stream. Low, guttural chants drew her closer. She recognized Swift Foot's voice; the despair in it snagged her heart and touched her. Mesmerized by both the sight and the sound, she crept nearer.

Bathed by the silvery glow of moon and stars, her husband's hair hung wetly over each shoulder. His face was tipped to the night sky, and his arms were outstretched. He turned in a slow circle. The pain etched on his face matched the sorrow in his voice as he begged for the spirits to give him wisdom and strength. He then begged for healing for his people.

A lump formed in Small Bird's throat. Though Swift Foot had tried to hide his emotions before, she'd already seen the depth of feeling inside him: first in the heat of his eyes during their wedding dance, then after, when she'd felt his passion and desire during their kiss—a kiss that seemed to have taken place a lifetime ago.

Moving silently among the brittle brush, thick bushes and trees lining the bank of the stream, Small Bird couldn't take her eyes off her husband.

Leave him, a small voice whispered. *He needs to be alone.*

No! How could she leave him? He needed comfort.

He needed *her*.

As she needed him.

Staring at the sleek beauty of his body, Small Bird needed him in every way. Earlier he'd given her a glimpse and taste of the passion between a man and a woman; right now she felt it rise again inside her. She felt torn between her need for him and the need to restrain herself. How could she be feeling carnal desires at such a time? She should be ashamed of herself. But her body couldn't help responding to the sight of him.

Her gaze scanned his upper body. His wet chest gleamed in the moonlight, each thick muscle fully defined. Her fingers crept up and over her own tunic to the soft swells of her breasts. She remembered the hard wall of his chest against them when he'd rested his body over hers.

She moved her left hand up, felt the sudden hammering of her heart. Her right hand touched the spot on her right breast where his heart had pounded. She longed to wade into the water, to rest her palms on his shoulders and dig her fingers into the hard ridge of his shoulder muscles. She wanted to skim her hands down over his massive chest and the taut plane of his flat, hard abdomen. Her gaze dropped to the water lapping against him, hiding that part of him she'd felt grow and harden against her.

Her chest tightened, her breath caught in her throat, and her palms grew moist. She slid them down the sides of her leggings to dry them.

Reflected light from the moon and stars rippled in the water that encircled his body as he continued to move in a circle. When he turned his back to her, she tried to take control of her desire, but that wide expanse of flesh stirred Small Bird as well. His long hair trailed downward, leading her gaze along the curved indent of his spine and farther, to the water hiding the swell of his buttocks.

He continued to turn, and her gaze went to his face. The anguish written there made Small Bird take a step back. She was intruding. This was a private moment, very personal, very emotional. Few men would want witnesses to such a display of pain and emotion. Especially the proud man she knew her husband to be. But the lines of pain etched around his mouth, and the silent prayers he mouthed, kept her from leaving.

As if he felt her eyes upon him, Swift Foot suddenly dropped his arms and stared into the shadows where she stood. He didn't speak, but Small Bird knew he sensed her presence.

Her heart pounded. Fearing his rejection, she bravely left the shadows and walked down the gentle slope of the bank to stop just shy of the waterline. For long moments neither spoke. Finally Swift Foot broke the silence.

"I will seek revenge so that your father will not be forced to roam the shadows of this land. Our enemies will pay." His voice held a promise, determination, and the need to prove himself worthy.

Small Bird frowned at the last thought. This man had no need to prove himself to anyone. Or did he? She regarded her husband with a steady gaze and sought the truth. Perhaps he, most of all, would feel a great need to prove himself. For a chief, he was young. Swift Foot had not experienced life to the same extent as most men who became great leaders. Add to that the merging of their two tribes, and the attack that had resulted in the loss of many lives, and Small Bird understood her husband's need for vengeance.

She sighed. Revenge meant more bloodshed on both sides. Yet the spirit of her father could not rest until avenged. In his ghostly form he'd roam the shadows of the *maka,* unable to journey to the spirit world. Staring at

Swift Foot, Small Bird knew her husband must honor her father.

Yet the killing had to stop. If he killed on her father's behalf, then the enemy would retaliate. In a vicious circle, the killing would never cease.

"This war must end," she said softly, stepping closer, ignoring the squishy mud of the stream beneath her feet. "This killing, these battles over something that happened before your birth, must be put to rest."

Swift Foot waded closer, then stopped. "It will never end," he said, his voice harsh with bitterness. "Talks of peace with our enemy have proven a waste of time."

Trying not to notice how the water lapped gently against her husband's hips, Small Bird forced her gaze back to his face. "There has to be a way. If not, we will all be destroyed."

Swift Foot smacked the water with the flat of his hand. "You do not speak anything I do not already know." He pushed forward, moving toward her, his body revealed in splendid gleaming nakedness.

Turning slightly out of respect and a sudden maidenly shyness, Small Bird refused to be silenced. "Then we must think of other solutions. There has to be a way to atone for the past that does not involve bloodshed."

"There is."

His whispered words, filled with sorrow and conviction, brought tears to Small Bird's eyes and a lump to her throat. "How?" The very way he'd spoken made her heart skip a beat.

Swift Foot shook himself. He turned his back to her, his wide shoulders flexing as he did. "It is not your concern," he replied. His voice was harsh, its tone warning Small Bird that he had no more to say on the matter.

He walked up the riverbank to pick up a clean breechclout and fasten it around himself.

Small Bird narrowed her eyes then stalked over to him. She moved around him until he was forced to acknowledge her presence. "You are wrong, my husband," she said. "It is as much my concern as yours. Your people are now my people. We are all at risk. Our *children* are at risk."

Swift Foot recoiled as if Small Bird had physically struck him. "There will not be children," he said in a snarl. "Not ours."

Small Bird's words brought back demons: the loneliness of his childhood, the regrets of a small boy who understood why his parents had died, and the sadness of a man who knew that he posed a risk to everyone around him.

He strode away from Small Bird. Earlier, with the storm bursting around them, with passion exploding between them, he'd almost forgotten his vow not to bed his wife. He'd decided long ago never to have children, because he refused to put any child through what he'd suffered. And there was no question that his own children would be caught up in this war.

Of course, he'd also once vowed to never marry; a hunted man had no business taking a wife. But while that decision had been taken from him, this one would not. He might not have been able to control his marital obligations; but bringing a child into this violent world was entirely within his power. Even if the making of such a child would bring him some pleasure. Looking into Small Bird's dark eyes, he acknowledged that there would be great joy in bedding her. But that was precisely why he could not.

He turned to leave, heading not back toward camp and his tipi, but away. Away from his wife and any temptation of claiming her as his own.

Small Bird followed and grabbed his arm. "I am your wife. You may not have wished for a wife, but you now have one. And as my husband, your life is now my concern." She paused, her chest heaving. "We *are* man and wife."

"You do not need to remind me of that fact," was all he said. He raked his eyes over her.

She tipped her chin up defiantly. "Then why do you say the future of our people is none of my concern? What affects one affects both. As your wife, I can help you. I can help *us*."

"I have no interest in what you have to say."
Swift Foot tried to look away and appear unmoved, but the wild fury in her eyes, the stubborn set of her mouth, drew him. The strength of her resolve made him burn with desire. Oh, how this dark beauty was different from the blond and timid Emily!

"I will have my say," his wife demanded. "I am also entitled to walk at your side. It is my duty and my desire to take care of you, to tend your wounds and ease your pain." Her voice softened. "Please, Swift Foot. Let me be your wife! Let me take care of you."

Swift Foot was overcome with emotion: rage at her demands and admiration for her strength. He advanced on her and took her in his arms. Her eyes glinted more brightly than the stars overhead.

"You wish to be my wife?" he asked.

She glared at him. "I *am* your wife."

"So you are." Swift Foot pulled her hard against him.

Small Bird opened her mouth to protest his rough handling, but he savagely brought his mouth down on hers. He would show her what she was requesting.

The kiss was filled with the intensity of the earlier storm. Violence poured between them. Small Bird took his fury, though, swallowed it and gave it back in the form of love. Understanding and compassion seemed to radiate from her—as well as a hunger he could taste.

Her mouth moved with his. It pressed back hard against his lips, bit when he bit. His tongue stormed her mouth. She welcomed it, tried to soothe him and drain his anger away. She held her own against his furious onslaught, and when she felt him withdraw, she pushed her way into his mouth. Her kiss held the same intensity and passion his had.

Hot. Furious. Explosive. Passion ripped the air between them like a bolt of lightning blasting a tree. Small Bird dug her fingers into his shoulders and hung on. Not once did she protest or pull away. She seemed to understand Swift Foot's blazing anger, knew it stemmed from guilt, sorrow, and his feelings of failure.

He didn't need to tell her. She knew. And she was sure she was right. Just as she'd been sure Swift Foot needed her, even if he protested against it.

Though it seemed a lifetime, their explosive kiss lasted no more than a few overwhelming heartbeats. Then Swift Foot's worry, fear, and anger transformed into simple need. His brutality became wholly passionate. The savage wildness that Swift Foot was always careful to keep leashed on the battlefield broke loose. He took from Small Bird. She had asked for this, and he would take from her.

He needed, so he would take.

He needed more. He took more.

He groaned beneath the weight of his need, feared it would consume and destroy him. Then Small Bird moaned—not in protest but wholly with husky desire. Somewhere deep in the red haze of his passion, it registered that his wife wasn't resisting.

Stunned, he realized that her passion matched his, that her lips were pressing just as hard against his, that her teeth were nipping at him in a frenzy of desire. He had not scared her away with his anger, nor with his passion. That calmed him faster than anything.

He shoved her away from him, held her at arm's length until she regained her balance. Then he released her. Their ragged breathing filled the air as they stared at each other. Her burning black gaze lowered to his mouth then shifted back to his eyes. He took in her bruised, swollen lips and his desire almost overcame him again.

"Go," he whispered hoarsely.

Nothing scared him more than losing control. In fact, he could not remember having done so since he'd turned seven. Until now. He ran a hand through his hair and realized it was shaking. He wanted to run far from this woman who threatened to destroy so much. But he could not. He'd never run from anything. He'd always faced his pain and anguish.

Even when he'd been forced to leave Emily behind, which was one of the most difficult things he'd ever had to do, he'd faced his pain. Once he'd left her, he could easily have run away. He'd known she would be found, had left her to the care of another of her kind. But he hadn't run. Instead of sparing himself the emotional pain of listening to her sadness, he'd hidden himself close by and had watched over her, sharing her agony. He'd felt that was his duty.

Staring at his wife now, he told himself that this time was different. He had no heart to break. This time it was pride—pride and a fierce need to be alone—that was making him take a step back. And while he desired this woman, it was wrong of him to make love to her like this.

Small Bird moved toward him. "No," she said, as if reading his mind. She came ever closer, resting her palms flat against his chest. "You are my husband. It is your right to take what I offer."

Swift Foot stilled. He didn't dare move. The gentle touch of her fingers, their unconsciously soothing motions, were like the soft glow of many tipis on a cold, dark night: They drew him in, made him feel safe.

He rejected her offer of comfort. He didn't want it.

No. He did want it. Yearned for it desperately. But he didn't deserve it.

Clamping his hands around her wrists, he pushed her away. "I take you in anger, not love. I have no love to give. I have *nothing* to give." His voice deepened as his pain grew.

"You are wrong," Small Bird argued, her eyes gleaming with unshed tears. "This is meant to be. The past—"

Her blind trust, her unwavering faith— both traits he'd lost a long time ago—sapped what remained of his control. Words burst out of him like water through a broken dam: "The past repeats itself. I am no better than my father. I have brought death to my people—"

"No," Small Bird interrupted, her eyes furious. She yanked free of his grasp. Her hand slashed downward. "You are not to blame for your father's actions."

Swift Foot laughed bitterly. "My father's dishonor is mine. I am no better." Grief, guilt, and a bone-deep exhaustion washed away his anger, and suddenly nothing could hold back the painful words he had to say. He had much to account for and live with. He would not add lies, or allow his wife to believe falsely of him.

He held up one hand when she opened her mouth to protest. "My father fell in love with a white captive. She had hair like the sun and eyes like the sky. He loved her and risked everything for her. He gave up his arranged marriage and offended the Miniconjou tribe, who wars with us to this day."

Small Bird looked confused. "This is not new to me."

Glancing for a moment at the flowing stream, Swift Foot forced himself to look his wife in the eyes. "I too fell in love with a white girl. She has hair paler than the morning sun, and like my mother, her eyes are the blue of the sky." Sorrow overwhelmed him. He did not hide the anguish of his broken heart from her; he revealed all to Small Bird, knowing that the truth would send her fleeing. Hoping that it would.

Small Bird gasped. Tears gathered in her eyes. Her mouth opened but nothing came out. Shocked, she broke away and paced along the river bank. Finally she turned back to him. "Do you plan to bring her here and make her your second wife? Will you choose her over me?" Her voice broke. One hand rose to press against her mouth.

Swift Foot closed his eyes against the obvious pain in his wife's eyes. All residual anger and resentment drained away. She had not asked for this marriage any more than he had. And no matter his own feelings, he had no right to hurt her. She was innocent. The blame lay with him.

"No. She is gone. I returned to fulfill my duty. But I cannot love again. You must understand."

Anger and resentment welled up inside him as he continued. "I have also vowed never to allow any child of mine to go through life with the guilt I suffered. Or the danger. No child of mine will have to endure dishonor or war. What my father did wrong will end with me. It will not be passed on."

Though Swift Foot had been cared for by his aunt and uncle, he'd always been aware of the taint inside him: The white man's blood that flowed through his veins. The knowledge of his family's weakness. Those things would not be passed on.

Staring briefly up into the night sky, he returned his gaze to Small Bird's face. He forced himself to share her pain. "The only way to prevent the past from repeating itself, the only way to end further bloodshed, is to end it with me. I will release you from our marriage come morning. I do not wish to burden you with my family's curse."

But would he have burdened Emily—risked her life—by bringing her back with him if he had not been promised to another? He didn't know. Would never know. Emily hadn't made him lose control like Small Bird, so . . .

Visibly shaken, Small Bird backed away. Tears streamed from her eyes and down her cheeks as she stared at him in disbelief. Then she turned and ran. Away from him. Back toward camp. Back toward their tipi, which he would never share with her.

After tonight he would never be able to trust himself around her. Though he had not said as much to her, Small Bird had freed the beast within him. And losing control over his emotions scared him far worse than twenty more years of war with the Miniconjou.

Chapter Ten

Small Bird ran, dashing away her tears as she stumbled back toward camp. "How can he be so cruel?" she whispered to herself. His words stabbed her heart with the same sharpness as the blade that had left open wounds on her husband's body.

Stopping well before reaching the outer ring of her people's tipis, she sought to calm her emotions. Desperately she tried to hang on to her waning faith. Her belief in the future, in the path she walked as being her true path, had taken a beating. Yet in her mind, heart and soul, Swift Foot felt so right. Their joining still felt preordained.

Closing her eyes, she looked inward. So many emotions had burned there in the last few days, she felt lost and confused. Focusing on her heart, she counted each beat, felt each breath she took. Deliberately she slowed her breathing. Then she concentrated on her other senses. The night wind brushed against her skin, cool against the tears on her face, soothing against her arms and throat when she tipped her head back.

Calmer, her thoughts still chaotic but no longer desperate, she wrapped her arms around herself and stared up at the bright, twinkling stars. "What is it you want of me?" she asked the four spirits above the earth. Moon, sky, and stars were the only ones visible, but she included sun in her request for answers.

Her gift of seeing and speaking the truth had always been respected by her people. Knowledge came to her when she needed it. She felt it as surely as anything, even when others disagreed with her. Even when Swift Foot disagreed with her.

Her father had listened to her words; he'd believed in her gift before he died. Her tribe's young medicine man also respected the truth of her dreams, and had agreed that her life be joined to Swift Foot's. Her husband's uncle, even, the old chief, and others—they all had believed as she did that this vision was meant to be.

But if she was right, why was it so hard to believe? Why was she forced to suffer and have doubts?

As if her thoughts had conjured him out of thin air, Wind Dancer appeared in her path. "You are troubled," he stated after he looked her over.

Small Bird glanced up at him. Perhaps he could give her the answers she needed, tell her she was right. "How do you know truth when you have no proof?"

Smiling, the shaman approached. "Listen to your heart. Have faith in what you believe."

"It is so hard to believe sometimes. It is so hard to know what's right." Small Bird sighed. "What if I'm wrong? What if I am choosing to believe what I want rather than the truth?" Though many others believed as she did, Swift Foot did not. And that he doubted made her doubt herself.

Wind Dancer lifted one hand to the night sky. "What do you see?"

She searched the heavens. "I see moon and stars. I see the one star that does not move. It is always there. The others dance around it."

"When you cannot see them, when clouds hide them from view, are they still there?"

Small Bird cocked her head to the side. "They are always there." She frowned, then glanced back up to the dark heavens. She could see the spirits now, but whether or not she could, she knew they were always there. They were eternal. Moon and stars appeared with the calm, soothing darkness of night, and sun and sky provided the renewal of light, life, and color during the day. Their colors and hues might change, clouds might hide these spirits, but for eternity they were there. That was an undeniable truth.

Truth.

Glancing back to Wind Dancer, she found him gone. Spinning around in a slow circle, she saw no trace of him. Then she smiled. She'd found her own answers. Resolve shoved the hurt from her heart. Though she still ached, she knew what she had to do.

Hurrying back to her tipi, she grabbed a large parfleche. Having done so, she retraced her steps, gathering her courage as she went. She found Swift Foot sitting in the same spot where she'd left him, knees drawn to his chest, arms wrapped around them as he stared blankly out over the stream. He sat so still and stiff, he looked close to shattering. He looked lonely and lost.

A small seed of jealousy sprouted in her heart when she realized her husband looked like a man with a broken heart. She recognized the look, felt the same pain: he looked as empty as she felt.

He loved another.

The knowledge whirled through her brain. Around and around, whipping her sadness into a froth it went, sending the shattered pieces of her heart to the four corners of the earth. Like his father, Swift Foot had fallen

in love with a white woman. An outsider.
How could she compete with an unseen, unknown enemy? He loved another, wanted another, but was stuck with her. In such a
situation, how could she gain his love, trust,
or respect? It was impossible, wasn't it?

She held a hand to her stomach to still the
nervous fluttering. Swift Foot had the wealth
and the means to support more than one
wife. It was an accepted practice. He could
have returned with this woman, made her
wife number two after marrying Small Bird.
Why hadn't he?

No, she realized with sudden insight. He
would not have—could not have brought her
back. His whole life, all his problems,
stemmed from a battle that centered around
a white woman. He had meant it when he
said it was too late for him and this white
woman. But his loss had bred resentment and
affected their future together.

Standing there, feeling the despair ema-
nating from him, Small Bird wanted to go to
him. She wasn't the woman of his heart, but
he was the man of hers, and she couldn't bear
to see him suffer so.

She smiled sadly. Swift Foot was her husband. He was a great warrior, a respected
leader, a man of principal and one of his
word. After all, he'd married her as he'd
promised. The truth of his feelings in this
matter had not changed his actions. She won-

dered if she would have been as strong if someone asked her to leave Swift Foot for her duty.

The girlish love she'd carried for Swift Foot for as long as she could remember, suddenly changed. It became deeper as she understood him better. She now knew one thing: she cared for this man wholly and could do no less than offer care for his wounds and whatever other comfort she could provide. No matter what he wanted, she still wanted him.

Shoving aside all her feelings of the heart, Small Bird left the shadows. The slight tensing of Swift Foot's shoulders told her he knew she'd returned. He didn't speak. Kneeling behind him, she rested her palms on his shoulders. He shuddered, then stilled.

Slowly she gripped the tight cords of muscle around his neck and pressed, using her thumbs to smooth away the knots. He tried to resist by leaning forward. "No. Allow me," she said. "You cannot change what is meant to be."

Swift Foot remained silent.

"You blame me for losing your white woman," she said softly, trying to show she understood his anger and resentment.

"There is nothing to blame you for. What is done is done."

"Yes, what is done is done," she whispered.

The fact that her grip and words held him where he sat attested to his exhaustion, phys-

ical and mental. Seeing again the image of
her husband standing in the water, chanting
and beseeching the spirits to give him
strength, Small Bird knew each death, each
injury had added additional burdens to the
already huge load on Swift Foot's shoulders.

"You have many injuries," she said. Her
gaze roamed down his arms, over his back
and his shoulders, to a large cut on his thigh.

"They are nothing," he said.

"I will treat them." Her tone brooked no argument. She unfolded the quilled strip of
leather she'd brought, revealing herbs and
powders tucked into smaller pouches. Some
mixtures had been made with grease and
were encased in a length of buffalo intestine.

Using a small piece of hide that she soaked
in water from the stream, she gently bathed
each cut. They were mostly already clean
from his bath, but a few were very deep and
needed to be rewashed. She tended the cuts
on his back and arms first, giving him time to
gain control over his emotions.

Slipping around, she knelt before him in
order to tend his chest. The tips of her fingers
stroked over his hard flesh. When her small-
est finger brushed one tiny male nipple hardened by the cold, Swift Foot jerked.

Heat flared within Small Bird. Quickly she
finished, but she couldn't resist one last
stroke of the firm flesh along his side. Next
she tended his thigh. First with the cloth she

dabbed gently at its hard, flat top, then slid inward, moving the edge of his breechclout aside. The gash there faded to a small, thin line halfway up his thigh. He gasped when she ran the cloth along it.

This time, when her fingers smeared bear grease onto the injury, her own breath hitched. His skin felt hot. Firm. The pads of her fingers itched to explore more, to discover each difference in their bodies.

"Enough." Swift Foot's voice, low and husky, drew her gaze.

"No. There are cuts here . . . and here," she argued, running a clean corner of her cloth down one cheek and along his jaw. His gaze darkened. Small Bird saw her reflection in it, and she felt the heat simmering there. Unable to resist or deny her desire, she stroked the backs of her fingers along the unblemished side of his face, then down across his full lower lip.

"You could have been killed today," she murmured.

"It would have been best," he responded emotionlessly. "It would have ended this fighting."

She shook her head, not shocked by his words but saddened by them. "No. It would have solved nothing."

"My death might be the only thing that spares your life."

"If they intend for me to die, they intend

for me to die." She placed her finger lightly against his lips. "What will happen will happen. We can only stay on the right path and be prepared. Had you died today, the need for bloodshed would have grown. Your people would have been given even more reason to retaliate. A life for a life. Vengeance."

Swift Foot grabbed her wrist, his fingers wrapping hard around her flesh. "My path *is* one of vengeance. These new deaths must be avenged. With each attack, a new cycle begins."

Small Bird drew a shaky breath, and a tear escaped. Her husband reached out to trace its path. "We must break the cycle," she pleaded. "Together."

"I do not think it is possible."

The starkness of his words gave Small Bird the courage to cup each side of his face. "You must have faith. You must believe. Our past brought us together. It brought us together for this. We must end the violence. Our future depends on what we do with the present."

Swift Foot sighed. More than ever he longed to believe. But after today he'd lost his courage, his will. All he wanted was peace and solitude.

The idyllic weeks of the summer seemed so far away, as if they had been nothing more than a sweet dream. He closed his eyes and searched his heart for Emily. He called her, wanted to see her. But she didn't come to him.

His eyes shot open, and he stared over the top of Small Bird's head, searching for his old love in the night sky. There was nothing there but the bright pinpoints of the stars. He could not summon her image. Confused by his tumultuous emotions, he glanced down and saw the silvery gleam of the moon in Small Bird's dark hair. When she met his gaze without hesitation, he saw the stars in her eyes.

Hope.

Fearing he'd lose control once more, he tried to look away. But the soothing touch of her hands, the gentleness in her eyes, and the promise of passion in her parted lips dragged a groan from his throat.

Many years ago, violence had brought them together and begun his quest to become a great warrior.

Violence had demanded he marry this woman, and it had denied him the love of another.

Violence now brought them together on a riverbank beneath the moon and stars. Would it consume them and end their lives? He feared he knew the answer. Yet despite his worries, he suddenly felt a strong pull to give himself over to her. He could not resist any longer the comfort his wife offered.

Sliding his hand around her neck, he

brought her close. "You should not have returned to me."

Her breath warmed his lips. "I could do nothing else."

Swift Foot wasn't strong enough to push her away. A deep need surfaced for her touch, her kiss; he needed to lose himself in this woman as he'd never before done with another. He wrapped his arms around her.

Forcing her face back, he skimmed his lips over it gently, tenderly. Her fingers inched into his hair, held his head close. Her lips kissed whatever they could find—sweet, comforting kisses that stirred Swift Foot's blood and released his pent-up hunger.

Their mouths met. Lips and tongues flirted. Swift Foot's arms moved to Small Bird's shoulders, crushing her to him. Her fingers dug into the back of his head, pinning him where she wanted.

At the same moment, each pulled slightly away. Their heavy breathing fogged the air between them. "Be sure, wife," he said, his voice hoarse with the effort to control himself. "Be sure of what you do."

Small Bird reached up on tiptoe to kiss him tenderly on the corner of his mouth. "I ask you the same, husband. You are mine. I will share you with no other. Nor will I allow distance between us." Her hands slid down the column of his neck, her fingers smooth on the taut muscles there.

"It may be death I am sentencing you to." In echo of her movements, his fingers traced the side of her face, lingering on the hollow below her cheeks.

"We are married. I am already the enemy in our foe's eyes." She took his fingers in hers and kissed the backs. "I give myself to my husband. No regrets."

Still Swift Foot held back. Even if he took what she so freely offered, what he was beginning to be sure he wanted, this was simply one more thing to be taken from him. He closed his eyes, remembering all the men who'd just died in battle, knew some of the others would never be the same. The price of his life was high. He didn't deserve this. Or her. He tried one last time to drive her away.

"Your father—"

Small Bird's fingers stopped his protest. "My father knew the dangers. He also believed in this union. He died a warrior. He died a father proud of his daughter, and confident that there would one day be peace."

"I wish I shared his belief." Swift Foot pulled her close. He hardly understood what was happening. Yesterday and before, the sight of this woman had only reminded him of the love he had lost. But somewhere he'd realized that there was something more being offered here: a chance at happiness and redemption.

Even had he not been promised to Small

Bird, he could not have brought Emily back. Not with the war between the two tribes. His people would have objected, for it would have been a daily reminder of his father's choice to put himself first, over the well-being of his people. Swift Foot could never do that, *would* never do that. His love for Emily had been doomed, for he would always put his people first and seek ways to atone for the past. Small Bird offered him a chance at both, and to be happy.

She pulled away. "One day you will believe. Our destiny is linked, and that truth, and the truth will be revealed."

He stared at her intensely. "I wish you to show me. To prove the truth of your words." His head drew closer. "But later. Much later." Then he kissed her.

Small Bird leaned into him, but Swift Foot kept his passion under control as gently and tenderly he explored her. He moved slowly. He teased and tasted, nurturing her growing need. When his wife's breathing turned erratic, he left her mouth to explore the slender length of her throat. His hands roamed over her; one pressed against her lower back, fingers splayed wide; the other supported her neck.

Reaching down, Swift Foot slid both his hands down the soft swell of her buttocks. His fingers gripped her thighs and he lifted.

221

"Wrap your legs around my waist," he whispered.

Small Bird felt light as the morning fog floating across the stream bank. Above her, the sky was lightening. Her legs hugged Swift Foot, bringing the part of her that throbbed up against the hard ridge of his manhood. The feel of him sped her heart and made her mouth go dry. He rocked against her. Beneath her tunic she wore leggings, but her womanhood ground against his breechclout, felt the swelling flesh of his desire.

One of his hands massaged the back of her neck; the other caressed her buttocks. "I feel strange," she whispered. The fluttering in her belly didn't hurt, nor did the pulsing of her sex. But with each slow rub of fabric against her body, her unrest grew.

"You feel desire," Swift Foot murmured in her ear. He pulled her lower body tight against him. "Feel what you do to me."

He held her in place until Small Bird thought the hot pulsing and throbbing of her body would drive her crazy. She squirmed. Though they touched intimately, it wasn't enough. Using her hands, she brought her mouth to his.

"Do not tease me any longer," she begged.

Swift Foot returned the urgency of her kiss with his own. He moved against her slowly. She moaned. Then his grinding grew fast, which made her pull away; the intensity was too much. He slowed, moving ever so softly, forcing her to tighten her legs around his waist in order to maintain contact. Then came a hard thrust that made her cry out and shiver in his arms. Surely she'd burst apart from the intense feelings coursing through her body!

Swift Foot lowered her to the ground and knelt before her. Small Bird shuddered at the feel of his fingers creeping up her thigh beneath her tunic. When he reached her waist, he made quick work of releasing her left legging. It fell.

"Turn," he said.

With his hands still on her waist, Small Bird turned to allow him access to her other side. The brush of his fingers across her buttocks made her gasp. Again the warmth of his flesh was shocking. A moment later, the second legging fell. His hands did not leave her. They spanned her waist until they found the ties that held the leather belt around her waist, to which each legging had been tied.

His gaze burned into her as his fingers skimmed her belly to undo the knot. Then the belt, too, was loose. Instead of whipping it off of her, he lowered his hands slowly. The belt inched down and off of her in a manner that had Small Bird's heart pounding in time to the throbbing between her legs.

Swift Foot dropped one end, reached between her legs, and removed the belt entirely—stroking it over her heated flesh as he did. Small Bird leaned on her husband's shoulders, overcome.

Sensations assailed her. She'd had no idea. She knew how a man and a woman mated, knew what went where, but these feelings and the growing ache inside her were foreign. "What is it you are doing to me?" She gasped.

Swift Foot stood and wrapped her belt around his fist. He lifted it in triumph. "I am making you want me as much as I want you. Do you want me, wife?"

Tears streaming down her face, overcome by happiness, Small Bird nodded. She held out her arms. "Yes, husband. My need is great."

Swift Foot took her fingers in his and lifted her hands over her head. He grabbed the hem of her tunic and slowly raised it. "Look at me as I look upon you. Know that I desire you."

Small Bird didn't even think to be embarrassed as he slowly revealed her to the world. She did as he commanded. She watched him and saw the way his eyes darkened, focused on his parted lips, heard his ragged breathing. Then, as if he could stand it no more, he drew her garment over her head.

Standing naked before him, Small Bird smiled shyly, then stepped forward. "I will see my husband, too," she said.

His flesh was hot when her fingers slid beneath the cloth of his shirt to find the knot of his leather thong. As he'd done for her, she slowly loosened it, allowing the breechclout to fall lower and lower, revealing her husband inch by inch.

At last, he grabbed her hands. "No more teasing," he said, his voice thick with desire. His breechclout fell. He scooped up her tunic, swung her into his arms as well, and carried her away from the muddy stream. He found a patch of grass, set her down, and spread out her tunic.

Small Bird took the hand he held out, and knelt in front of him. When her husband pulled her close, then forced her back, she obeyed, loving the feel of his hard, muscular body pressing against hers.

"I will be gentle. I promise." Once more he bent his head to kiss her.

Small Bird gave herself up to the pleasure, waited for the wildness that had overwhelmed her before. But it didn't come, for Swift Foot remained gentle. He was controlled, and her frustration grew. She wanted the beast within him. The beast she'd seen. Not this controlled person he presented to the world.

She knew the truth, knew violence lived deep inside him. And it was that part that made him so passionate. She pulled his head back. "Kiss me. *Really* kiss me. As before. I want all of you." She pulled her knees open and wrapped her legs around him as she'd

225

done while they stood. "I want all of you."

Swift Foot stared down into her eyes. He didn't want to lose control. He feared that he would hurt her. "No. Slow. Easy," he said. He tried to resume their kiss, but Small Bird bit his lower lip. She tugged on it, suckled and stroked it with her tongue. Her hands roamed his back, and her legs tightened, bringing them naked flesh to naked flesh.

Her hips lifted and circled against him. He felt the springy curls of her womanhood on his sex. He jerked his hips, unable to stop the involuntary movement. Then he felt her heat, and the moistness that proved her need.

"No," he moaned. "Slow. Controlled." His hands bunched in her hair to keep from going to her breasts. He had to bank his desire.

Small Bird ignored him. Her body continued to rub and press hard against his. She tipped her hips up, trying to merge their bodies. On his back, Swift Foot felt the sharp sting of her nails. "Now. Make us one," she said. "Be the man you are. Do not pretend. Not with me. Not in this." The scrape of her teeth against his throat, the stroke of her tongue along his collarbone, shattered his control.

He needed this woman, had to have her now. He couldn't wait to initiate her with the slow gentleness she deserved.

Raising himself up, Swift Foot pulled his hips back. Small Bird's legs spread wider before him. Positioning his shaft at her wet entrance, he fell slightly forward, his weight on his hands. "Hold me. Hold me tight." He moaned. He had not entered her.

Her arms went around his neck, her legs around his hips. Swift Foot stared down at her. As though embarrassed or afraid, she tried to close her eyes, cutting the bond between them. He stopped her. "Watch," he said. "See what you do to me?"

She gripped him with her thighs, pulling the tip of him an inch into her. "Show me," was all she said. "Make me yours, Swift Foot."

The sound of his name on her lips, the renewed fearlessness in her eyes, and the throbbing heat of her left him no choice. With one swift stroke he entered her, tearing through her maidenhead.

Small Bird bit her lip to silence her cry of pain, but she never took her eyes off him. Swift Foot ordered his body to go slowly. To show his wife that he could be gentle. But the violence of the day, the raging fury storming through him, along with years of being forced to maintain control at all times, overpowered him.

His hips surged forward. Then again. And again. Faster and faster. Harder and harder he thrust until his lungs hurt and his body knew of only one thing. He sought release in becoming one with this woman.

Chapter Eleven

Small Bird flinched at the first tearing of her maidenhead, but watching her husband, seeing the veins on his temple and forehead, the look of surprise on his face as he lost control, fascinated her. The sensations of hurt and burning faded with each thrust until she felt something primal clawing within her.

She tried to still it, wanted to watch her husband, needed to see this part of him—but with each of his rapid thrusts, her breathing grew shallower, her head rolled back, and her eyes closed. She tried to fight it, to watch him, but she couldn't.

A wave of need built inside her. It was like a storm. Without ever realizing it, she was raising her hips to meet his thrusts, her moans and soft cries contrasting with the harsh, guttural sounds coming from between his clenched teeth.

Her fingers dug into his back, and she held him tightly. Supported by his arms, he pushed up his torso stretching away from her, their bodies now touching only where they were joined. Cool air rushed between them.

When Swift Foot tossed his head back and let out a moan, Small Bird gasped and held her breath. For one heartbeat she stared at him; then she felt him shudder and saw some unknown emotion take control. Then pleasure overcame her. Her body stiffened, her head rolled back, and her eyes closed. With one last deep thrust, Swift Foot sent her spiraling from her body into ecstasy.

Her lower limbs tightened as she convulsed around her husband's throbbing member; her body pulled him to her, held him inside. Flashes of light brighter than any star exploded in her brain as the world fell away beneath her.

Floating, exhausted, but incredibly satisfied, Small Bird lay still, her eyes closed, trying to find words to describe the wondrous experience that had just occurred. Swift Foot slumped down, his body blanketing hers, protecting it. Around them, cool air swept over their sweat-drenched bodies.

"That was . . ." Small Bird shook her head. How did one put into words the experience of leaving one's body to float through the heavens?

Swift Foot lifted his head and stared down into her face. "Unforgivable. I took you with no tenderness. No consideration. I caused you pain."

Small Bird trailed her fingers down the side of his cheek, careful not to touch the bruised and scraped flesh there. "You are wrong, my husband. I gave myself to you. I wanted no false emotion or feeling. Yes, there was pain, but it was the most wonderful experience I've ever had." She paused, feeling suddenly shy.

"I flew," she said at last.

Swift Foot lowered his forehead to hers. "We flew together."

Remembering the lines etched in his features, the concentration, she traced the side of his face and asked, "Did it cause you pain?"

Swift Foot chuckled. "Once I took your maidenhead, did *you* feel pain?" He stared down into her eyes.

Frowning, Small Bird sought to remember. "No. I wouldn't say it was pain. Yet I needed so badly, it hurt."

"That is how I felt," Swift Foot agreed. He marveled. Small Bird had accepted that uncontrolled part of him he revealed to no one— not even Emily. He'd taken his new wife with such violence yet her own response had more than matched his. She had equaled his passion and even encouraged it.

Faced with the knowledge that Small Bird not only accepted the unseen violence and lack of control within him, but encouraged it, Swift Foot paused. He had to think about this. But before he could examine all that had happened, he had to get some distance.

He went to pull out of her; but a surge of renewed desire shot through him at the feel of their slippery congress. Groaning, he slid back into her.

Her eyes widened. "Can we do this again?" she asked. "Can I fly again?"

Grinning, knowing he could not, at least this morning, deny either of them the release they both needed, he tucked a stray strand of hair behind her ear. "You can fly as many times as you wish, wife. I will lift you."

Pulling her off of him, he drew her onto his lap. He slipped one finger inside her, then two. Her head rocked from side to side. "I want you," she said in a gasp. "Fly with me." As he stroked her, her words slurred.

"I will. But right now you will fly for me."

Small Bird felt odd as her husband used his fingers to pleasure her. And he watched! She felt his eyes upon her. She should have protested. But while she felt embarrassed, her body surged with the need to fly. She bit her lip, trying to silence her cries of ecstasy.

His fingers slid through her woman's curls and found the sensitive nub therein. She gasped.

"Do not hold back," he urged. "Let me hear how much you want this. I need to know you want this."

His words freed her. Her breathy moans grew. She urged him on, crying out as he sent her higher and higher. His fingers inside her stroked long, hard, and fast. The one finger on the bud of her sex circled faster and harder. At last, something touched just the right spot; she burst apart. Her hips jerked and shook. Her back arched and her fingers dug into the ground seeking something to hold.

But she was free. Flying. Soaring among the stars.

Swift Foot entered her quickly. She felt his hot length slide into her, and he groaned as once more her body convulsed around him. The walls of her sex gripped him and urged him to find his own release. He thrust deeply, over and over.

"More," she said softly. "I can feel it building." She sobbed beneath him.

The knowledge that she wanted him so much, was responding so completely, sent Swift Foot over the edge. "Yes, fly with me," he cried out. Then he grabbed her, and slanted his mouth over hers.

"Yes," she said into his mouth. "Yes."

And she did fly with him. Together they left the world and their problems to soar as one to the heights of pleasure.

*   *   *

Willow Song sat in her tipi. The continuous wailing and lamenting all around her had released her own sorrow. Though she could take no part in the preparations for the dead, or console the grief-stricken, she felt the grief of each woman, man, and child as her own.

Also having just learned from her brother that Small Bird's father had died, Willow Song especially wished that she had the courage to go and offer words of sympathy to her.

She glanced over at the parfleche she'd made to give to her cousin's wife. Like most of what she made, it would find no good home but her own. Or maybe her brother would take it to trade the next time trappers were spotted.

Had she been a true Double-Woman Dreamer, her skills at quilling would be revered, sought after for their good medicine—even though the women would still not touch or get close to her. But that was not so. Instead, she lived in a half state. It didn't matter. She worked for her own satisfaction, not for a sense of worth. With her disfigured body, her worth to anyone except her brother, and perhaps Swift Foot, was less than that of the pups who were often killed for special feasts.

Concentrating on the intricate design of the yoke of a man's shirt, she tried to blot out the sounds of grief raging around her. At last, when she had had to remove the same quill three times, she set the garment down. Running her fingers over the soft elk skin—it had been tanned until it was thin, supple, and soft—she thought how nice it would look on Lone Warrior.

She grimaced. There was as much chance of him accepting a gift from her as of her being made whole again. Even though he'd been kind, she refused to believe he'd actually wear anything she made. Staring out the slight opening of the doorway, she thought of how he'd come upon her, and heard her singing.

He hadn't been afraid. Hadn't been repelled or repulsed.

There is beauty in you that none has seen before.

Her hands lifted to her face. One side was smooth and soft, but the other remained rough, covered in scar tissue.

I think I am falling in love with you.

Willow Song felt ill—sick with fear. Lone Warrior hadn't been serious, could not have meant his words.

Walk with me.

But she had walked with him. And though she'd kept him to her good side, waiting for him to tell her he was playing a horribly sick joke, but he hadn't. They'd walked in silence.

She closed her eyes and tried to smile, ignoring the stiffness of half her mouth. As much as her brother loved her, she knew he couldn't bear to look upon her ugliness, for it reminded him of their mother's death. She

understood and needed him too much to resent that. As he accepted her flaws, she accepted his.

Outside, the night air felt fresh and soothing. She longed to step out and leave her
small enclosure, but even under the cover of
darkness she didn't dare. Not with so much
grief ravaging her people. Any who saw might
blame her for the deaths of their loved ones.

A sudden cramp in her thigh made her cry
out. She stretched her leg and rubbed the
knotted muscle. Fear wasn't the only thing
that kept her inside; the long and arduous
night of travel had left her muscles screaming
in pain and her body weak with fatigue. It
would take many days before she recovered.
By then they'd likely move camps again, and
leave the dead behind.

A sound outside her tipi made her tense.
Who was it?

"*Hau*," a low voice spoke.

Willow Song held her breath. Lone Warrior? Here, in the early predawn hours when
most were asleep?

"Willow Song. I've come to see if you are
all right."

The man's voice, deep and husky, rich with
tenderness, made her shudder. "I am fine,"
she whispered, hiding her pain from him. She
couldn't move to the doorway to see, and
couldn't allow him in. She didn't want him to
see her like this.

"Will you come out so that I may speak to you?" he asked.

Tears gathered in her eyes at the concern in his voice. She still feared he played a game—a cruel one that would break her heart and crush her spirit. It seemed no matter what she told herself, she'd started to hope he cared for her.

"No. I cannot. Please go. It is early." She longed to see him, wanted to offer him sympathy over the loss of his father, but she didn't dare. His sister was wife to their chief, and he was also an important member of the tribe. There could be no relationship between them.

Why had she forgotten that fact? She tried to scoot over to the doorway to close the flap. She couldn't allow him to see her again. As soon as she moved, the knot in her leg went into a painful spasm. She cried out, then bit down hard on her lip to silence herself.

Lone Warrior pushed inside. "What is wrong?" he asked. He took one look at her leg, then dropped to his knees. "You are in pain."

"It is nothing." She gasped. "It will pass." Her fingers twitched over her thigh.

"Let me," Lone Warrior said, moving her hand out of the way.

Willow Song realized two things at once: her head was completely uncovered, and he was about to touch her thigh and the ugly scars caused by the hooves of the horse that had trampled her.

She pulled her hair over her shoulder to hide the ugly side of her face, and reached out a hand to stop him. "Please do not." She couldn't bear for him to see so much horror, let alone to touch it. He was so beautiful. So perfect. His long, black hair was parted down the middle and fashioned into two thick braids hanging over his broad shoulders to his gleaming skin. His good health, good looks, and sinewy body took her breath away. Her throat clogged with emotion.

He was as perfect as she was marred.

As beautiful as she was ugly.

As strong as she was weak.

He deserved someone whole. A woman he could be proud of. Someone who could walk at his side. Willow Song was not that woman and never would be.

But as he had the other night, Lone Warrior ignored her protests. His hands, warm, firm, and gentle, slid her dress up just past her knees. Then he leaned down, putting firm pressure on her thigh. Slowly he worked his way up from her knee, easing the muscles as he went. When his fingers brushed the ridges of her scars, she tensed.

"No. Relax. Let me help," he said. His voice soothed yet commanded her compliance.

At first his firm massage hurt—as her own clumsy fingers would have. But after a few minutes, magic flowed from his fingers into her thigh. The warmth of his hands and the strength in them were far more potent than had been Willow Song's attempts to ease her own pain. She relaxed.

As she stared at him, watching his dark, perfect fingers knead her flesh, Willow Song truly feared that she was falling in love. He glanced up at her, and their gazes locked. His hands stilled.

"Soon it will be day. When darkness bathes the land once more, I will come for you. Will you walk with me again?"

Willow Song wanted to shout yes. But fear held her back. She withdrew into herself. "I cannot."

Lone Warrior lifted her chin with his finger. "Why? Are you afraid of me?"

Slowly, she nodded, for she was. But that wasn't the only reason she told him no.

He reached out and tucked her hair behind her ear. "I have looked upon your face. Do not hide from me." He slid his finger down her disfigured cheek. "Please let me come to you tonight. I have need of your company. I mean you no harm."

Ashamed, she drew a deep breath. "I cannot walk tonight. My . . . my leg—"

Lone Warrior cursed. He took both her hands in his. "You will not have to walk. I will carry you, and we will find a quiet place to sit."

The thought of him carrying her made Willow Song blush. "It is not proper," she protested, even though her heart begged her to accept. His eyes held sadness, anger, and need. She responded to his need by lifting one hand to the side of his jaw.

"Are you afraid of what the others will think?" he asked.

"No," she replied softly. "Of course not. I fear what they will say of you. You are important."

"And you are not?" he wondered. He held up his hand. "No, do not answer, for what you say will anger me." He smiled to take the sting from his words. "It is settled, for I care not what others say, or think." He forced her to lie back, then covered her with a fur, saying, "Now rest."

He stood, then without giving her a chance to talk him out of returning, he left, giving her no chance to argue.

Though it hurt to move, Willow Song threw off her cover and pulled herself to the doorway. Slowly she lifted the flap and watched Lone Warrior walk away. Had she lost her mind? Her life had always been a solitary one, though she might desire to be with others. As a child she'd borne her isolation bravely, for that was the least she could do for her people. But she'd cried at night when there was no one around to see or hear.

Pulling herself back to her pallet, Willow

Song lay down and stared out the top of her tipi. Softly, so no one would hear, she sang a song of healing. Those for whom she sang would not hear, nor would they know she sang for them. But *Wakan Tanka*, who commanded the other spirits of their world, might hear her song and bring healing to those who suffered.

Chapter Twelve

The dawn turned into full morning. Lying between two furs, Swift Foot knew it was time to rise. From outside his tipi came sounds of people leaving their homes: the clearing of a throat, low murmurs, steps walking past, even the sound of horses greeting the day.

Normally he'd have been up, bathed, and planning his chores by now. But today the cozy bed made warm by the body snuggled against him kept him from rising.

He told himself that he didn't want to disturb Small Bird. The day would start soon enough, and it would be emotionally draining as she dealt with the death of her father, just as so many had lost their loved ones. Today the damage from last night's battle would be fully realized. In the harsh daylight they would all see the ravages of grief. And he would learn what other warriors had died during the night.

The day would be busy and emotional, and he wanted to postpone it as long as possible.

Rubbing his chin over Small Bird's head, he closed his eyes. Their lovemaking had been unlike anything he'd ever known. Remembering his loss of control, he sighed. No one had ever won that from him—and there had been plenty of times in his life when he had been given the opportunity. He'd carefully nurtured his control, knowing how easily he might otherwise give in to resentment or bitterness.

Usually he solved things by running: when things became too much, when he feared that his control was in danger of snapping, he ran. But last night he hadn't been able to escape. And he hadn't been able to stop from taking all that his wife offered.

Even now, when his shield of logic was firmly replaced, his body hardened with need for her. But such desire couldn't be given free rein again.

Using his hand, he smoothed strands of midnight-blue hair from Small Bird's face. Regret filled him. Fear assailed him. The enemy *would* try to kill her. And if he'd gotten her with child during their wild night of loving?

Pain clutched at his middle. *No!* He

couldn't think about that. He'd never allow that to happen. Yet it had happened to his parents. And sooner or later an attack would be launched against his family that he couldn't fight off.

The urge to protect his wife overwhelmed him. Had he been able, he'd have taken her away and hidden her somewhere safe. But there was nowhere they could hide safely unless they wandered alone for the rest of their days. And that wasn't much safer. Only in numbers would they be able to defend themselves amply, pool their resources to survive.

Small Bird shifted in his arms. One hand rose over her head, and she rolled onto her back. Her fur covering slipped, revealing one bare breast. Swift Foot stared.

He hadn't seen much in the night and early predawn, only felt the softness of her flesh. As he watched, cool air kissed the nipple. The small bud tightened. His loins swelled along with it.

He closed his eyes and tried to clear his mind. He could not allow himself to get emotionally involved. She could be just his wife. A wife took care of the tipi. Cooked. Saw to her husband's needs.

He gulped. He had one need that continued to grow.

No!

In his mind he told himself over and over he was risking too much. The more he touched Small Bird, made love to her, the greater her chances of conceiving—if it wasn't already too late. And also, deep down, he knew the real reason he strove to remain distant was that he feared falling in love with her.

After Emily, he hadn't thought another woman could enter his heart. But Small Bird had found her way inside. Her courageous spirit, her unfailing belief in their rightness, her determination and her fierce need to be with him instead of leaving him to be alone, her compassion—all had won him over.

Worse, after last night he wasn't sure he could bear to be alone again. But he had to keep his distance. Becoming emotionally involved with Small Bird would do neither of them any good. With that thought in mind, he tried to ease away from her. She woke.

He froze at her innocent, sleepy gaze, her flushed cheeks; and once more his gaze slid down to her bared breast. He swallowed hard. The small, fleshy mound tempted him. He wanted to bend down and cover it with his mouth. He wanted to lave her nipple with his tongue, and most of all he wanted to hear her soft, breathy cries fill his ears.

"*Hau,*" she said softly.

"*Hau,*" he replied, his voice deep and low.

When she saw where he stared, she blushed and tried to cover herself.

"No. You are beautiful." He pulled the fur

down, revealing both of her rounded breasts to his gaze.

Get up and leave, his inner voice demanded. *Do not risk more than is already at stake.* Listening to that voice, he pushed away.

Her arm went around his neck and stopped him. "Stay a few minutes," she cajoled.

"I have work to do. I am needed."

"Yes, husband, you are needed. But a few minutes won't make a difference."

Swift Foot shook his head. *Control,* he reminded himself. *Control.* That was all he had.

Small Bird traced his lower lip with her finger. "You are trying to run. But you cannot. It is too late to change what we did."

Swift Foot closed his eyes. "You mean if you are with child."

"Yes. If I am with child."

The image of a small girl who looked as Small Bird had at age three slid through his mind. She'd been a cute child with big, trusting eyes and a sweet nature. He remembered how she'd clung to him, how she'd followed him around for days and how he'd held her close and comforted her. The thought of one day having a daughter who dogged his heels or looked up at him with big, trusting adoration turned his resolve to mush. The image appealed—greatly.

But there was one problem: he had to keep everyone safe. "How can I bring you any further into danger?" he whispered.

Her hand cupped the back of his neck, and she smiled. "Can we decide that after we fly again?"

Swift Foot felt shock at her casual dismissal of danger, but he took in the hunger in his wife's dark brown gaze. "Perhaps there is no more within me to give," he said. But he knew he wouldn't refuse.

She smiled again, even more hungrily. "There is more in you than even you can see, my husband."

He growled low in his throat. "All right. For now, then, I want to see my wife. All of her."

Small Bird flung the covers off them both. "Look, my husband. Look all you like."

Swift Foot bent his head to her breast. "I plan to do more than look, wife."

Small Bird rose. Sore and stiff, she bathed with water from a skin and scrubbed with a piece of softened hide. She dressed with care.

As wife to Swift Foot, she had many new duties. Food had to be arranged, and with so many deaths, everyone would pool their resources together and help out everyone else. Also, they would have to determine who would help out those families who had lost their men.

Taking a deep breath, she paused at the door of the tipi. The sounds outside brought back the nightmares of last night—the memories of the dead and wounded. Last night she'd taken comfort in Swift-Foot, but today he'd be busy with his own duties. She was on her own and too old to run and hide from emotions she didn't enjoy.

"I still don't understand," she whispered, feeling sick at heart over the loss of her father. "He can't be gone." It seemed impossible that one day he would be planning her wedding, and the next he would be gone.

Resting her forehead against the pole to one side of the doorway, she tried to make sense of the tribe's many horrible deaths. So many. The loss had been great for each side.

Shoving aside the flap, she peered out of her tipi. Wails filled the air. Across from her, two small children huddled near another home: a small boy and his older sister. Both looked scared. Small Bird knew how they felt. Even as a grown woman she longed to have Swift Foot's comforting arms back around her. But she wouldn't see much of him for the rest of the day.

Stepping outside, she crossed to the children. Inside their tipi, soft sobbing spoke of death. Small Bird held out her hands. "Come. We will find you something to eat."

The girl simply stared at her. The little boy, in desperate need of comfort flung himself into her arms. He slumped against her as Small Bird picked him up, and she rubbed his back. Tears stung her eyes. Had these two been out here all night, hiding in the shadows?

Small Bird asked, *"Waniyetu nitona he?"* *How old are you?*

The young girl drew herself up. *"Waniyetu mawikcemna!"*

Small Bird smiled. "You are ten? You are old enough to tend to your small brother, then. Come. I know just the person to help you."

She made her way to Yellow Quail's tipi, where she set the boy down. "Wait here." Stepping to the door, she called out, *"Hau."*

Shy Mouse came to the flap. The girl threw her arms around Small Bird. "I am so sorry, cousin," she said, sobbing.

Holding the younger woman close, Small Bird fought her own tears. She had no time to give in to grief. Especially with two frightened children behind her. Pulling back, she motioned with her head. "Their father is among our lost. They were huddled outside."

Shy Mouse stopped her. "Say no more." She walked around Small Bird, sank to her knees, and looked at the children. "I could use your help with the morning meal," she told the girl. "There are many who need to be fed. Including your little brother."

The little boy scrunched up his face. "I am not little. I am big. Like my father." He puffed out his skinny chest.

His sister bit her lip and looked ready to

cry. She glanced first at Small Bird, then at Shy Mouse. "He does not understand," she said, her lower lip trembling.

Small Bird brushed her fingers across the girl's cheek. "None of us understands, child. Let my cousin help you care for your brother until your mother stops grieving and comes for you."

The ten-year-old took her brother's hand and pulled him into the tipi.

Shy Mouse patted Small Bird on the shoulder. "I will watch them," she said.

Thanking her cousin, Small Bird left, heading for her mother's home. Stepping inside, she found Yellow Robe sitting next to her father, staring blankly into space.

Approaching, she knelt. "Mother?"

Yellow Robe glanced at her. Tears swam in the woman's eyes. "Your father is gone, daughter."

"Yes, mother. I know." She spoke gently, worried at the almost childish tone of her mother's voice.

"There is nothing left for me." Yellow Robe rocked back and forth.

"That is not true. You have me. And Lone Warrior. We both need you."

"No. You are married now. You have a husband, and soon you will have children of your own. Lone Warrior will also take a wife."

Small Bird gripped her mother's hand. "Yes. Then we will both have children who will need their *unci*." She glanced around and saw a bowl of weak broth. "Have you eaten?"

"I am not hungry," her mother said.

Small Bird picked up the broth. "You must eat and stay strong."

Yellow Robe shook her head. "I wish to be alone."

Small Bird set the bowl down. When her mother motioned for her to go, she stood. At the doorway she hesitated, worried, but at last she left. It was only right that her mother have some time alone before putting her father to rest.

Small Bird next went to check on Makatah. She had never experienced a miscarriage, and the memory of her cousin's left her shaken. How could anyone bear to lose a child before its birth, to have felt its life for just a short while? Her hand crept to her belly.

Had she and Swift Foot created a life last night? Would she soon feel movement, as her cousin had? She couldn't even imagine the pain and devastation of losing something so precious.

Matoluta answered her greeting. He stepped outside, his face ravaged by loss.

"How is she?" Small Bird asked.

"She is sick. Here." Matoluta jabbed his heart, his voice bitter. He turned away, hate in his eyes.

Small Bird put a hand on his arm. "I am not your enemy, Matoluta."

"No. Your husband is. I am taking my wife away. We will leave here, somewhere we will be safe." He stormed away.

Behind her, Lone Warrior appeared. He said, "Many are angry. Many will leave."

Whirling around, Small Bird glared at her brother. "And will you leave as well?"

He shrugged. "This is not a good place to be. There are bad spirits here. Angry spirits."

Small Bird moved over until she stood toe-to-toe with her brother. "Maybe they are angry at our people's lack of faith. It is not bitterness that is needed here, Lone Warrior. It is unity."

"Death is all that your husband brings to us," Lone Warrior responded. "Our own father died in yesterday's battle."

Pain seared Small Bird's heart. Only the knowledge that her father had wanted her union with Swift Foot, had believed in the joining of these tribes, and that he had been so proud of her during the ceremony kept Small Bird from becoming mired in guilt.

She held on to Wind Dancer's wisdom of this morning. "There are many things that are not clear to us, but there is a reason for everything that happen. Even if we cannot see it."

Lone Warrior stepped back. "Some of us seek reasons where none exist." He stalked away.

Small Bird sighed. "This is a wonderful first day as Swift Foot's wife," she said to herself. Of course, last night had been worse: the deaths, the late-night flight . . . Yet the coming of the morning had been wonderful. Her husband had shown her how the stars glowed in early morning. And he had made love, glorious love, to her. And the last time he had been slow and gentle.

Sighing, she turned and saw her cousin standing in the doorway of her tipi. "You should not be up," she scolded.

Makatah waved her concern away and said, "I feel fine."

Small Bird moved closer, noting her cousin's swollen eyes and the paleness of her face. "*You* are angry with me as well," she said. She swallowed the lump of pain in her voice.

Makatah limped forward. "No. I am not angry with you. You are my cousin. This was not your doing."

Sighing, Small Bird said, "Your husband does not believe that."

"My husband is angry. He will calm."

"How can you be so calm?" Small Bird knew she'd have been wailing and knocking things over.

Makatah took her hand. "Did you not hear your own words to your brother? Neither anger nor placing blame will bring my son back. And neither will harsh words heal your father. Or any of the others. We have to go on. We have to find a way to end this war before any more die."

Feeling a huge sense of relief, and an easing of her guilt, Small Bird asked, "Then you do not plan to abandon Swift Foot?"

Makatah shook her head. "This is where I belong, this tribe. My family is here. My husband just needs time to clear the anger from his mind. To see that his chief did what he thought was right."

Small Bird nodded. Overcome, she turned to go and see what needed doing. There was much to be done, building this new campsite.

Makatah tagged along. As she put it, if she stayed alone, she'd think of her loss. She needed to be busy. Small Bird welcomed the company.

Beginning her first day as the leader's wife, Small Bird found that her resolve to find a peaceful ending for this war was growing. Tipi after tipi revealed either injured men or grieving widows. Women had shorn their hair, mutilated their flesh, and now wailed in loud lament. Those cries filled the air and made her cringe.

The warriors who were uninjured had mostly ridden off to scout out the enemy, so the camp was sparsely populated with the living. Women helped their sisters, mothers, daughters, and friends prepare the deceased. Tomorrow those bodies would be laid out to rest on scaffolding. Some would be lashed to high tree branches, like her father.

By the time the sun rose fully, Small Bird was mentally drained. She never wanted to go through such bloodshed again, and she would do whatever it took to avoid it. How had this continued for so many years?

Far away, in another place, similar activities prevailed. Hawk Eyes had traveled long and far to return to his people's camp. His warriors had followed.

Now, in the first hours of being home, Hawk Eyes was overseeing the dead, the wounded, and the grief-stricken. Glancing up, he wondered where the storms were. Why weren't the spirits angry, slashing the sky with their fury?

So many deaths. He staggered to the water of a nearby stream and dropped to his knees. Defeat rested on his shoulders. Though his warriors claimed victory, said that the spirits had driven off their enemy, Hawk Eyes knew the truth: there had been no winner in yesterday's battle. All had lost. Casualties had been intolerable on both sides.

Angrily, he picked up a large stone and tossed it as far as he could into the river. He heard it splash, saw the wide ripples before the flowing water again calmed.

Like yesterday's battle: A few ripples and then all was the same. All for nothing.

"My husband."

Hawk Eyes stood and held out his hand to his wife. Seeing Eyes came to him. He led her to a large boulder. She sat.

"Our son?" he asked.

"He is with the other children," she answered. Her eyes were sad. "We must leave. There is danger here." Her eyes looked unfocused.

Hawk Eyes knelt before her. "What is it? What do you see?"

She glanced at him, worried. "I see violence. A red battlefield. And I see our son." Her voice dropped.

Hawk Eyes took her hand. "I will not allow anyone to harm our son," he vowed.

Tears streamed down Seeing Eyes's face. "You cannot control everything, husband. We are all in danger."

"Then we will leave. I will move our camp again, then return to meet the enemy."

Seeing Eyes seemed inconsolable. "I wish this all to stop. Let it go. Let there be no more deaths between us and them. Too many have already died for something that happened long ago."

Hawk Eyes bowed his head. "I tried to make peace. But I cannot allow to live a tribe that will come after you and my son. This must be finished. *Swift Foot* must be finished."

Seeing Eyes rose slowly, her sad eyes again

unfocused. "Then follow the voices of the spirits. She will come and lead the way."

Standing, Hawk Eyes opened his mouth to speak, but his wife cut him off.

"I do not know more than that." With slow steps, she walked away.

Hawk Eyes followed slowly. In the camp, he was met by a group of warriors with various cuts, gashes, and bruises. They were led by Many Horns. "When do we attack again?" the young brave asked.

"Have not enough died?" Hawk Eyes asked wearily. He knew he had sworn to carry this through, but the bravado in the other man's voice had drained him of his fury.

Many Horns drew himself up. "We are not cowards. We will fight. We will protect you and not allow the treacherous Swift Foot to harm you or your son. That is our creed."

The reminder that his son's life was threatened bolstered Hawk Eyes's sagging strength. "We will do nothing for now. There are dead to be laid to rest, injuries to heal, and strength to be regained."

Many Horns spoke up. "I will go and find our enemy, learn where they hide."

Ready to deny the younger man, Hawk Eyes paused. Many Horns *had* been able to track the enemy and report on its locations and numbers. And while the peace missions he'd been sent on had failed, he had been able to find out valuable information, including the wedding. It wasn't the warrior's fault the weather had not been in his people's favor, and that the last battle had gone so calamitously for all.

"I will send you and two others," he decided.

Many Horns shook his head. "One travels faster and blends with the land."

Hawk Eyes nodded. That was true: one man could often achieve what many could not. Too bad he couldn't achieve peace. "Go as soon as your wounds are healed."

Drawing himself up, Many Horns shook his head. "I will go now."

Hawk Eyes watched the young brave depart. He wished he could just let the past go, just leave honor to sort itself out and stop all the killing forever. But pride, anger, and the fate of his son made that impossible.

Chapter Thirteen

Tossing and turning after a long day of trying to rebuild his tribe, Swift Foot relived one of his greatest days—the one on which he'd exchanged a child's name for that of a mighty warrior. When he was troubled, the memory stole into his dreams to remind him of what and who he was.

One day you will be a great warrior, his uncle proclaimed to all at the ceremony. *Already you are cunning.* Charging Bull held up two pieces of rabbit fur. Mastinca *is fleet of foot and endures on long journeys; he is clever and cunning. When he bolts down his hole, he always escapes. Learn his ways and his secrets. Listen when he speaks to you, and carry his powerful medicine with you always.*

Charging Bull tied the bands of rabbit fur

around his young nephew's upper arms, then turned to his people. From this day onward, the son of my brother shall be called Swift Foot. In times of danger, his ability to think fast and run as the wind shall carry him from danger.

Newly named, Swift Foot threw back his narrow shoulders, feeling as big and important as any warrior present. In his hand he held an eagle feather—his first. By touching and wounding the enemy with just his hands, he'd counted coup and earned it. Though the tribe still mourned its dead, Swift Foot's victory was being celebrated and acknowledged. Out of death came the birth of a warrior.

When Buffalo Medicine Man shuffled toward him, waving his rattles, Swift Foot held his breath.

The elder lifted his hands. "For there to be life, there must be death. From death comes new beginning. The courage and bravery of a child will bring our people peace someday." The shaman then turned his back and held out his hand to the young brave named Wind Dancer.

Swift-Foot's eyes widened when he had seen a tall lance—taller than himself and the same size used by grown warriors. Dangling from the top of the lance, a leather thong with a piece of prized white rabbit fur, along with bits of fluffy eagle down fluttered in the cool breeze. Was it for him?

"You have earned the right to take your place among the warriors, and to ride at the side of our chief. One day you will become a great leader." Buffalo Medicine Man put his hands on Swift Foot's shoulders, and turned him to face his tribe.

Though his people had cheered, their recently ravaged, grief-stricken faces cut into him with the same stabbing pain as an arrow or an ax blade. In his sleep, he tossed. They'd been wrong! Death was not only a new beginning; it could also sometimes be senseless: And more lives would be lost, with Swift Foot powerless to prevent it.

As long as he lived, the enemy would seek him and those around him. More would die. More would know pain. Peace. He wanted peace.

"No," he muttered. No more war. No more deaths.

"Swift Foot," a soft voice crooned. "Wake, husband."

No. If he woke, he'd have to face the truth. But the hands caressing his forehead were cool, the voice compelling. His battle-weary mind and bruised heart needed consoling. He opened his eyes.

"You are dreaming." Small Bird stared down at him, worry shadowing her eyes.

Raking his hands through his tangled hair, he tried to turn away. "It is no dream." The grief in the faces of the past had been replaced by the remembered faces of last night. The pride he'd felt so long ago had turned to sorrow and guilt. Where once he'd thought he could achieve anything and everything, today he admitted to being a failure.

He'd tried hard to live up to expectations, but in his time as chief, he'd cost his people much.

"Tell me," Small Bird begged. Her soft voice was alluring, tempting him to share his thoughts and his heart. He closed his eyes, against the past and the future. His jaw hurt from clenching it so tight. He could never admit to her or to anyone else how inadequate he felt. The faith of his people had been misplaced.

"Go back to sleep," he said, too weary to match wits or words with her. She'd been asleep when he'd finally returned to the tipi and though he'd longed to hold her, he hadn't. Too many conflicting emotions rolled through him.

"I want to help," she said, sounding hurt.

The rush of emotion that he sought to keep at bay battled for release. Yesterday, in his wife's arms, he'd lost control. But everywhere else he'd buried all feelings. He'd been strong for his tribe, though it hadn't been easy. Each grieving woman was a reminder of his guilt; each warrior, laid out and prepared, was a renewed stab of agony. And the innocence of his people . . . They were all caught in a cycle that had begun only because his father had been weak.

But why wasn't his father allowed to be weak? Why wasn't he? Weren't the leaders of men allowed to seek happiness also? Each injured tribesman that he'd gone to see had threatened his self-control. This was all his fault. By his living, others died. He'd wanted to shout in anger, to rant to the spirits about the unfairness of the world.

But he hadn't. What good would it do his people for him to lose control. Control, his uncle had taught him, was the attribute of a good leader. And strength. These were the mistakes his father had made, giving those things up. And tonight, if Small Bird touched him, he wasn't sure he wouldn't make a mistake, too. He wasn't sure he'd be able to contain the anger he felt. Tonight he was weak and vulnerable.

He felt her resettle beside him. Relieved, he tried to lose himself in sleep, but too many thoughts raced through his mind. He closed his eyes and concentrated on tomorrow. Small Bird's shallow breathing intruded. He'd hurt her.

"I did not mean to hurt you, wife. I have had a long day. We both have. Rest now."

Small Bird twisted. After a long moment of silence, her voice broke the silence. "You still regret our marriage. You want *her*."

The pain in her voice drew him onto his

back. He'd never wanted to hurt this woman, yet he seemed destined to continue to do so. "It is not thoughts of that other woman that trouble me."

"You said you loved her." Small Bird's voice sounded small and uncertain.

Swift Foot sighed. At one point, thoughts of Emily would have taken his breath away. But now he felt nothing. Now, as the silence lengthened between himself and his wife, he realized that he no longer hungered for the white girl. Instead, he yearned for the time he'd spent away from his people, alone, wandering the *maka*. Then he'd been happy.

With a start of surprise, he realized that his time with Emily had represented similar things: peace, little responsibility, carefree happiness. Their time together had been a time of freedom, a dream, for it had been as far from reality as possible. In a sense it hadn't been real.

Well, what he had felt for her was real. But the path he walked—the path he'd always planned on walking—had made their love impossible. Unlike the love he could feel for one of his own people.

"I did love her," he admitted to his wife. He frowned into the dark then, saddened. He also tried to make sense of his sudden insight.

Small Bird rolled onto her side. He felt her eyes on him. "Did? Do you not still?"

Shifting, he faced her. Shadows hid her features, giving him the courage to bare his heart. "I loved her. Maybe a part of me always will. But it was not to be. She gave me something I needed at the time."

"What?"

Swift Foot felt the warmth of his wife's breath between them. It drew him closer. Reaching out, he traced her lips. "A safe haven. A world that wasn't real. A world I controlled." And that was the key, he thought. He'd been in control. Totally.

"You are chief here," Small Bird said.

"But I cannot control all that happens." His voice turned bitter. "As chief, I led our warriors into a battle that took many lives. Perhaps if my uncle—"

Small Bird stopped him. "No. The outcome would have been the same no matter who led our warriors. This battle was an inevitability."

"I wish I could believe that," he said.

After a pause, Small Bird snapped, "You say your love with this white woman was not to be. I do not believe it. Everything happens as it is supposed to. What happened yesterday was also meant to be. We don't know why, but perhaps it will pave the way to happiness. Perhaps everything will."

Swift Foot shook his head. It was too seductive to believe that. Too easy to accept the idea that he hadn't been anything but a pawn of destiny. He wouldn't release the guilt of dishonor from his shoulders. The deeds of his father were his to bear for all time. As was the guilt from his own mistakes. "What happened yesterday was a mistake. It will escalate the hatred. More lives will be taken. I have failed, though I know not what I should have done."

His wife inched closer. "Our world is a circle. You lost one woman, but you got me. You cannot have the good without the bad. There cannot be life without death. Everything renews. There must be balance." Small Bird's voice was a mere whisper.

Swift Foot snarled, "You lost your father! Your cousin lost her babe!" Perhaps he himself would even lose his own child. He refused to think of the possibility that he'd gotten her pregnant so quickly.

"Yes, I lost my father," Small Bird agreed. "Should I be bitter? Should I wish that another's father had died instead? Should a child of two or three years of age have died instead of one not born?"

Swift Foot listened to his wife. She was kind, forgiving him. But he was far older than his years. His innocence had been stolen long ago. He knew he was guilty, but she did not need that inflicted on her. "You are a strong woman, wife," he said. "I want no more death, either. If only so that you will lose no more people you love."

Small Bird reached out and wrapped her arms around his neck. "Then we will find the

way to peace, and give it to all as our gift."
She pulled him closer.

Swift Foot nuzzled her neck, unable to resist. His hand slid slowly up and down her
spine, the other pillowing her head.
Breathing in her sweet scent, he felt desire
spiraling inside him. He said, "Before you
asked what Emily gave me. You did not ask
what you give."

Pulling her head back, Small Bird traced
the length of his jaw with her finger. "Is there
something?" She sounded surprised and
pleased.

He reached down and started inching her
dress up. "You take my control away."

She cocked her head at him, then lifted
herself so he could remove her clothing. Unashamed, she rose naked before him, allowing his heated gaze to roam her face and
body. "Is this a good thing?" she finally whispered.

Gently, Swift Foot pushed her down on
their buffalo skin. He covered her body with
his, allowing his hard length to mold to her
softness. Arching his back, he leaned down to
suckle on first one breast, then the other. It
was a long time before he moved to her
mouth and murmured, "Absolutely."

Small Bird finished packing her tipi and her
belongings. She had two dogs and the mare
Swift Foot had given her. Finished, she went
to see who else might be in need of help.

Walking to the next tipi, she found the two children who'd lost their father. They sat on the ground. Their mother, with help, was folding her tipi to be loaded. "*Hau*," Small Bird greeted her. Several times over the last few days, the small boy had come to her for a quick hug, or just to see what cooked over her fire.

The girl still held sadness in her eyes. Bending down, Small Bird noticed two pups in her lap and realized the pregnant bitch she'd seen earlier belonged to these children. She reached out to stroke one pup's fat belly. "Are you keeping these pups for yourselves?" she asked. She hoped so, for she knew new life would help take the children's minds off their loss.

The girl shook her head. "No. We cannot. The mother died during birth. My mother does not want them." She looked sad and upset.

"There are only two? Were there others?"

Again the girl shrugged. "They are gone."

Small Bird's stomach clenched. She stared at the brown balls of fluff. One dark nose lifted. Its owner rooted around, his small squeaky cry wrapping around her heart. Making a decision, Small Bird reached out. "I will take them in trade."

"What will you give for them?" the mother demanded, turning at the proposition.

Small Bird met the woman's gaze. She kept

her voice soft. "I will give one horse for the two pups." She'd noted that the family had no horse of their own, that they were borrowing horses for the move.

The boy's eyes sparked like a star exploding in the sky. "A horse?"

The mother nodded in pleased surprise, then went back to her work. Only the girl eyed Small Bird with wariness. "What will you do with them?" she asked.

Small Bird knelt. "I will raise them." She eyed the two squirming beasts. "But I might need help feeding them."

The girl drew herself up. "*I* will come and feed them, then." She pulled a small basket from behind her. Soft scraps of bear fur lined the basket. She held up a bit of deerskin fashioned into a bottle with a small nipple. "You must use meat juice."

Small Bird smiled, knowing she had done a good thing. "*Pilamayan*," she said, thanking the children.

"What have we here?"

Startled, Small Bird turned, a pup cradled in each hand as she faced Swift Foot. She smiled weakly. She had no idea if her husband liked dogs or not. "I just traded one of our horses for these two motherless pups."

A brow lifted. "And what do you plan to do with these pups?" he asked.

Small Bird's eyes narrowed and her chin lifted. "Raise them to be strong adult dogs."

Swift Foot eyed the two children and their hard-working mother. "I think two horses for two pups is a fairer trade. When the pups are strong adults, they will be of great help." He motioned to a young brave who was accompanying him. "Take these children to the herd. They shall each be allowed to choose a horse from amongst my stock."

Small Bird grinned as the two children raced off. Their laughter eased the gloomy pall over the tribe. Adults stopped to watch, small smiles hovering around their mouths.

"My wife has a kind heart." Swift Foot said softly behind her, his hot breath stroking the back of Small Bird's neck.

"My husband is generous," she said softly.

"They are in need," he agreed. "And we have much." He stared at the two mewling pups. "Take them to Gray Woman's tipi. Her dog just gave birth. She does not give her pups away to be eaten. She will allow your pups to nurse and keep them safe for you." With that he walked away.

Small Bird turned to go find Gray Woman's tipi. She nearly ran into her brother.

"It is easy to give when one has more than enough," he said. Contempt lingered in his words.

Narrowing her eyes, Small Bird glared at Lone Warrior. "My husband's heart is kind. He is generous."

"Because he feels guilty," her brother spat.

"No, Lone Warrior. Because he *cares*." And that was the truth. Swift Foot cared about his people—even to the point that she knew he sometimes considered turning himself over to the enemy in a trade: his life for peace. He hadn't said the words, but she'd heard them in his voice, and she recognized his intent. He sometimes believed it was the only way.

Lone Warrior opened his mouth to protest. Small Bird held up her hand. "Careful, brother. Do not insult my husband further." Without giving him a chance to respond, she walked away.

He caught up with her. "Wait." When she stopped, he glanced away. "I am sorry. He *is* your husband."

"And our chief." She held his gaze.

"And our chief. My chief. I should not speak so openly in anger."

"Speaking of it is not the problem. Acting on it or allowing it to rule you is the difficulty. That will only give your unhappiness power over you."

Lone Warrior grinned ruefully. "When did my sister become so wise?"

Small Bird smiled back. Then, noticing the gaunt look of her sibling, she glanced around to make sure none were listening. She said, "And when is my brother going to admit that he is in love?"

Lone Warrior's smile faded, and he glanced down at his feet. "She is afraid," he said.

Reaching out with one hand after shuffling her pups into her basket, Small Bird gave her brother's arm a comforting squeeze. "Then you must prove there is nothing to fear."

Brother and sister stared at each other for a long minute. Then Lone Warrior said, "You are right. But it will have to be dealt with later. We have much to do before reaching our new camp tonight."

Glancing down at her new puppies, Small Bird grimaced. "That we do, my sweets," she said to them. Then, with a nod to her brother, she hurried off to finish her preparations.

In a short amount of time, the tribe was retracing its steps. With the ground hard—there was no rain today—the path up the ravine was easily navigated. At the top, Small Bird glanced downward. One day she hoped to return to this place. Hidden away in this canyon, many dead had been laid to rest. Though it was a place of sadness, Small Bird also held precious memories of her time here. This was where she and her husband had first become one.

With mixed feelings, she fell into line, choosing to ride with her mother, aunts, and cousins. Up ahead, she spotted the two children she'd helped, sharing the back of one horse. Their mother sat proudly on the other. When the children spotted Small Bird, they turned to wave.

Small Bird waved back. She belonged—not

only at her husband's side, but among these people. She vowed to find the path to peace for all of them.

A shadow trailed the tribe. Unseen, unheard, like a snake in the grass, Many Horns kept himself concealed. From the battleground he'd followed the signs left in the trampled earth. He'd found this ravine just that morning, having spotted the warriors guarding it.

He could have killed them and sneaked down to count their numbers and eye their camp, but he didn't want to alert Swift Foot to his presence. Traveling on foot most of the way, he'd been able to arrive undetected. Swift Foot was not the only one who ran fast. Endurance was something Many Horns had worked hard to achieve. But he also had a horse sheltered a safe distance away.

By midday, he was particularly glad he hadn't tried to take the guards. The enemy was on the move. This was good, for it meant he'd be able to spy from a distance. He patted his bundle of clothing and prepared to follow. Finally the last person left the ravine, and the boulders were replaced to hide the path down. Many Horns collected his horse and rode out after them.

For three days he stayed well behind. He had the advantage of being able to easily spot the large tribe on the move. No one had spotted him. He was clever. Cunning. Shrewd.

When the Hunkpapa tribe finally halted and began unloading travois, he grinned. They were many miles from the ravine and the battlefield, but he knew the way back to his people. Crawling up to a man-sized boulder to watch the tipis be erected, he planned and plotted.

The eastern horn was far from him. The herd of horses who might spook at his presence had been taken far to the north. The tipis closest to him belonged to the outcasts. Everything suited his needs well.

Darkness finally came. People came and went, but he waited. When he deemed it late enough, he donned a woman's dress and covered his head. Since he was dressed as a *Winkte*, no one would bother him.

Chapter Fourteen

Lone Warrior embraced the night as he followed the snaking river; it gave him what he desperately desired. Cradled in his lap, Willow Song rested her head against his chest. Whenever she rode with him, she insisted on placing her scarred cheek so he could not see it.

Reaching down, he stroked his fingers through her hair. Over the last few days the tribe had headed south for flatter, grassier land. With winter coming, they needed to hunt and prepare for the cold months. Slowing his horse, Lone Warrior rejoiced in the feel of the woman snuggled against him.

"Where do you take me?" Willow Song asked, lifting her head.

"Somewhere special." He grinned. Each

night he came for her, and they spent much time together. Already he'd received many comments—and unwanted advice. Kills Many Crows had even tried to order him away from Willow Song. But Lone Warrior ignored them all. He loved this woman, and anyone who could not see the beauty he saw was blind.

When he arrived at a low overhang of rock with dry brush on either side, and several large boulders that formed a small, secluded enclosure, he stopped his horse and dismounted. He'd found the spot earlier, and thought it perfect to try to convince this woman to be his wife.

His mouth went dry. So far any mention of the future had sent her into a panic. Holding up his arms, Lone Warrior helped Willow Song down. Instead of setting her on the ground, he carried her across the rocky terrain and into the enclosure. He'd brought furs, food, and water. This would be home away from home.

Setting Willow Song down, he allowed her length to slide over him slowly.

She glanced around. "You went to much trouble tonight, Lone Warrior."

"You are worth it, Willow Song." He bent his head and kissed her. Then he just held her tenderly. Finally he gathered his courage and tipped up her chin. He stared into her dark eyes. "I want to make you my wife, Willow Song," he said.

As he'd expected, she stiffened. "I cannot." She gasped, trying to pull away.

"You can. You love me. As I love you." And he did—deeply, desperately.

Willow Song's eyes filled with tears. She glanced away and stared at the furs, pouches of food, and wood for a fire. "Please, Lone Warrior. Do not ask again. You deserve better." She turned away, her shoulders hunched.

Lone Warrior stepped close, but he didn't pull her back to him. His heart sank. "I deserve the woman I love," he said. "I want no other."

"I cannot marry. Ever. You know this."

"I know no such thing." He turned her gently back to face him. "You deserve happiness, too, Willow Song. Marry me."

Sobbing, Willow Song fell into his arms. But she said, "I cannot give you what you want."

Frustration rumbled low in Lone Warrior's throat. "What *do* I need, Willow Song? Tell me."

"A child." She sobbed, her hand resting on her abdomen. "I will never have children." Tears streamed down her face.

Lone Warrior had had no idea that her scars, her injuries, were so extensive. But he found it didn't matter to him. Only she mattered. "Then we shall not have children."

She glanced up, uncertain.

He cupped her face. "I want you, Willow Song. I want to make you my wife. Now. To-night. This is a good time. Our warriors will be hunting and will not break camp for a week. Come with me. And when we return, we will be man and wife in the eyes of all."

"I may be your wife, but they will still not accept me."

"*I* accept you. I love you and want to take care of you."

She glanced down. "You feel sorry for me."

Lone Warrior laughed softly. "No. I feel sorry for me. I want someone to take care of me as well." He rested his chin on her head and stared off into the night sky. "What do you say? Can we take care of each other?"

Willow Song sighed. "I am honored . . . but so afraid."

"Of what the rest will say?" Lone Warrior led her to the furs he'd laid down. He felt her trembling. He knew her leg bothered her. Sit-ting, he pulled her down into his lap.

"No. That you will see the rest of me." She hesitated. "There is no beauty here." She hugged herself.

"There is beauty everywhere that counts, my love." He shifted. Holding her gaze, he grabbed the hem of her dress. "Show me what you fear. Let us get it out of the way, so that you will see that I love the woman inside this body."

Willow Song shifted and lifted her arms. She closed her eyes and bit her upper lip.

Slowly Lone Warrior lifted the hem of her dress. "Look at me, my love," he said.

Holding her teary gaze, Lone Warrior slid the dress up her body and over her head. He waited, staring into her eyes for a long time before allowing himself to look at her body. She lowered her arms to her sides, but did not try to hide herself.

Scarred flesh puckered her neck and collarbone and one shoulder, and covered half of one breast. The other side, like her face, was nearly perfect. Her other breast *was* perfect: a small, round globe tipped by a rosy flower.

His fingers trailed down both her sides. Then he stared at her belly. Deep scars, wide and silvery-white, crisscrossed her entire abdomen, and more puckered flesh padded her hips. He saw where the horse had trampled her. Saw the slice where either a knife or sharp war ax had nearly killed her.

"I don't know how you survived," he whispered. "You were but a child."

Considering all the damage that had been done to her, he knew he stared at a miracle.

"I should have died," she said.

Lone Warrior stepped closer and ran his hands over her shoulders, across her back, and down to cup her buttocks, drawing her close. "No. You were saved for me. You are my miracle. My love. For now. For always." This time when he kissed her, he showed her the truth of his words. "I want you, Willow Song. I love you."

"I love you, too, Lone Warrior," Willow Song whispered. "But I am still afraid."

He smiled down at her. "Do not be afraid, Willow Song. Not with me. Not ever."

When he took her lips once more in his, Willow Song relaxed and gave herself up. When his fingers stroked her flesh, she felt beautiful. And when he entered her and made their bodies one, for the first time in many years she felt whole.

Swift Foot sat in front of a fire outside his tipi. Small Bird served him, his uncle, and his cousin. Kills Many Crows set his bowl of rabbit stew down untouched.

"I don't see why we have to miss the Sun Dance. There will be many tribes gathered. Always we have gone."

"Our enemy has never been so bold," Swift Foot explained. For days Kills Many Crows had complained bitterly, and he was sick of it. "And it would be a dangerous trip."

"Then perhaps only those of us who feel it is safe should go," Kills Many Crows snapped.

Charging Bull waved his son to silence. "We will have our own Sun Dance ceremony for those who wish to participate. Swift Foot is right. The grassy plains are far, and the many weeks of travel will make us and our wounded vulnerable."

Swift Foot nodded to his uncle. "There are still many warriors healing. Many grieving widows. Such travel is too much to ask of them. There will be no more discussion on this matter. The council agreed."

Kills Many Crows glared at Swift Foot. "They always agree with you. You can do no wrong."

"If my husband can do no wrong, then perhaps you should agree with him." Small Bird set a bowl of boiled greens down before the men. She sent Kills Many Crows a pointed look. "Of course, those who seek to find fault can always do so."

Kills Many Crows snarled, but quieted.

Swift Foot sighed, yet he was glad to see his cousin silenced. He met the unrepentant gaze of his wife. It was no secret among the men that whenever anyone was heard complaining about the running of the tribe or criticizing her husband, Small Bird stopped to give an earful. She challenged them to come up with better solutions. They never had. Action, she swore, spoke louder than words.

When she'd heard that some of the poorer men planned to take their families away, she'd organized the women into groups, making sure that those who had much wealth willingly shared with those families who didn't. None of the women would leave tight-knit family units or friends, and she'd created many.

This had all pleased and astounded Swift Foot. His wife's love for their people, her willingness to step in where needed and take control, had eased the anger and bitterness of many. He owed her much. She was as a mother bear protecting her cubs—or a mother dog determined to see her pups grow to be adults.

He smiled. She guarded those pups she'd gotten as fiercely as she protected him. She checked on their progress several times a day, even carrying them with her in a sling over her shoulders when they were tired, so they'd bond with her. She found reasons to talk to him frequently during the day, even entering the council lodge sometimes.

Kills Many Crows, embarrassed to have been lectured by a woman, got to his feet and left. Small Bird smiled with deep satisfaction, picked up the steaming bowl, then sat down apart from the men to eat.

"Your woman is sharp-tongued." Charging Bull looked amused.

"Sharp in her mind as well." Swift Foot laughed. "She sees what is truth and does not hesitate to speak it."

Charging Bull smiled. "I felt guilty once for forcing this marriage on you, but now I see that I was wise in the decision. She is good for you. And our people."

"Unlike another woman," Swift Foot said. Silence fell.

He broke it after a moment. He'd allowed this to hang between them for too long. It was time to see the truth spoken. "You were right, Uncle. Small Bird meets the needs of our people. The other met only *my* needs." It didn't hurt to say the words. They were true and he could accept that. He could even see now that perhaps he'd needed the time with Emily to become a better man, a better leader, but that they hadn't been right for each other in the scheme of things. It was with Small Bird at his side that he excelled. They were a team.

Charging Bull adjusted himself on his seat. "And does this wife of yours meet your needs, my son?"

Knowing it wasn't physical needs his uncle spoke of, Swift Foot nodded. "Yes. She meets needs I had not known existed."

Charging Bull sighed. "Then all will be well. Time will reveal all. Your past and hers have joined to provide a new future."

"I just hope we all survive to see it," Swift Foot joked. His attention went to his wife. A quick glance at the purple, blue, and golden sky revealed the setting sun. Soon it would be night.

His uncle got slowly to his feet. "I see what is in your eyes. You are not interested in dinner. Take your wife. Go ride. Share the sunset." His gaze sharpened. "We have no guarantees of tomorrow. Only today. Now. So don't waste the gift of time." Then the old man walked off.

Swift Foot hurriedly finished his meal. He tried to remember his aunt and uncle together, but it was so long ago, he couldn't. Had his uncle not spent enough time with his wife? Did he have regrets now that she was gone? Standing, Swift Foot decided his uncle was right. He would not waste the time he'd been given with Small Bird.

He went to her and held out his hand. "Come."

Startled, she glanced up. "What is wrong?" She set her food down.

He smiled. "There is nothing wrong. Can a husband not ask his wife to walk with him? Can we not go find a quiet spot to watch the sun as it sets?"

She smiled. "I think I should like to walk with my husband," she said, taking his hand in hers.

Swift Foot led her away from camp. They moved toward the sun, that ball of fire hanging low in the sky. When he found a secluded place, he pulled her down in front of him.

The horizon sparkled with golden flames. Red fingers streamed overhead, mingling with the dark blue sky. As the sun sank lower, the red grew more vivid, the blue turning nearly purple. For a brief moment the world seemed to stand still. The birds held their breath, the water froze, and across the heavens, all color intensified. At last the faint round image of the moon came slowly into being as the golden fire of the sun disappeared from the sky. The reds merged into the purples until all was the murky shade of dusk.

"That was beautiful." Small Bird sighed.

"No, the beauty is here, before me. Swift Foot turned his wife around and made her straddle his lap.

As one, they came together in a kiss that started soft and slow and ended hard and hot. When he pulled back, Small Bird framed his face in her hands. "I love you, husband."

Swift Foot's throat seized. The first and only time he recalled *saying* those words had been to Emily during their last night together.

"Do not say anything," his wife said. "When the words feel right, they will come." She slid closer, pressing his hardness against the vee of her thighs.

Her heat branded him. Swift Foot lifted her dress, whipped his breechclout to the side, and in one swift move he pulled her down onto him. He slid easily inside her.

"Yes." She moaned. "Show me what you cannot tell me."

Swift Foot went out of his way to show her that he loved her. Even if he could not say the words.

*　　*　　*

Long after darkness had claimed the sky, Swift Foot stirred. "We must get back."

Small Bird sighed. She had no energy, no desire to move. "I don't think I'm ready to get up yet." She snuggled deeper into her husband's arms. She felt his lips against her temple. He was smiling.

"Then I must help you," he said.

She giggled. "And how will you help me, husband?"

As he stood, she hoped it would be to love her again. And again. Twice he'd sent her flying toward the stars.

As he stretched, she frowned. "We cannot go back undressed," she said.

"We cannot return until we have bathed, either," he said.

Small Bird's eyes widened. He reached down and grabbed her, and her arms wound tight around his neck. "It will be cold," she said in a squeak, the warm, cozy cocoon of sleep gone.

"What better way to revitalize ourselves?" he asked. Carrying her down to the stream, he strode in, immersing them both to their chins.

Small Bird pulled away, but he held her tight. His lips came down on hers.

Sighing when at last he broke the kiss, she stroked one wet finger down his cheek. "Kiss-

ing like that will lead to more—" She broke
off, blushing.

He shifted her until her legs were wrapped
around his waist. "Loving?"

Feeling the hard tip of him against her
belly, she deliberately moved her body up and
down until Swift Foot held her still. "You
seem to have need of me, my husband," she
said.

"That I do, wife. That I do."

Moon Fire slipped through the darkness.
She'd almost given up on Many Horns coming for her. Each night, she strode around the
back edge of camp, but he didn't come. His
absence, she feared, meant he'd died in the
battle.

The thought brought tears to her eyes and
anger to her heart. She paced, keeping to the
shadows, then paused to stand with her back
resting against a willow. Another wasted
night. If Many Horns didn't come soon, it
would be too late. Her parents were planning
a double wedding.

An arm snaked out and covered her mouth,
and she tried to scream. "Quiet," a voice ordered.

Moon Fire sagged with relief. Then she
turned. "Many Horns! You are alive!" His
hand motioned for silence. Grabbing her
hand, he pulled her from shadow to shadow
until they were far from camp. He pulled her

down into the flat, grassy space behind a boulder.

Whipping off his head covering, he stared down at Moon Fire. She wrapped her arms around his neck. "You came for me," she said. "We will go away. Tonight."

Many Horns kissed her. He nibbled her lips. "Not yet."

Moon Fire shook her head. "It must be. My time grows short. My father has accepted a marriage offer. We must elope."

"We will, my lovely one. But in good time. We have plans to make."

"What kind of plans?" she asked. But Many Horns didn't answer. His hand had already found her wet and willing.

"Later," he whispered, easing himself out of his breech clout into her. "Later."

Moon Fire gave herself over to his demands. Whatever he asked, she'd do. She loved this man, and needed him desperately.

Chapter Fifteen

Over the next two weeks, Swift Foot organized daily hunts. Two bands of warriors rode out each day and usually returned before dark. Normally hunters followed the game and were often gone for long stretches at a time, but with the unease and fear of another attack, none of the men wanted to be away for much more than one night.

Small Bird watched her husband ride away. It had been more than three weeks since the battle that had done so much damage. Most everyone believed that the Miniconjou had left to return to their homelands and wouldn't return until next summer. But her husband refused to let down his guard. He would not make the mistake of underestimating his enemy again.

Spending the morning tanning hides, Small Bird straightened as several children ran past. A small smile lit her lips. She'd missed her monthly flow, which she hoped meant she was with child. Just the thought of Swift Foot's babe growing inside her made her feel like dancing.

Across the way, Makatah and Shy Mouse worked side by side, stretching out a hide to dry. "Look at her," Shy Mouse called, and giggled. "She is thinking of her husband again."

Small Bird met Makatah's gaze. Her cousin studied her, then smiled in understanding. "Pull harder, sister, and leave our cousin to her work."

Unable to resist her own bit of teasing, Small Bird grinned. "I have seen you, too, staring off into space often enough these last few days, Shy Mouse. Who has caught *your* eye?"

Shy Mouse blushed and busied herself.

Makatah laughed. "I think more than one warrior has caught my sister's eye. Every night a different suitor comes to visit."

Moon Fire's arrival ended the good-natured teasing. Breathless, the young beauty stopped in front of Small Bird. "Your mother needs you, cousin."

Small Bird, along with Makatah and Shy Mouse, stood. "What happened, Moon Fire? Where is she?"

"She fell and injured her foot while gathering wood. Come quickly."

Wiping her hands with a wet cloth, Small Bird felt her heart race. Her mother hadn't done well since losing her mate. She had remained in a terrible depression, though it had eased some in the last few days. "I will come," she said.

"We will come with you," Makatah suggested.

Moon Fire shook her head. "My mother is with her. She asks only for her daughter."

Small Bird nodded. "Wait here," she told her cousins. Hurrying away, she turned. She didn't want them to think she didn't appreciate their concern.

Makatah waved her onward. "Go. Do not keep Yellow Robe waiting."

Moon Fire led the way from camp, following the stream. Small Bird frowned. Her mother normally stayed close, as they all had been ordered to do.

"Are you sure she came so far, Moon Fire?" she asked. They had left the vicinity of camp and were well out of sight of any of her people.

"Yes." Moon Fire pointed. "She is resting near those trees."

Small Bird hurried. Why had her mother come here?

When she got to the small stand of trees, she stopped and glanced around. "*Ina? Ina?*"

she called to her mother, worried. Had the woman wandered off? Where was Moon Fire's mother?

Glancing over her shoulder, she saw her cousin hanging back, a strange look on the girl's face. "Help me find her," she called out.

Going between two trees, she screamed when a large arm wrapped around her neck from behind. It tossed her to the ground. "Run, Moon Fire!" she cried. "Get help! Get—" Her voice was muffled as her face was pushed into the dust.

Small Bird kicked out and tried to roll free, but a large body held her effortlessly. In short order, her assailant had her bound, then yanked her to her feet. To Small Bird's shock, she saw Moon Fire still calmly standing there. Her cousin stared at her with a satisfied expression on her face.

"What is going on, Moon Fire?" she asked. Glancing over her shoulder, she frowned. "Who is this? Many Horns?"

Laughing, Moon Fire shoved Small Bird, sending her crashing down across the rocky ground. As Small Bird regained her feet, Moon Fire hung on the strange warrior's arm. "Yes, this is Many Horns," she said. "He has come to take me away." She stared at the warrior with adoration.

Small Bird studied Many Horns. She hadn't seen him but had heard of his attempts to bring peace. But that had all gone sour. She turned her amazed glare to Moon Fire when she realized her cousin had lied to her, drawn her to the enemy. "You are a traitor!" She gasped.

"Now don't be difficult, cousin. You got what you wanted. Why shouldn't I have what I want?"

"You have betrayed us. Your own family!" Shock was turning to anger. "Swift Foot will deal harshly with you," she promised.

Moon Fire dismissed Small Bird's words. "He has to find us first," she scoffed.

Many Horns interrupted. "Enough. We have far to go." He shoved Small Bird toward the trees in the distance. Picking up a sack, he pulled out an arrow and tossed it down several feet from where he stood. He picked out a small medicine bag and dropped that as well. Then he strode over to Small Bird. He studied her.

She refused to show fear. Her husband would find her.

When Many Horns reached out and tore the feathered thong from her head, yanking out a hank of hair, Small Bird winced, tears springing to her eyes. The feathers she wore matched the ones Swift Foot did. Many Horns tossed those feathers and strands of hair where he'd dropped the other items.

Returning to her, he grabbed Small Bird's arm and started walking, dragging her with him. Soon they reached a tree where two horses were tied, and he swung her up onto one and mounted behind her. To her shock, she saw a small boy bound and gagged on the ground.

"Get on the other horse and take the brat," Many Horns ordered Moon Fire. "We need to get out of here."

Moon Fire glanced from her lover to Small Bird. She frowned, her hands going to her hips. "Why can't *she* hold the brat and ride this horse?"

Many Horns smiled grimly. "Your cousin might try to ride off, love. The plan has been set into motion. We cannot risk anything going wrong."

Unhappy but following orders, Moon Fire mounted. She gave her cousin a jealous look. "Just remember that you are mine, Many Horns."

He lifted a brow. "Do you doubt me?" he asked. Anger edged his tone.

"No." Her eyes went to him, then returned to her cousin.

Small Bird saw the doubt and the jealousy there. "Swift Foot will come," she said in a snarl. "Make no mistake of that."

Behind her, Many Horns tightened his hold. "I am counting on that, girl. I am counting on that."

After a disappointing afternoon and having to return empty-handed, Swift Foot stalked through his camp. The buzz of usual activity reassured him that nothing had gone amiss in his absence: women prepared meals; children ran and laughed. Already things were returning to normal—as normal as possible with so many recent deaths.

His gaze shifted to his tipi, where there was no cookfire burning. He looked around the camp. Though he didn't see Small Bird, he wasn't worried. Since becoming his wife, she'd taken her tribal duties seriously, dividing her time equally between helping her mother and others in need and her spousal duties such as cooking his dinner.

After caring for his horse, Swift Foot turned the animal out into the herd. Skirting the camp, he paused at Willow Song's tipi. Seeing the flap open, he stopped. No one answered his call. Poking his head in, he saw that his cousin wasn't there.

He shook his head. No one had seen Lone Warrior since last night. Likely the pair had run off. He smiled. Though Kills Many Crows spoke angrily of Lone Warrior's attentions, fearing the man meant to use Willow Song for some odd reason, Swift Foot wasn't worried. He trusted Lone Warrior.

Cutting through the camp, he spotted Gray Woman tending to her dog and puppies. He stopped, easily picking out the two that belonged to his wife. Their bellies were rounded and they slept contentedly.

Bending down, he stroked their backs. "I am surprised to find them here," he said to Gray Woman.

The old lady finished giving the mother dog her meal of fat, bones, and broth. "She has not come for them yet."

"She must be busy today," he guessed.

"The wife of our chief is kind and generous," Gray Woman agreed. "That always keeps her busy."

Swift Foot continued on his way. As suspected, Small Bird was not in their tipi. He went to her mother's. No one was there, either. Perhaps, he'd find his wife and her mother with their female relatives.

Walking away from Yellow Robe's tipi, he almost bumped into Makatah, who was headed his way with a big bowl of steaming meat. "How is my aunt?" his wife's cousin asked. "I bring her food so she does not have to walk on her weak ankle."

Swift Foot tipped his head to the side. "She is not home."

"Oh. Then she must be with Small Bird in your tipi."

Glancing around, Swift Foot spotted Shy Mouse and Yellow Quail leaning on their willow backrests as they ate. In front of the tipi beside theirs, Moon Fire's family was also eating. There was no sign of his wife, or of his mother by marriage.

"What is this about her foot? Did Yellow Robe fall?"

Makatah nodded. "Moon Fire came to fetch Small Bird to help her."

"Do you know where they went? What time?"

"That way." The woman pointed. "Is something wrong?"

"I don't know." Worry suddenly churned Swift Foot's gut. He'd told Small Bird not to leave the immediate vicinity of camp—even to bathe. But she would have left if her mother needed her, or if anyone else did. He pondered his choices.

"Something is wrong," Makatah said. She stumbled as she walked up to him.

Steadying her, he took the bowl of hot food from Makatah. "I will go search for them."

Matoluta, coming up behind to see what was going on, asked, "What is going on?" Though he'd threatened to leave the tribe, as had several others, none had carried out the threat. But anger still vibrated through him. It was in his voice.

Makatah took the bowl back from Swift Foot. "My husband will go with you to look for your wife. If something is wrong, you will need help."

Swift Foot nodded, but waited for Matoluta to give his consent.

When Makatah elbowed her husband none

too gently, he drew himself up. "I will go with my chief," he said.

"Let us go, then."

Matoluta began calling out to others, telling them that Small Bird was missing. Before Swift Foot got out of camp, he had half a dozen warriors marching at his side and behind him.

He found footprints from where his wife had been working, and he followed them. When he arrived at a stand of trees, he called out. He saw signs of a struggle. His blood went cold. Lifting feathers that matched the ones he wore in his hair, fingering the long strands of blue-black hair, he brought it all to his face. "We will find you, wife," he promised.

"Look at this." Matoluta held up an arrow and pointed to a medicine bag lying on the ground.

Swift Foot stared down at the small pouch with a hawk's profile painted on it. Red fury streamed through him.

Hawk Eyes had taken Small Bird!

Turning, Swift Foot ran back to camp. The rest followed but could not keep up. He did not wait. He had no time to lose. He had to find Small Bird. His heart raced. Fear burned through each vein in his body.

This enemy had killed his parents. They had killed so many to get to him, and now they had taken his wife. He knew they would not hesitate to kill her.

Hawk Eyes rode hard, and his men followed the clear tracks. They headed north, toward the enemy—toward where Many Horns had tracked them. Fury pushed him. Far into the night they'd gone. Somehow the enemy had found them, and they'd taken his son.

Once and for all, it was time to put an end to this battle. No one harmed those under his protection—especially his family.

His wife had been found, knocked unconscious. She'd been taken far to the south and abandoned. But his son was gone. Hawk Eyes knew who was responsible. The false trail did not fool him; only Swift Foot had the guts to do such a deed.

Many Horns had been right: Swift Foot wanted war. He would get it. To the last man if need be.

Chapter Sixteen

Small Bird was tied to a tree, bait to lure her husband into a trap. Worse, she knew it would work. Swift Foot would come for her; he'd die; and it would be her fault for going so far from camp when he'd told her to stay close. At least her mother was all right. Moon Fire had told her that Yellow Robe was assisting in a birth and had not been harmed. She supposed her cousin had no reason to lie, so her mother was probably fine.

Unfortunately, she and the small four-year-old boy tied beside her were not. According to Many Horns this was Golden Eagle, the son of Hawk Eyes. The child wore a stoic expression, but Small Bird knew he was terrified. As she herself was.

Many Horns continued to sharpen his knife

while Moon Fire prepared a simple meal. Watching Many Horns, Small Bird had to admit his plan was good: kidnap the son of one chief and the wife of another, and let the two sides blame each other and fight. But she didn't understand his reasons. He was Miniconjou. Why take the son of his chief? All he'd needed was her to lure Swift Foot into a trap.

They'd ridden for two days before stopping here. But why?

To still her nerves and fear as Many Horns ran his finger over his blade, Small Bird asked, "Why the child? What purpose does it serve to scare him? And why did you take him? You don't need him to lure my husband into a trap."

"I am not scared," Golden Eagle spoke up. But his voice quavered.

Many Horns threw his knife. It slammed into the tree trunk inches above Small Bird's head.

She refused to cower. Now more than ever she needed to retain her faith in herself, had to believe that all things happened for a reason. Giving in to terror would do no one any good.

Standing and retrieving his knife, Many Horns bent down and pressed its blade to her cheek. Yes, I have you. So your husband will come." He paused to stare at the child. "But the boy will bring his father." He walked over to where Moon Fire sat.

"My father will come, and he will kill you." Golden Eagle's youthful boast brought laughter to Many Horns. Moon Fire joined in somewhat less enthusiastically.

"Your father will be killed by Swift Foot," Many Horns answered cruelly.

Moon Fire moved over to her lover and ran her hand down his back, but Small Bird noticed Many Horns seemed barely aware of it. "Then you plan to kill us," she guessed.

Many Horns looked unrepentant. "Yes. You will both die. Then I shall know peace. Revenge will be mine." His eyes were filled with some unknowable rage.

Moon Fire frowned. "You said you weren't going to hurt anyone. Not seriously. Bring them together and make them talk, that is what you said."

Many Horns laughed harshly. "They will never talk. Those two will come together and die trying to kill each another."

Small Bird spoke up: "You underestimate both Hawk Eyes and my husband. They will learn of your treachery and come after you."

Moon Fire looked nervous.

Once more, Many Horns's knife flew toward Small Bird. This time she felt the blade strike close to her head. He hadn't hit her, but he had come about as close as he could: she felt the blade, cool against her scalp.

The man pulled Moon Fire into his arms, and Small Bird saw her cousin swallow hard.

"Do not go weak on me now, my love," he said. "They all have to die. You know that."

"So that we can start anew somewhere else?"

"They cannot be allowed to live. I will have my revenge. And if we let these others go, they will point their fingers at us and we will never know peace." His voice drifted. "Do not feel sorry for any of them. They are all responsible for the loss of my father."

Moon Fire pulled away, seemingly surprised. "You didn't tell me that."

"Would it have mattered? The important thing is that we have our revenge. Then we will go away. Just like you wanted."

"Oh, Many Horns," Moon Fire crooned, resettling in his arms.

Small Bird took a deep breath. The longer Many Horns talked, the longer they rested here, the more chance Swift Foot would have to save her. She just prayed he would not fall into the other man's trap. "Who killed your father? If I am to die, you can at least tell me why."

Many Horns narrowed his eyes, but he kept hold of Moon Fire, his fingers stroking the outer edge of her breast. "My father wasn't killed, exactly. He loved the mother of Hawk Eyes, but she was promised to Runs with Wind. He was angry that she wouldn't run away with him. When Runs with Wind rejected her, my father tried again to marry her." His voice grew hard. "Again she rejected my father."

He rubbed the strands of Moon Fire's hair between his fingers. Small Bird wanted to know more, but she didn't dare risk angering him. He was silent a long while. Finally he continued.

"My father left the tribe. He married my mother who was the daughter of another chief in a different tribe. He never loved her—all he wanted was to prove he was a worthy warrior. After I was born, he left and never came back. We had no one. My mother lived with the shame of his rejection. Not wanting to go back to her own tribe, she took us to that of Hawk Eyes' father. But they did not want us."

"My mother took me away. Along the Big Muddy river, two white men found us. One of them kept us with him. He took my mother to his bed. Then she started drinking his poisoned water and turned mean like him."

"So you are trying to punish both tribes for your past?" Small Bird interjected, astonished that so much hate could live in one person.

"I ran away when I was twelve winters. I'd been beaten, my mother had been beaten . . . but she didn't care. All she wanted was more of that firewater. The day I left, I swore I'd kill the men who did this to my mother. The men who destroyed our family—as I will destroy theirs."

"What does this have to do with Swift Foot or his father? By not marrying the woman your father loved, Runs with Wind gave your father a chance to win her."

"My mother could not live up to what my father wanted! He only wanted Hawk Eyes's mother! And your husband's father spurned her! And Hawk Eyes's father had her! They laughed at my father, drove him away, made him miserable. And that made my mother miserable. And now I will visit that upon their children!"

Looking to her cousin, Small Bird shook her head. "He's mad. You cannot allow him to do this, Moon Fire."

Sneering, Many Horns lowered his face and kissed Small Bird's cousin. "She will do as I wish. She loves me." Standing, he carried the girl a short distance away. Then, though it was only dusk, Many Horns took Moon Fire on the ground there in full view, uncaring that he had an audience in the early-evening light.

Small Bird closed her eyes. Next to her, she felt the child slump against her as he slept.

"Come for me, my husband," she whispered. "Come for me. Find us before it is too late. And do not fall victim to Many Horn's trap."

The clear night sky was kind to Swift Foot; it helped him see to track his foes. Night turned to day, and day again into night. His party stopped only to rest, and to water and feed the horses. During these times, Swift Foot gathered his warriors and formulated several plans.

As they did so, he listened, he kept thinking of Small Bird. *Hang on, my wife. I am coming.* He sent the prayers up into the sky. It was midafternoon on their second full day out.

Night Thunder used the tip of his finger to draw a path in the dirt they'd softened. "We have come from here." He drew their path. "I think they are heading here. They go south, back to their own lands." He marked an area far off.

Swift Foot frowned at his friend. "When we battled, we were here." He marked the site, then where his scouts had told him the Miniconjou had camped before the fight. Likely they had moved; since. He had a smaller group of warriors with him this time. Though he longed to attack directly, to get revenge, he felt he had a better chance of getting Small Bird back alive with stealth. Especially if those who had taken his wife managed to reunite with their tribe. "If they came from here, knowing the land, they will most likely be here." He marked where he thought his enemies would be taking Small Bird.

Murmurs of agreement followed. One voice dissented.

Swift Foot sighed. Kills Many Crows had insisted on coming along. To his surprise, his cousin pointed to a region most avoided.

Susan Edwards

"They'll stop here. In *Mako Shika*."

The badland. Swift Foot considered. Hadn't he sought refuge there after the attack. Because the earth was so barren, it made a good place to hide from an enemy. Most tribes avoided the stark place, but Swift Foot had always seen not only a beauty, but a practical purpose to the area. What better place to set a trap than among a maze of rocks, hidden valleys, and deep ravines? Perhaps his foe thought as he did.

He said, "That is a large area. It will be hard to find them if they go there. Especially if they cover their tracks."

"But they do not cover their tracks. And there are only two of them." Kills Many Crows looked smug.

Which worried Swift Foot. Was he riding into a trap? "There will be many others," he promised. "Perhaps they lie in wait." He studied their dirt map, considering his cousin's assessment.

Glancing over at Kills Many Crows, he was surprised to find no bitterness there. There was intensity, but it was not directed against Swift Foot.

His cousin met his stare. "No one harms a member of our family."

Swift Foot nodded, pleased. "Then let us ride. We will head to the badland."

As he mounted, he focused his rage, drawing on his inner strength. He had control. He would find his wife. Then he'd make sure he never lost her again.

Dumped in an exhausted heap on the hard, dusty ground, Small Bird tried to move. She felt so sore. Her arms ached. Her feet felt numb and her tongue was swollen. She was so thirsty.

Somewhere near her, she heard Golden Eagle whimper in his sleep. Her captors had been more generous with him. Twice she'd seen her cousin slip him some water while they traveled. Small Bird continued to ride with Many Horns, though, and he gave her nothing.

Struggling to sit, Small Bird fought a wave of dizziness. Her eyes felt gritty. She tried to wipe them with her shoulders, for her hands were tied behind her back, but it was useless.

Bleary-eyed, she stared up at the night sky. The stars winked down at her. She found the one that never moved. She found the seven stars of the seven councils. Then she remembered Wind Dancer's words. He'd said reason was always there, reason for all things. Like the stars, or the sun. He'd said that she had to have faith—she had to believe.

Stifling a moan, she wasn't sure she had any faith left. Surely she'd die long before Swift Foot found her. Her eyes were scratchy. She couldn't even cry for the much needed moisture. She tried to close her mind to her physical discomfort and her mental anguish, and she shut her eyes too.

Another whimper made her scoot over to the child. "Hush," she said in a croak. "They will come. They will come," she murmured until her throat closed.

Golden Eagle rolled closer, seeking comfort.

Please, she thought over and over. *Please save us*.

Staring up at the sky, Small Bird continued to pray. The night blurred. The star she'd been focusing on split into two above her head. She blinked, then realized the one star really had split into two. Two trails of light zoomed down toward where she lay. Her aching eyes followed the shimmering light until comets winked out.

"Find me, husband," she wished on the shooting stars. "Find me."

Chapter Seventeen

Riding, his body bent over his horse, spent with exhaustion, Swift Foot still refused to give in to the need for rest. He had to find Small Bird before it was too late.

Night Thunder caught up with him. "We must stop."

"We cannot." He couldn't stop. Not until Small Bird was found.

"You will do your wife no good by killing the horses."

Sighing, Swift Foot nodded. His friend was right. Both man and beast were beyond exhaustion. "Give the signal." He slowed.

Dismounting, he found that fatigue nearly brought him to his knees. Beside him, his horse hung its head, blowing softly through its nostrils. It had been hours since they'd last found water. Swift Foot opened his pouch, and poured the precious liquid into his palm for the horse.

Afterwards, he sat. He didn't bother to hobble his mount. Like him, the animal was too tired even to think of wandering. Knowing they had to rest for several hours, Swift Foot lay back and closed his eyes. Just for a few minutes—he would not sleep, he told himself firmly. He could not sleep until Small Bird was returned to him and those who'd taken her punished.

That was his last thought. Soon he was dreaming of Small Bird: the love in her eyes and in her voice, and her compassion toward his people and toward him. It swept away all the pain of his past. Whether making love, defending him, or seeing to the needs of others, his wife put her heart into all that she did. And he loved her deeply for that.

Yet, of everything he held dear, most dear was the way she believed in him. Nothing he'd ever said or done had swayed her from the determination that they were meant for each other. That knowledge soothed him. It made him happy. He woke.

With all her faith in him, he refused to fail her. They could believe in destiny, but they could not sit back and wait for it to happen. "I'll find you, my wife," he promised.

In the deep dark night cloaking the sky above him, stars blinked down. Small Bird loved the stars. Swift Foot smiled, remembering that first night he'd shown them to her. Suddenly two stars shot across the sky. Swift Foot's heart hammered as he watched the stars fall and fizzle out like flames doused with water.

A sign. It had to be a sign. "She's alive," he shouted, conviction ringing in his voice. He jumped to his feet. The stars would be his guide.

Night Thunder rushed to his side. "What is it?"

"A sign. The spirits sent a sign. We go. Now."

Knowing the rest would follow as they could, he rushed to his horse and rode off.

Rough hands shook Small Bird awake. "Shh," a voice said.

Lone Warrior! Her throat too parched to do more than croak, her eyes too dry to cry tears, Small Bird struggled to sit. If her brother was here, then it meant Swift Foot was near. For just a moment it hurt that her husband hadn't come for her himself. Gathering her pain and burying it deep, she concentrated on getting herself and Golden Eagle free from their captors.

Something sharp slid between her wrists, slicing through the leather thongs binding her arms behind her back. At first she couldn't feel her fingers; her arms hung useless and heavy. Then the blood began to flow, and excruciating pain shot through her. Small Bird bit down hard on her lip to keep from crying out. Her feet were untied.

"Come, I've got to get you out of here." Lone Warrior slipped his arms under her.

Small Bird protested. "The boy. We have to take him with us."

"What boy?" Lone Warrior asked.

"The son of Hawk Eyes. He is here." But where? She looked around.

Lone Warrior grabbed her shoulders. "We have to get you away. Forget him."

"No. We cannot. Where are the others?"

"The others? I don't know. I saw the camp-fire and came over to see what was happening, then had to wait till it went down to speak closer. Why is Moon Fire here? And who is this other—"

Small Bird shook her head. "Many Horns. He is responsible—"

"Ah, the enemy." Many Horns's voice rose behind them.

Small Bird whirled around.

Lone Warrior stepped forward, his knife outthrust defensively. "You will die for your crimes," he promised.

"Not so fast," Many Horns said with a sneer. He moved into the moonlight, holding Golden Eagle in front of him.

Small Bird tried to get around her brother, but he blocked her progress. When Moon Fire stepped out of the shadows, Lone Warrior shook his head in horror, he couldn't believe that his cousin had truly betrayed her tribe.

"What is going on?" the girl asked.

Narrowing her eyes, hating to have to say anything, Small Bird lifted her voice. "Moon Fire is the one who is responsible for the deaths in our tribe. She told Many Horns about my wedding; she informed him of our camp's defenses, and told him when to attack." Her throat was so dry, the accusation made her cough and fall to her knees.

Many Horns glanced into the darkness, then eyed her. "Get up," he ordered, waving his knife. He pointed at Lone Warrior. "The child dies if you do not toss your knife to the ground." To show he was serious, he brought the sharp edge of his blade to the boy's throat.

Small Bird's heart stopped. She stood. "We cannot allow harm to come to him," she whispered to her brother. No sound came from the child, and the darkness kept her from seeing his features clearly.

Lone Warrior tossed his knife to the ground. Many Horns laughed. "Good. But you will all die, anyway. Warriors from both tribes ride into my trap. What better revenge than to let them do my killing for me? I left a false trail for each to find. The mighty Hawk Eyes and Swift Foot will soon clash, and they will kill each other and you."

"And you can allow this, cousin?" Lone

Warrior obviously couldn't believe the girl's duplicity.

"It is no crime to want happiness, cousin," Moon Fire said, her voice full of anger and disgust.

"Take his knife," Many Horns barked.

Small Bird watched her cousin bend down, placing herself in the way of her lover. Many Horn's view was obstructed. Seeing their only chance for freedom, she nudged her brother with her elbow, then glanced once at him, and once at her cousin. Moon Fire grabbed the knife, stood, then turned and started walking back.

"Now," Small Bird said in a hiss. Springing forward, she threw two fistfuls of dry, dusty soil and pebbles at Many Horns, then tackled her cousin. Behind her, Lone Warrior charged forward. "Run," he yelled.

Moon Fire screamed. Many Horns dropped his hostage as wind blew dust into his eyes. Lone Warrior knocked him to the ground.

Small Bird held her breath and crawled to where Golden Eagle had fallen. He grabbed her, whimpering.

"Run, Small Bird."

Lone Warrior's voice spurred her to her feet. Weakened, she staggered as she lifted the child to carry him. She turned back to her brother. "I can't leave you." She jumped out of the way as the two warriors rolled toward her, locked in a life-and-death struggle.

"Go. Find the others. Let them know you and the boy are safe, or it will be too late for everyone. The killing will be worse."

Realizing that neither tribe knew the truth—that Many Horns and Moon Fire were behind the kidnappings—Small Bird turned and raced off. Along a narrow fissure that split off from the main part of the ravine, darkness overwhelmed her, closing in on her. She moved forward blindly, stumbling over large boulders in her path, which forced to slow in order to avoid a fall that might injure the child. At last she reached the wide main body of the ravine, but she couldn't figure out which way to go. She didn't know where Many Horns had led the two tribes to fight.

Tears streamed down her face. Fear for his safety demanded that she return to her brother; but fear for her people kept her going. Small Bird searched desperately for a path leading out of the deep ravine. Around her, its sides rose smoothly and sharply upward. There was no way out. Knowing that if Many Horns killed her brother, he would come after her, Small Bird let out a frustrated sob.

"Where do I go?" she cried to the stars above. "Help us," she sobbed.

As if in answer, she heard a clear voice lifted in song. It came from the left.

"The spirits hear you," Golden Eagle whispered. "They sing for you." Awe filled his voice.

Small Bird crossed the stream and followed the voice of the spirit.

Swift Foot entered the ravine from the south, followed by his men. There were two main entrances to this canyon, and several paths leading up the west side. The east was a sheer rock cliff.

He rode slowly, unable to see any tracks. There were many recessions along the walls of the ravine. Small Bird had to be here somewhere, yet he dared not call out. He stopped often to listen, but heard nothing. Frustration and fear made him edgy. He was afraid to go on. His warriors spread out; they checked every where.

By the time the darkness turned to the gray of predawn, he was afraid he was too late. Then he spotted a cloud of dust coming toward him. Stopping, he grabbed his bow and motioned for his warriors to regroup. Out in the open, they were unprotected, and there was no place to hide—just dry, dusty land and a riverbed that was half-full with autumn rain.

An approaching group stopped a short distance away. Like Swift Foot and his warriors, the Miniconjou war party had no cover. The two tribes sat with arrows nocked and aimed. Given the short distance from each other, one volley could kill nearly every warrior present.

"Where is my wife?" Swift Foot finally called out.

Hawk Eyes shouted back, "I know nothing of your wife. You have my son. Return him to me or die!"

Night Thunder and Kills Many Crows flanked Swift Foot. "They seek to trick us," Night Thunder guessed.

"If you have harmed Small Bird, your tribe and mine will *never* know peace!" Swift Foot promised. Anger roiled inside him, but he kept it under control. Before he killed his enemy, he had to find his wife.

"You do not wish peace, or you would not have taken my son." Anger emanated from Hawk Eyes's entire tribe.

Confused, recognizing that something wasn't right, Swift Foot stared into the fury of his enemy. He tried to explain: "It is you who seek war. You attacked my people at my wedding. You stole my wife. The people of Hawk Eyes speak falsely when they say they wish to talk of peace."

"We speak falsely? Do you think I did not learn of your plot to attack and kill my son?" Night Thunder shook his head, furious. "We have two women missing. And we have proof you are the one responsible."

"Proof?" Hawk Eyes lowered his bow and arrow, and held up something else. "I have here the foot of *Mastinca*. It was found near

321

my wife. You tried to kill her, then took my son, and now you lie about it. I ask one more time: Where is my son? Release him to me unharmed and I will spare your lives this day. I am tired of violence. However, kill me and the many warriors I left behind will seek out the people of Swift Foot forever and kill them."

Intrigued, Swift Foot lowered his own bow and removed the medicine bag from the bundle tied before him on his horse. "I know nothing of your child, Hawk Eyes," he called. "I only know my wife is gone. This medicine bag belongs to you, does it not?" He threw it over to the other chief.

Hawk Eyes caught the bag and stared at it. "This has been missing for many weeks. You took it from me when we battled. This is not proof."

Once more both chiefs readied their bows and arrows. Beneath the pale dawn, arms trembled, eyes blurred, and anger blazed.

Just before Swift Foot loosed his first arrow, the first act toward total bloodshed, he heard a sound.

A song.

Blinking in surprise, he listened to the wind sing a sad melody. It was compelling: He wanted to lower his bow. Had exhaustion claimed his mind, or were the spirits already mourning his death?

"What trick is this?" Hawk Eyes called out.

Beside him, Kills Many Crows and Night Thunder both stiffened. Swift Foot realized they heard it also. Warily, he glanced around.

"Look," someone cried out.

Swift Foot swung to the right. High on a rocky shelf, a lone woman stood with arms outstretched, her pale dress fluttering in the wind. High above, moon, stars and sun illuminated all. Long, flowing hair streamed around the woman's head as she sang—of peace not war.

Swift Foot glanced at his warriors, unsure what to do. Neither did the enemy seem to know. Bows on both sides were lowered, all attention focused on the woman. Then she stopped and stood there, as if watching them.

"A vision," Hawk Eyes whispered.

"A message," Swift Foot said, equally stunned.

"*Unhcegila.*" Someone gasped as a hunched, monstrous shape crawled out of the shadows and toward the vision. Gasps rose from the warriors.

Held by the surreal play of spirits, Swift Foot urged his mount forward. He held his breath as the monster reached out a hand and pulled itself up over the ridge. The monster became two shapes as something fell off its back.

A gasp left his mouth when the first figure stood. It was a woman. A child was the other shape. Swift Foot galloped forward. It couldn't be. He prayed it was. "Small Bird," he shouted.

Spotting the gathered horde, Small Bird held out her hands. "Do not fight," she called down, in a hoarse voice. "Do not fight!" She slumped to her knees.

The child beside her dropped also and stared down at them. "Father. Father," he called, his voice weak as well.

The woman who'd sung her song of peace stood above, as if guarding Small Bird and Golden Eagle. Without thought to his enemy or fear of receiving an arrow in his back, Swift Foot jumped down from his horse, ran to the sloping side of the ravine, and started pulling himself up.

Below, he heard someone climbing after him. It was Hawk Eyes, and he was murmuring, "My son, my son," as he followed.

Twice, both men lost their footing and slid down the steep slope.

At last, Swift Foot reached the top. His first thought was to run to his wife. Then he hesitated, knelt, and held his hand out.

Hawk Eyes grasped his wrist. When the other chief came over the top, both men eyed each other briefly, then rushed to their loved ones. Swift Foot fell to his knees to make sure Small Bird was unharmed. Hawk Eyes gathered his boy into his arms.

"My wife. Tell me you are unharmed," Swift Foot said. He cradled her close, his lips on her hair, his hands sliding over her arms, searching for injuries.

"I am fine." She tried to lick her lips. "Lone Warrior—." Her voice broke off.

"What about him?"

"He is here. He saved us."

Swift Foot glanced around, just then realizing it was Willow Song who stood nearby. It had been her voice that had stopped the killing. With a sick feeling, he realized just how close to total destruction they'd all come. In the short time it had taken Small Bird to climb up, he and Hawk Eyes could have decimated each other's tribes.

"Where is Lone Warrior?" he asked his cousin. She'd again covered her head. Below, the warriors of Hawk Eyes stared in horrified fascination.

"He comes." She pointed.

All eyes turned to the north: there a warrior struggled out from a narrow gap where the earth had split, and formed a hidden trail.

Small Bird covered her mouth with her hands and cried out. "He's safe!" She tried to rise.

"We will see to him," Swift Foot promised. Down below, several warriors had already ridden off to collect him.

In his arms, his wife leaned closer. She licked dry lips, and he realized he had no water to offer her.

"Here."

Glancing up at the strange voice, Swift Foot saw one of the enemy. The man had obviously climbed up behind his chief, and now he held out a water pouch.

Swift Foot took it and gave his thanks. Then he offered the skin to Small Bird. She drank greedily.

"Not too much," he warned. Closing his eyes, Swift Foot realized that he'd nearly lost this woman. Tears sprang to his eyes. Unashamed, he let them fall. Suddenly, in this respect, control didn't seem to matter. "I nearly lost you," he said. He bent to kiss her temple. "I love you, Small Bird."

"I know," she whispered. But he had never seen her look so content. "I am sorry I left camp," she added a moment later.

"You should be, wife." Swift Foot's voice shook as he once more considered what might have happened.

"It was Moon Fire and Many Horns—" she explained, breaking off to cough.

"Do not talk." Swift Foot stood.

Sighing, his wife tried to obey. "Thirsty. I'm so thirsty and tired."

"And I'm hungry," came the voice of Golden Eagle behind her.

Looking around, everyone laughed—nervous laughter, but laughter all the same.

"My son will be all right," Hawk Eyes said, his voice thick with emotion.

Swift Foot felt his wife's arms wrap around his neck. "I think we all will be all right," she said. And he had a feeling she knew how to achieve peace between the two tribes.

Chapter Eighteen

Small Bird stared at the two chiefs. "Well? Is that not a good solution?" They'd been here for four days, and each had summoned his entire tribe. They were all now camped out on the plain. An uneasy truce had been reached between Swift Foot and Hawk Eyes in order for each party to care for their loved ones. Now they were speaking of peace—and they were nearing an answer.

Hawk Eyes sat across from Small Bird, his son sleeping beside him. The poor child refused to leave his father's side. Wind Dancer and three elders, along with Lone Warrior, sat between the two chiefs. Warriors from both tribes were gathered around, watching the talks warily.

Realizing that neither man had answered,

Small Bird leaned forward. "Joining the two tribes by marriage will *end this war.*" Her tone brooked no argument. She looked to Wind Dancer for support, for the two chiefs still said nothing.

The medicine man spoke. "War started when such a vow was broken. Peace will be restored by righting the wrongs of the past."

Hawk Eyes finally nodded. He glanced over at Small Bird, some small admiration sparkling in his golden eyes. He addressed Swift Foot. "Your wife is as clever as she is brave. She tells us the simple solution, something we should have done long ago: we shall merge our families as they were once meant to be."

Swift Foot nodded at the sleeping boy. "You have a son. He is brave. I pledge my eldest daughter to him. And if we are not blessed with a daughter, then my son will marry your firstborn girl."

Hawk Eyes nodded as he stroked his son's hair. "It is time to put the past behind us, to look to the future. I agree to join our families."

Wind Dancer stood and returned with a ceremonial pipe. He lit it, then offered it to the spirits before passing it to Hawk Eyes. Once it was given to both chiefs and each council member, the shaman proclaimed the marriage promise binding. Peace had been restored.

A cheer rose around them. Swift Foot

stared at Small Bird, his eyes filled with both admiration and worry. "I think it is time for my wife to return to her tipi to rest."

"Your wife is fine," Small Bird said. For, truthfully, she didn't want to be alone. Her husband had a duty to see to yet—the bodies of Moon Fire and Many Horns had yet to be dealt with—and she wanted to be at his side.

"Then let us eat," Swift Foot said, standing up and taking his wife's arm. A feast had been set up in the warm autumn evening. The scent of roasting meat filled the air. Women laughed and men talked. A group of boys ran to Golden Eagle and coaxed him away to play.

"If you insist on staying up," Swift Foot whispered, "then you will stay by my side." He sounded pleased.

Small Bird smiled. "I have no problem obeying your order, my husband." Still weak from her ordeal, she was content to eat and observe. Dancers had already formed lines, and this celebration would last long into the night. She sat.

Lone Warrior reclined across from her and Swift Foot. He had wide bandages wrapped around one upper arm, a deep gash in his shoulder that stopped him from using his other arm, and two deep cuts in his thighs. He'd fought Many Horns to the death.

Then Small Bird thought of Moon Fire, her cousin. Rather than face her people after her treacherous actions, she'd jumped off a cliff and fallen to her death.

Despite all that had happened, the knowledge that her cousin had killed herself saddened her. But deep down, she knew that Moon Fire had chosen her own destiny. She'd done wrong, and now perhaps she'd atoned.

Shoving away the sad thoughts, Small Bird met her brother's twinkling eyes. "Married life seems to agree with you, Lone Warrior," she said.

The big man grinned and accepted a bowl of steaming meat from Willow Song. He pulled his new wife down beside him and held the bowl between them. "As it does with you, my sister."

The siblings smiled at each other. Small Bird glanced over at Willow Song. Half of her face was as perfect and heavenly as her voice. And the other half, the half nearly everyone else had found so repulsive, was now hidden beneath a beautiful mask of feathers.

The mask, made by Small Bird and blessed by Wind Dancer, was the perfect solution. Her bravery had not been enough for the tribes to entirely accept Willow Song. The woman's voice had prevented the two clans from killing each other, but the tribes had both insisted she keep her face covered whenever she was in public.

Shuddering, Small Bird sighed. She'd wished for a more open-armed acceptance of her new cousin, but she supposed the tribes would grow to accept Willow Song as she herself did. Thinking of the girl's courage, Small Bird recalled those frightful moments when she'd clung to the steep slope of the ravine with Golden Eagle's small arms wrapped around her neck. She'd been unable to call down to let her husband know she was safe. Any distraction on her part might have sent her and the child tumbling. Finishing that climb, knowing that at any minute the two groups of warriors might attack and kill each other, had been the hardest thing she'd ever done. And Willow Song had forestalled that violence. The others saw that, and they would accept her more as time went on.

Leaning back against her willow backrest, Small Bird felt happiness seep into her. The warmth of the fire, the rumble of her husband's voice, the singing, laughter, and sounds of peace, lulled her into a light slumber.

When Swift Foot scooped her up some time later and declared it was time for her to retire, she didn't protest. Nuzzling her face into the warmth of his shoulder, Small Bird wrapped her arms around his neck and smiled. If her husband thought he could just put her to bed, then leave and return to the feasting, he was mistaken. She wasn't *that* tired.

Glancing up into the sky, seeing streaks of dusk racing across it, she sighed. Soon the stars would come out and light up the night like clouds of fireflies.

Inside their tipi, Swift Foot lowered her gently to their bed of furs. Small Bird kept her arms wrapped around his neck, refusing to let him go.

"We have guests, wife," he said. But desire turned his brown eyes into twin pools of dark honey: sweet, enveloping, and irresistible.

"Our guests will not miss you, my husband. Not as much as I will."

Sliding his length alongside her, Swift Foot stared down into her face. "Then I will stay for as long as you need me."

Grinning, Small Bird pulled his head to hers. "Then you will be here long, my husband, for I will need you for the rest my life."

"As I need you, wife. As I need you."

Epilogue

His sharp eyes scanned the flat-topped buttes where patches of scraggly brush clung tenuously to the vertical sides. Deep ravines of sandstone, shale, and clay reflected the bright sunshine.

The hot wind carried him effortlessly over miles of golden prairie, rocky formations, hills, and valleys. Waves of heat blurred the land. Nothing moved. Patiently he scanned the many tributaries snaking away from the river. Most were dry, the nearby vegetation brown and brittle—but here and there, gullies of dark green contrasted flatly with the bleached earth.

Tendrils of smoke rising from the far side of a large outcropping of mounded rocks drew his attention. Yellow pine fought for life in the inhospitable soil there, adding color. Dipping one wing, the eagle followed the wide prairie that wrapped around the rocky formation like hands cupping a delicate flower.

Down below, Small Bird felt the eagle's shadow glide over her. Glancing up, she smiled softly. Once, she'd believed the presence of an eagle to be a bad omen. Things were different now. Perfect.

Another shadow slid over her, blocking the heat of *Wi*. She glanced over her shoulder at her husband, a man as powerful as *Wambli*.

"You have returned," she said. She jumped to her feet. He caught her in his arms. Small Bird buried her face in the warm slope of his neck. He'd only been gone for a week, but it felt like a lifetime.

"Did you miss me?" He claimed her mouth before she could answer.

Breathless when he released her, Small Bird giggled. "Perhaps not as much as you've missed me."

His gaze lingered on her face. His fingers swept over each side and slid into her hair. He pulled her back to him. This time he nuzzled the soft hollow of her throat. "I plan on showing my wife just how much I missed her. Starting now. And tonight. And tomorrow. We will make up for the time I was gone."

Small Bird laughed gently. "Husband, if we were to make up all the time we miss when you hunt, we would not eat or sleep."

"You do not hear me complaining." Swift Foot's tongue began a light tickling across her collarbone and up the side of her neck.

"No, I would not mind, either. However, our son would be most displeased."

Reluctantly, Swift Foot pulled away. "I am most eager to share my wife's mat again. It has been far too long."

"Is that all you can think of?" Small Bird relished the brief flicker of repressed need that crossed her husband's features. She loved him so much, and had missed the intimate sharing of their bodies as well. Lowering her gaze, she couldn't help but notice how much Swift Foot wanted her.

"I do not lie when I say I have missed you, my wife." Reaching out, he took hold of Small Bird's hand and began walking.

"How is my son?" Pride filled his voice and shone from his eyes.

"He complains as much as his father," Small Bird said. She loved walking with her husband: just the two of them, moving as one with hands twined and shoulders brushing close.

"Waiting does that to a man," he answered wryly.

Stopping, Small Bird took Swift Foot's other hand in hers and stared up into his loving eyes. Hunger rose from deep within her. "You don't have to wait anymore. You're back. *We* don't have to wait anymore," she whispered.

Swift Foot's gaze slid to her mouth, then back to her eyes, his own gaze as hungry for her as she was for him. "You are sure you don't want to go back to the tipi, wait for privacy?" he asked, his hands lifting to frame her face.

Small Bird leaned into him. "I am sure."

Sighing, Swift Foot drew her close. "It would have been hard to wait for dark, my wife."

Grinning, she slid her body close to his, her hips sweeping over the bulging front of his breechclout. "I know. For me, too. But my mother is tending our son. He will be fine until we return."

Grinning, Swift Foot swung her up into his arms.

"We shall go and watch the sun set."

"I would like that." She loved this man so much, she couldn't imagine life without him.

"And after, we can catch a star or two." Swift Foot followed the twisting stream away from camp, leading her quickly.

Snuggling close, Small Bird laughed. "I like stars," she whispered. "The more the better."

SUSAN EDWARDS

White Dove was raised to know that she must marry a powerful warrior. The daughter of the great Golden Eagle is required to wed one of her own kind, a man who will bring honor to her people and strength to her tribe. But the young Irishman who returns to seek her hand makes her question herself, and makes her question what makes a man.

Jeremy Jones returns to be trained as a warrior, to take the tests of manhood and prove himself in battle. Watching him, White Dove sees a bravery she's never known, and suddenly she realizes her young suitor is not just a man, he is the only one she'll ever love.

___4890-6 $5.99 US/$6.99 CAN

Dorchester Publishing Co., Inc.
P.O. Box 6640
Wayne, PA 19087-8640

Please add $2.50 for shipping and handling for the first book and $.75 for each book thereafter. NY, NYC, and PA residents, please add appropriate sales tax. No cash, stamps, or C.O.D.s. All orders shipped within 6 weeks via postal service book rate. Canadian orders require $2.50 extra postage and must be paid in U.S. dollars through a U.S. banking facility.

Name_____
Address_____
City_____ State_____ Zip_____
I have enclosed $ _____ in payment for the checked book(s).
Payment <u>must</u> accompany all orders.☐ Please send a free catalog.
CHECK OUT OUR WEBSITE! www.dorchesterpub.com

DON'T MISS THESE HEART-STOPPING HISTORICAL ROMANCES BY LEISURE'S LEADING LADIES OF LOVE!

Lakota Renegade by Madeline Baker. Alone on the Colorado frontier, Jassy can either work as a fancy lady or find a husband. But what is she to do when the only man she hopes to marry is a wanted renegade? For Jassy, the decision is simple: She'll take Creed Maddigan for better or worse, even if she has to spend the rest of her days dodging bounty hunters and bullets.

_3832-3 $5.99 US/$7.99 CAN

White Wind by Susan Edwards. Searching the Old West for her father, lovely young Sarah Cartier doesn't make it far before she crosses paths with Golden Eagle, the brave who rescued her years before. Golden Eagle has already pledged to marry another when Sarah comes back into his life. But with Sarah provoking him like no other, he vows no obstacle will stop him from tasting her sweet lips, from sharing with her an unforgettable ecstasy as he forever claims her as his own.

_3933-8 $5.50 US/$7.50 CAN

Dorchester Publishing Co., Inc.
P.O. Box 6640
Wayne, PA 19087-8640

Please add $1.75 for shipping and handling for the first book and $.50 for each book thereafter. NY, NYC, and PA residents, please add appropriate sales tax. No cash, stamps, or C.O.D.s. All orders shipped within 6 weeks via postal service book rate. Canadian orders require $2.00 extra postage and must be paid in U.S. dollars through a U.S. banking facility.

Name_____
Address_____
City_____State_____Zip_____
I have enclosed $_____ in payment for the checked book(s).
Payment <u>must</u> accompany all orders. ❑ Please send a free catalog.

CHASE THE WIND
CINDY HOLBY

From the moment he sets eyes on Faith, Ian Duncan knows she is the only girl for him. But her unbreakable betrothal to his employer's vicious son forces him to steal his love away on the very eve of her marriage. Faith and Ian are married clandestinely, their only possessions a magnificent horse, a family Bible, a wedding-ring quilt and their unshakable belief in each other. While their homestead waits to be carved out of the Iowa wilderness, Faith presents Ian with the most precious gift of all: a son and a daughter, born of the winter snows into the spring of their lives. The golden years are still ahead, their dream is coming true, but this is just the beginning. . . .

Dorchester Publishing Co., Inc.
P.O. Box 6640
Wayne, PA 19087-8640

_5114-1
$5.99 US/$7.99 CAN

Please add $2.50 for shipping and handling for the first book and $.75 for each additional book. NY and PA residents, add appropriate sales tax. No cash, stamps, or CODs. Canadian orders require $5.00 for shipping and handling and must be paid in U.S. dollars. Prices and availability subject to change. **Payment must accompany all orders.**

Name: _____

Address: _____

City: _____ State:_____ Zip:_____

E-mail: _____

I have enclosed $_____ in payment for the checked book(s).

For more information on these books, check out our website at www.dorchesterpub.com.
_____ *Please send me a free catalog.*